THE
WITCHING
TIDE

A NOVEL

MARGARET
MEYER

SCRIBNER

New York London Toronto Sydney New Delhi

Scribner
An Imprint of Simon & Schuster, Inc.
1230 Avenue of the Americas
New York, NY 10020

First Scribner hardcover edition September 2023

SCRIBNER and design are registered trademarks of The Gale Group, Inc., used under license by Simon & Schuster, Inc., the publisher of this work.

For information about special discounts for bulk purchases, please contact Simon & Schuster Special Sales at 1-866-506-1949 or business@simonandschuster.com.

The Simon & Schuster Speakers Bureau can bring authors to your live event. For more information or to book an event, contact the Simon & Schuster Speakers Bureau at 1-866-248-3049 or visit our website at www.simonspeakers.com.

Interior design by Davina Mock-Maniscalco

Manufactured in the United States of America

10 9 8 7 6 5 4 3 2 1

Library of Congress Cataloging-in-Publication Data is available.

ISBN 978-1-6680-1136-2
ISBN 978-1-6680-1138-6 (ebook)

For Michael
and
For the women who fell victim
to the 1645–47 East Anglian witch hunt:
in these pages, you are remembered.

Suffer me that I may speak; and after that I have spoken, mock on.

—JOB 21:3

Search diligently therefore for it in euery place, and lest one bee deceiued by a naturall marke, note this, from that. This is *insensible*, and bring pricked will *not bleede*. When the mark therefore is found, try it, but so as the Witch perceiue it not, seeming as not to haue found it, and then let one pricke in some other places, & another in the meane space there: its sometimes like a little *teate*, sometimes but a *blewish spot*, sometimes *red spots* like fleabiting, sometimes the *flesh is sunke* in and hollow, as a famous witch confessed, who also said, that Witches couer them, and some haue confessed, that they haue bin taken away; but, saith that Witch, they grow againe, and come to their old form. And therefore, though this marke be not found at first, yet it may at length: once searching therefore must not serue: for some out of fear, some other for fauour, make a negligent search. It is fit therefore searchers should be sworne to search, and search very diligently, in such a case of life and death, and for the detection of so great an height of impiety.

—Richard Bernard, *A Guide to Grand Iury Men*, 1627

PART ONE

YELLOW BILE

ONE

S he was in the garden at first light. There were herbs to cut: rosemary for the roast meat, mint and mallow for her cough. The house and the street and the hill beyond it were dimmed by a thick, flame-coloured haze, and as she crossed the grass she saw how the morning star was swathed in the vapour. A single magpie flew from it, so close that its wing-beat stirred the air by her face. It landed on the roof's ridge and mocked her in its grating voice.

Two bad omens; but what was she to make of them? The day would unfold as God intended.

The mallow grew full and fierce at the street's margin. Martha crouched and cut handfuls. Over her shoulder she saw three men approaching. She stood. The men faltered and fell back as though they had seen a hell-fiend rise: that hag was her.

When they recovered they came on apace, right up to the house. Then she knew them—Hesketh's lads from the smithy at the far end of the village, and Herry Gowler from the gaol. She ran for the door and was almost through it when they reached her. They had the blunt look of men uneasy with their task and their fear told itself in needless force. They shoved her aside and she went down like scythed barley, lying over the threshold while her lungs pumped noise like punctured bellows. They stepped over her and went in. She turned her head and saw Simon coming from his bed under the stairs with his hands raised: part greeting, mostly alarm. With their staves they felled him and then turned for the kitchen. Martha pushed herself onto her knees and crawled after them, trying to call Master Kit's name. The curtain rail splintered as they wrenched it. Cloth poured onto the floor. Prissy had been shelling peas into a dish. Martha heard the dish break, the hail of green beads, Prissy's animal wail. Accusations—unconscionable, shocking—issuing harshly from the men's throats. They left dragging Prissy between them like a heifer bound for the slaughter-house.

Martha got to her feet and watched them go. The front door was ajar and the mist seemed to clot and fold in, as if to veil what had happened.

Simon came and stood by her. "It were only time," he said thickly. One of his nostrils had split and the red ran into his mouth. "For our turn," he said. "In Cleftwater." They looked at each other in silence. His eyes were dark and glassy, fixed on her. In them she saw her own fear reflected.

She made a wide circling gesture, to the kitchen, the house, their village.

"Right enough," Simon said. His voice was flat with misgiving. "Nothing's safe now. Nothing."

All the black of the world rose then. In it was a vision of the Archer babe—his blue mouth, his waxy pallor. Dread grew through her body like a vine. Simon saw her sway and grasped her elbow and brought her to the kitchen stool, making her sit while he went to bring the master. His steps flustered away over the flagstones to the stairs. Droplets of blood marked his route. After a moment she heard his hesitant knock on the bedchamber door and Kit's voice, deep and with the husk on it that it always had in the first of the morning. And then Mistress Agnes's also, high with alarm.

———

Gone Prissy. Taken Prissy. They had wrenched her from here so roughly, from her hearth and her home, Prissy's hard-won places. Everywhere there were reminders. Proving bread dough in a bowl in the hearth embers. Gold hairs, glinting from the floor rushes.

Martha forced her legs to move, hauled herself upright, pulled back the kitchen shutter. Meagre light seeped in and she found the ewer and drank straight from it, so fast that ale runnelled from both sides of her mouth. The fire was all but out. She raked it, coaxing the embers by blowing on them. Her breath was short and the flames took a long time to catch and were weak until she fed them, pine cones and a piece of salt-wood from one of the wrecked boats on the beach. She sat on the stool again. The sun wrote strips of light on the wall and for a long time she studied them, unsure of their message. Her cheek was smarting where she had fallen, the split skin puffing up on either side like lips. It felt bad, like some judgement, to be marked in such a way. Through the kitchen window she could see the back yard's dimness beginning to thin, and through it came the faint repeating pulse of the sea, regular as breathing. She listened to it until her heart began to slow.

Maybe she dozed or maybe it was just that her eyes closed. Her thoughts were dark and running and she did not like to be in them. Why Prissy, and not her? And what of the other taken women, from the villages not far south of here? Women in Salt Dyke and Holleswyck, a mother and daughter among them. More in Sandgrave, not a half-mile away. Some of them dead already of gaol fever and some still to die, if the courts willed it so. Kit said a London lawyer had been hired to try them, a man known to take coin in advance of a judgement; a man not known for clemency.

She was Cleftwater-born and knew many things, but not the true nature of this new terror that had until today been safely distant, a rumour only. Now it had arrived. Now it was real. Prissy's arrest would not be the first. The kettles hissed over the fire and their noise mingled with the ripe waft of the slops bucket, setting off a queasy current that ran from the base of her throat to her guts. The same anxiety came and went and nudged again. When? When would they come for her? If they came, what then? Nothing then. She would be less than nothing. Disowned. Stateless. Worse than that: she would be reinvented, made monstrous; every one of her misdeeds and defects—real or imagined—magnified a thousand-fold.

God help her then. God help them all. All the taken women.

A hand was on her shoulder, anchoring her with its grip. She opened her eyes.

"How do you, Martha?" Kit said.

She looked at him, then at her hands. They must talk for her. Inside her were unvoiced words—so many—that shoved and bobbed in her head and chest. That could not be sounded because of the thing in her throat—a thick, throbbing form that stole her voice and used her breath for its own. Something lived in it: a serpent, a worm. Since childhood it had been there. The herbs she took damped the coughing but did not stop the worm's work. It hurt to talk. Because of it she rarely spoke. Now her hands drew the shapes of their language, soundless signs and gestures—made up more than thirty years ago between Kit and herself—that was their way of speaking to each other.

Well enough.

He put some fingers lightly under her chin and tilted her cheek to the light. *I will bring the doctor*, he shaped back.

Nay, she motioned. *I have my herbs.*

He brought the jug and a beaker and poured more ale and squatted beside her while she drank. "What did they say? When they came. What reason did they give?"

She shook her head. *None.*

"They must have reason to enter a house—any house— like this."

Her cheek throbbed. She found she could not look at him. Life with Kit had gone along of its own accord, she had lived it more or less content, had never thought to question it. Or be questioned, in her turn.

"Martha?"

She let out a breath she hadn't known she was holding. Kit was a good man and a kind one. He had rescued Prissy— their comely, golden-haired cook—from a life of whoring on Salt Dyke docks. Similarly with her, Martha. She had been his boyhood nurse and he had kept her on, given her the dignity of work and a home. It was impossible to lie to him.

She made her hand into horns and brought it to her forehead.

"They said . . . what? That she is of the Devil?"

Aye . . . aye. His servant. She circled her ring finger. *The Devil's bride.*

He looked uncertainly at her, then past her. His expression hardened, decided itself. "Rest here a while," he said. "Mistress Agnes is still abed. Simon and I will see about Prissy."

He squeezed her shoulder and went. She tried to stand but all her strength had drained away and she had to lean against the kitchen table. The house was quiet except for familiar sounds; the constant soughing of the waves and over it the grunt of the hogs, which were beginning their day's foraging in the unyielding dirt of the yard. The window showed the wash-house and her physick garden and behind all these the far flint wall with its gate that opened onto Tide Lane. Beyond the lane was the sea: flat, listless, the colour of polished pewter. With Prissy gone there would be so much more to do. Ale to be brewed. Meals to prepare. Mistress Agnes would soon rise and want help getting dressed.

There was a ringing numbness on the hurt side of her head and for some minutes she stood without moving, trying to steady herself in the kitchen's disarray, scattered pans and plates and drying herbs, shards of broken dish, the slew of peas on the floor. Hearing Kit's voice upstairs as he conferred with Mistress Agnes; knowing with utter certainty that Prissy's arrest was the beginning, had set something in motion, some pitiless mechanism that could be neither stopped nor diverted.

———————

The prospect set her in motion. She went upstairs and along the narrow passageway that passed the main chamber, then up another flight of stairs to her room in the attic. Its one small window looked out over the back garden to the sea.

Mam's small cedarwood casket was under the bed. She lifted it onto the mattress and unlocked it. The hinges complained as she raised the lid. On top was a layer of yellow flowers that crumbled to dust at her touch. The casket held the past, the difficult past: heirlooms from Mam mostly. One by one she took them out. Mam's rosary beads. Mam's scissors. Mam's thimble, carved from a walnut shell by one of her lovers. Mam's best bodice of wine-coloured damask, too small now for Martha. Pins, needles, three wood bobbins, an awl, two shallow dishes of beaten brass, and a copper cross that had once been set with chips of blue glass, all but one of them gone. Pieces of fabric: thin pennants of silk and an oblong of green velvet, cut from some lady's gown and still bearing the traces of rotted embroidery, which held some tiny yellow teeth and a coil of brown hair. Whose? Hers, most likely. Baby teeth and hair.

Underneath all these was the chamois pouch. For years—decades—it had lain in the chest. She had never needed its contents. The pouch held all Mam's charms, ones she'd been gifted as well as those Mam had made herself. Martha loosened the drawstring. The first charm was a tiny, wizened organ, grey-pink and dried to a nut-like hardness: the gallbladder of some field creature—a vole or shrew. She threw it on the bed, mouthed a soft curse, brushed her fingers clean. Went on with the unpacking, discovering a tiny lidded jar holding a handful of nails, a corn dolly, some dried trumpets of foxgloves, a shrivelled sprig of white heather. Then a toad, crushed flat as paper, with a crushed collar of briar-thorn wound around its neck.

———

Blood sang in her temples and ears: these things occurred when Mam was near. She put the dried toad on her bed with the other charms. The worst of her panic had subsided but still she paused, needing to gather herself. She regarded the charms. Not these. None of these. What she needed was still in the pouch.

She looked at it again. From its open mouth she thought she heard a tiny sound leaking, a sinister, persuasive hum. She took a breath, steeled herself to reach in, brought out the package. The linen wrapping was frayed but otherwise as she remembered. She unwound it. The contents fit neatly in her palm. A prickle of feelings went over her; the lancings of memories and old grief.

The doll was ill-made and lumpen, crudely fashioned from a stump of candle, egg-shaped where the wax bulged at its hips. Remnants of burnt wick were still in it.

She turned it in her fingers. It had two aspects, she remembered now. The two faces. One without eyes or only pinpricks for eyes, the nose a pinched-out nub, the mouth barely discernible—a sickle-shaped nock made by some woman's fingernail. This side, this face, quite peaceful. Closed-looking. The face on the other side was more formed and more frightening, the burnt-in eyes widely staring, the O of its mouth agape, as if it were trying to scream. The hands looked splayed, their fingers crudely scratched into the wax. The legs likewise, suggested only, a carved line.

The doll seemed to cling to her skin. Mam had taught how a left eye was the witching eye, able to see things not readily visible but present nonetheless. She turned the doll to one side and studied it aslant. Light haloed it, put a sheen on the dingy yellow wax, kindling the recollection of its purpose. It would need rousing if she were to use it—make use of its powers.

———

She took the doll down to the kitchen. A fly on its back spun frantically on the windowsill and she watched it without really seeing before pulling the shutters closed. Her apron with its map of stains hung from a peg and she put it around her neck. Prissy's skillet swung from the beam, and she lifted it down and put it on the trivet and lit the big candle beneath. The copper flushed as it warmed. She pressed the doll's legs first into the pan and after a moment the wax began to yield. She turned it upside down and repeated the process, holding the doll's head to the heat until the wax was doughy. She took the pan off the trivet, set it aside. With her thumb she stroked the curve of the head.

Her body felt cold and partly vacant, as if her own solid self had been nudged aside to make room for something other— a force, a spirit. It coiled up her, very chill. The doll's wax skin was clouding. Its eyes as yet were blind. A small draught toyed with the flame of the trivet candle and the strands of hair that hung about her face. The flame died. With its disappearance came hesitation and she put the doll quickly down and stepped back, wrapping her arms about her ribs as if to reassure herself of her own substance. Her undershift needed washing; her own musk came from it, reassuring.

Surely, always: it was better to do something. To take things in hand.

From the table the doll looked out. Already it was cooling, firming its purpose. She relit the trivet candle and held the doll's nether end over the heat until the wax softened again.

Then inserted her cuttings knife, slicing longways up until the blade came to a nub of wax. Let that be its groin. She teased the segments apart. Let these be its legs.

She propped it against the ale jug. It was done. Was it done?

In her chest excitement and alarm jostled, speeding up her heart. She picked it up again to study it. The thing seemed to quiver; she felt air moving around her as though people—women—were brushing past; she could hear rustling skirts, felt the touch of hands on her face. There were sounds also—she brought it to her ear—an echo of voices—cries and protests and shrieked entreaties, Mam's warnings—coming from its open mouth.

She held it away from herself, at arm's length. The noises stopped. Her heart calmed a little.

The doll was just that—a child's toy, a stick of wax. All the same: she brought it again to her ear and heard it once more: a thin, reedy keening.

———

A hammer of thoughts in her head; the doll in her fingers, which now she dropped, as if it had stung her. What was it really, this deformity she had woken? What had she woken in herself? She squashed her hands together, as in prayer. *Forgive me, forgive my trespass, O Lord.* Wax flaked from her fingers. The doll was for using, that was its truth, the essence of its nature. As much as she feared it, she needed it.

She went back upstairs and searched in Mam's casket for a bodkin, pulling it gingerly from a square of plain linen. Downstairs she was struck with fright, threw down the bodkin and put her hands to her temples. Felt her own flesh, her pulse that was quick with a springing excitement.

She wanted to live, and live freely. Prissy must live, and live freely.

She pressed the needle to the doll's bloodless skin, working the tip to make a wound.

Prick, aye she must prick the hardening wax, pierce the rind of the poppet's throat. On her neck and arms the hair stood up, responding to some unfamiliar, alien current: revulsion, attraction, a variety of awe.

Wax doll.

Witching doll.

Poppet.

TWO

She wrapped up the poppet and hid it in her apron, then went out of the kitchen and the house, crossing the yard as fast as her stiff knee would allow. Yesterday's unnatural heat was still trapped in the brume. The street was full of Thomas Archer's cows that had pushed down their fence to get at the clumps of grass that fringed the road. In the wash-house she stood on Kit's old birch stool and hid the doll in a join where a rafter met the wall.

She came down off the stool and went to the tub. The sheet was where she'd left it from the night before. She lifted it from the pink water. Mostly the blood was gone. There was only the suggestion of it, faint red marks on the cloth. She worked the handle of the pump up and down but carefully, so that its metallic bray wouldn't wake Mistress Agnes. New water came in gouts into the tub. Thoughts of last night crammed her head and she pumped harder to try to rinse them away. The harsh soap worked into the grain of her skin as well as the linen. As she scrubbed she considered the remedies for different stains. For wine, salt, to draw up its redness. Wax could be got out by heating and blotting, but it would oftentimes leave an oily mark. For blood, cold water was best. She pumped again, rinsed the linen, and wrung it into a twist that she carried like a swaddled babe to the rope strung across the far end of the yard. The sun would reach here soon. The sheet was heavy to lift and she mouthed a protest at the pain in her gullet that came with any effort, no matter how slight. She stood back, rubbing her throat. The street ran beside the garden wall and beyond it was the long strip of wasteland where nothing but campion and sea poppy grew, and beyond that the shale beach sloped gently down to the sea. The water was mute and grey and very still. From the width of it a big orange sun was crowning, burning away the mist.

———

Last night's birth had come before time and on a tide of mother's blood.

Her neighbour Jennet Savory had come knocking very late, after the household had gone to bed. Simon had woken Martha and she'd gone to the back door. Jennet's face was whey-coloured in the lantern light. She was gabbling, gesturing down the street to where her sister Marion Archer lay, exhausted from trying to birth her first babe. The child would not come.

Martha had gone to the kitchen and roused Prissy, a maid keen to learn the arts of birthing. Together they went to the physick garden, working quickly to cut the necessary herbs. When they got to the Archer house Marion was lying utterly spent on the pallet, her mouth opening and closing with hoarse screams. Her friend Liz Godbold was crouched by, stroking Marion's head. The light of the bedchamber was dim and uncertain and Prissy had lit the lantern and more rushlights, and by them they could all see the too-much blood of Marion's labour and the obstinate bulge of the babe. Martha knelt at the mother's thighs and saw that a single tiny foot was through; a first bad sign. *Take hold of it,* she'd told Prissy, who'd pulled while Martha eased the rest of the body out, in rhythm with the mother's straining. The shoulders came and then the head, face down into Martha's cupped palms. She lifted the child and wiped away its skim of blood and muck. Red and white—love colours, life colours—that she rubbed off with an old cloth, and she kept on chafing its head and spine until she heard its first in-drawn breath, the first thin cry. A cry for the beginning. A cry for itself.

Then she turned it over. What she saw stopped her breath. She crossed herself. The child had ears and eyes and an abundant thatch of dark hair but that was the best to be said of it. There was almost no neck; the head grew straight out of the torso, angled up to the sky. A stargazer babe, its milky eyes fixed on heaven. Its top lip was over-large and riven, unnatural, wrong.

She had seen such babes before. Always they were a shock. Of their own accord her lips prayed, *Yea will I fear no evil, for Thou art with me*, and she wrapped the babe tightly to stop the flail of its stringy arms, shielding it with her body from the view of the others. They were busy with Marion, who was asking again and again for her child, a first look at her first-born. Her voice was weaker than before. The pallet was soaked through, dark with blood. It would have to be burned.

Martha moved away, out of the lurching rushlight to the dimmest corner of the room. She sat on a stool cuddling the babe, rubbing the small cage of its ribs. Feeling the quiver of its heart, its moth breath. A rush of feeling went through her; she was tender for him, this innocent runt of a boy, this wrong babe. He was turning his face blindly this way and that, already wanting to suckle. Wanting to live, as all babes did. Gently she examined his lip and nose. How would he suckle? He might live for a day, two at most. He could not survive; she could not see how he would survive. Already his fists were cooling, his mouth turning blue.

She thought of all the infants helped into the world at her hands. It had pleased God to put skill in her, the necessary gifts for this birthing work. Fast, slow, healthy, sick: every babe mattered to God as they had mattered to her. Often they were healthy and survived and sometimes they were sick or born dead, called straight away to the Lord; regardless, she had delivered them all in a bliss of yearning and envy, oh, countless, longed-for babes; this child of Marion's among them.

A knowledge nudged and nudged again, like an insect battering at a flame. She could feel it arriving even as she tried to hold it at bay. Some evil must have found its way into his mother's bride bed. He must have been cursed, to be born so ill-formed.

Her bowels writhed. How dreadful it was, how unworthy, to harbour this singular terror—primitive, ancient—that among them, these women, her friends, there could be a witch. The thought spread, consuming, eclipsing all things of grace in the world, dawn light on a pearly sea, the various golds of an autumn harvest, the miracle of a newborn, the kindness of neighbours. Which of them was it? Which?

She held the boy closer, tighter, closing her eyes as she cradled him. Mouthed a rapid prayer, for courage as well as protection. When she opened her eyes she saw the babe's blank ones. She brought him to her ear, listened for his breathing. There was none, or none she could discern. Godspeed. Godspeed him, tiny boy. She wrapped him in the birthing cloth and got up.

The mother was still bleeding, well on her way to death. Martha handed the boy to Prissy. "Oh, but it is ill made!" Prissy said, low-voiced. A look went between them that was itself infected. *Say nothing,* Martha motioned. Liz had gone out to tell Tom Archer he was a father; they could hear him in the passageway, anxious for news. Jennet came to Prissy for a glimpse of the babe, catching sight of it and gasping, "Save us, Lord, save us!" She struck her breast and began to sob, a quiet choking. The fire was low and a strange dusk had got in the room. Lithe shadows bred in it. Martha lit a handful of dried sage and bay leaves and its small smoke worked around the bedchamber, masking the raw smell of blood and horror. The mother asked over and over for her child until Jennet made a cradle of Marion's arms and put the body in them. They wept with their foreheads together; two sisters, one with her life bleeding away. Martha worked quickly to make a stemming tincture. There was nothing to be done for the babe except bless him and bury him, and no salve except prayer for his mother's broken heart.

———

On the way home a gull had come with them, its wings fanning white against the night.

"Why does it happen? When little lives are gone so quick," Prissy said. Her expression was unreadable in the dark. "It was so marked . . . I've never seen the like." Her hands knit together, clenching and unclenching. "Was it my fault? Did I do it wrong? Did I pull too hard and damage him?"

Nay, nay, girl, Martha shaped. She patted Prissy's shoulder.
You did nothing wrong.

"Then why did it happen?" Prissy said again, beginning to
be tearful. The night was clear and very still, stifling in the heat
that had lain over the village for days. The tide lapped, coming
in; moonlight glanced from it and from the shale that lay in big
shining drifts.

The gull was back. Three times it circled overhead. Martha
took Prissy's arm and they followed as it led them down to
the water. Their shoes made soft biting noises as they walked.
Near the tide's edge Martha scooped up a handful of stones and
handed them to Prissy.

Choose.

"What do you mean?"

Choose one. She made a cradle of her arms and rocked it.
For the boy.

Prissy studied the stones. After a moment she held one up,
egg-shaped. "Like this?"

Martha kissed the tips of her fingers, inscribed the shape of
the stone, then mimed casting it away. *Put your blessing on it*,
she wanted Prissy to understand. *Then give it to the sea.*

Prissy hesitated. Then kissed the stone, once, twice—
"A kiss for the babe, another for his Mam"—and lofted it,
far out.

The stone arced and sank. Small dark waves lapped and
broke and came again: like certainty, like doubt. Martha set
down the soiled linens and crouched, rinsing her forearms in
the black. Let the water wash away the night's sorrows. Let it
wash away panic. *Trust in the Lord with all thine heart; and
lean not unto thine own understanding.* Let the Lord deal with

any witches. Foam came about her hands, quick with darting green lights that faded as she watched. The tide brought things and took things; the Lord gave life and took it. It was the order of the world, not for her to question. In time the mother would know this also. If she lived.

Almost at the house Prissy had said, "It'll never leave me. The memory of it," and Martha was suddenly testy, wanting sleep, wanting peace, impatient with the struggle in the younger woman's face. Roughly she'd grasped Prissy's shoulder, given her a long look. If the girl would learn birthing, she must learn death as well.

THREE

The worm roiled in her gullet and the painful scrape of it brought her back. How long had she stood here? Motionless before the stained birthing sheet, with her head lowered and the bruise on her cheek pulsing?

She opened the garden gate and went out into Tide Lane. The street was a dirt line running from the Cleft through the village to the harbour. She went along it, skirting Archer's cows. Their udders bulged. This afternoon she would bring Simon and milk them, leave the full jars at the Archers' door. If Marion could take food she would do well to drink off the cream. Passing the Archer house she saw that it was shuttered and their chickens still cooped. She went into their yard and freed the birds and scattered some grain. A clump of hollyhocks grew by the fence, tall spears of yellow. On an impulse she cut some before going on her way.

At the corner she turned right and along Slip Lane. The church spire rose ahead, butting a bleached, hard-looking sky. She wanted to go and she did not want to go; there were prayers that needed saying—that were overdue—for Prissy and the dead babe, also for her own immortal soul. Even so, her feet dragged. She crossed the High Street and began to climb. The street went up, gently at first and then very steeply; some long-ago wit had named it Wish Hill. It was lined with dark elms that cast long shadows over the street and as she passed a clamour of rooks lifted, circling over her in a noisy, lopsided figure-of-eight. Spirits seemed to swarm, around and through her. They were of her and also of the world beyond this one: sprites, boggarts, the souls of the unshriven dead. Of unbaptised babes.

How was it that such dark thoughts could prosper on a day so bright? But they did, and she could not be rid of them. They could only be quelled. The heat weighed and her shadow stepped noiselessly alongside. Her panting had a creak in it. The sound was not new but of late it was disturbing. It was caused by the worm. At times during the day and often at night she could feel its pressure in her chest and throat. It was eating her, stealing the vigour from her heart and making her slow and heavy. Even now it was stealing her breath.

Many times she had thought on how to halt it. The only certain way was to stop breathing for good. At the hill's crest she thought she was finished. She bent over with her hands on her knees.

Where she stood the road branched into three. Left for the track to Top Field and Oliver's Paddock, named after the donkey that once grazed there. Right for Psalm Cliff and All Saints Church. A traveller or a witch-hunter going straight ahead for another half mile would join the coast road that ran in both directions, north to Blythe Bay and Seachurch, south to Holleswyck and Sandgrave and then the bigger port of Salt Dyke.

She turned and walked the last short distance to All Saints.

Its door swung to, shutting out all noise. At the altar, late-harvest offerings of hops and barleycorns and squashes. Colour, pooling on the flags from the last stained-glass east window, the only one saved from soldierly smashing. She stood for some moments while her breathing levelled; hesitant; unclean because of what she was or what she brought here; the worm's taint, the stain of guilt.

Some redemptive reflex stirred. She crossed the nave, went up the aisle to the eighth pew, which was the place where she and Mam had always worshipped. Its kneelers were arranged in a line. Mam's was faded, a white dove stitched on a yellow ground. She lowered herself onto it. Closed her eyes and steepled her hands and waited for the swarm of thoughts to abate. It didn't. Her agitation grew. A parade of images welled pinkly against her eyelids: Mam, Prissy. The dead babe, its blind eyes open. In them was a lament. Her lips began to move: *I will call upon the Lord, who is worthy to be praised: so shall I be saved from my enemies. From myself.*

The prayer faltered, clotting on her lips. Too many times it went this way: short-lived. Prayer was necessary, a habit like sleeping or breathing. Faith was different. Hers was not like other people's. It had some basic defect, its restless inner needle always roving, from conviction to disbelief to shame and around again, moved about by some unseen current, the source of which she didn't know. Mam had always said to pay no heed to how it worked; where the needle came to rest was a matter twixt a woman and her soul. In the end it was deeds that counted. In life Mam had been loud, practical, earthy. Her faith shallow-rooted, carried lightly even on Sundays; failing entirely at the end. Martha's was similar, leaning to solid things that could be seen and heard and handled. Such as hollyhocks. Such as stones kissed for dead babes.

Such as, a little wax poppet.

————

A shadow had assembled in the corner of her closed left eye. She opened it. Father Leggatt had edged into the pew beside her.

"Ah, no—don't let me disturb your prayer."

She unclasped her fingers and raised herself to the pew, indicated for him to sit. His cassock smelled of fire-smoke and old wool and onions. "How are you, Martha? I heard about Prissy," he said, not waiting for her answer. "These are dark days that we are in." His expression was unfamiliar, had lost its usual brightness. "She is fortunate to have good friends such as you, who pray for her. And a master and mistress who will surely speak for her. If she is innocent . . ." His gaze was on the altar, and then abruptly upon her. "What think you, Martha? Is she of the Devil? I hear it was her hands that marked the Archer babe. Could she . . . *Is* she capable of such a deed?"

Martha shook her head emphatically, kept her look on the priest while she inscribed the letters in the air. *Prissy did no wrong.*

"Prissy . . . ?" the priest said, puzzling out her meaning.

Did no harm, she told him, with large scything gestures.

"Nothing . . . ?"

Oh, he was slow. *No. Harm.*

"Nothing wrong? Prissy did nothing wrong?"

Aye. No wrong.

The priest's face relaxed. He was almost smiling; and then he wasn't.

"I'm told the babe was . . . a kind of monster. A terrible face."
He let out a breath. "You were at the birth, I think?"

Aye, I was.

"And which of you was it, who delivered the child?"

The needle skimmed: truth, treachery. She was dismayed
at where it had stopped. Her mind took up its whisper: careful
now, go careful. For Prissy. For herself.

I did.

He let out a breath. "That's good, Martha. I'm relieved." He
sighed. "Evil travels every road in these times. God be thanked
that the witchfinder rides after it, routing it from our homes.
From our lives. Though I confess, even last week I thought, he
will find nothing here. Cleftwater has its share of sin but it is free
of witches. I knelt and gave thanks to God for it." His voice sank,
as if burdened. "But now Master Makepeace is come with his
great knowledge of witches, and already there are tattle-tellers.
Master Makepeace has got evidence, I'm told." He turned to face
her, his mild blue eyes filled with alarm. "It seems that after all
there are witches in our midst. Of whom Prissy is just one, so
Master Makepeace declares."

Her voice made a noise, a refusal, that came out as a groan.
Nay. Not Prissy. Not her.

He watched, absorbing her message. Then turned away,
thrusting his hands into his sleeves. His profile was perfect, the
head of a young man in his prime, its skin clean and unblemished, its dark hair lustrous. He was known beyond Cleftwater
for the perfection of his sermons and his beauty, both. He had an
innocence, a sturdy faith so unlike her own. His reverie lengthened and her discomfort with it. She wanted to be away, to go
home; where Kit was, and Mistress Agnes. And the poppet.

Already there was need of it, of its powers, however slight. Prissy must have its help. She shifted, preparing to get up. The priest was blocking the pew. He had a puzzled expression, as if uncomfortable thoughts moved inside his head.

"Was the birth writ down? Have you put it in the register?" She shook her head.

"Then we'll do it now." He got up and went away to the vestry, where Cleftwater's ledger-book of births was kept. Her mind churned, muddying with concern. She must sign the register; she had hoped to avoid it—to leave no trace of her presence at the birth. She got quickly to her feet, wondering whether she might simply slip away, but already the priest was returning with a pen and the ledger-book that he balanced on the edge of the pew.

"Did the child have a name?" She held out her hands palm up.

"What was it? A boy or girl?"

A boy.

He nodded and passed her the quill. Brown ink leaked from its tip. She wrote: Creature. A blunt word for a blunted life.

The priest regarded what she'd written. "Creature." He sighed. "It will have to do. I will pray for him and for the family, nonetheless. Now you must make your mark, Martha, to show that you were there." Reluctantly she wrote it. He took the book and blew on it. She dipped to him, a small curtsey, *Good day to you, Father.* Took only a few paces and he was at her side again, taking her arm, turning her to face him.

"Was there anything else, Martha? Any matter you want to tell?"

The blue eyes were assessing her, very earnest.

No. Nothing.

"You are sure?" He still had hold of her arm. "Because you can, you know. Unburden your conscience. If you have need."

What was it that he knew? She arranged her face into a frown. His grip tightened. "I must tell you that Master Makepeace is a thorough man." He glanced about him, almost furtive. "His searches spare no one. Every Cleftwater woman should look to her safety. Prissy is not the only one to be accused— already there are others in the gaol with her—"

Her blood dropped. She lifted her hands into a V. *Who? Who?*

"You ask who they are? Well. Ellen Warne and Hannah Holland. Also Ma Southern, brought from Holleswyck. All of them now in the gaol." He rubbed his forehead. "I cannot believe that any of them could be so blighted or have done any wrong. But I'm told that Master Makepeace has gathered considerable evidence of their Devilish work." He looked away, into some distance, as though he were studying Cleftwater's quandaries. She could see how far he was in the clench of fear. "It does perhaps explain Cleftwater's recent afflictions. Last winter's storms. The sicknesses that have plagued us all year. And the deaths of our babes." His voice softened. "We are fortunate to have you, Martha, and your skills. But I pray you—in these times—make sure you are blameless. Search your conscience, be sure your every deed is utterly turned to God. Make sure that the witch-hunter can find no trace of wrongdoing, no stain on your record, for he will make more arrests, of this I am certain—"

The church door groaned open. Footsteps; feet scraping on the wad of sacking in the foot-well. Tom Archer coming in. At the font he halted and took off his cap. He was here no doubt to pray for his child's soul, to plead with Father Leggatt for a proper burial within the churchyard walls. For a moment she was seized by the unthinkable: that the minister had arranged it—some reckoning with the dead babe's father, here in the church. The needle spun, the worm lurched. She must get away, naturally and with ease, like someone clear of sin. Slowly she pulled her arm free of the priest's grip. She clasped her hands demurely and dipped her head. *I thank you for your concern, Father.* Then tapped her fingers to her lips and held out both blank palms. *I have nothing to tell.*

The font looked imposing, stark in the half-light of the west end. She could feel Tom's eyes on her, the burden of his grief. The pilfered hollyhocks fairly singed her hands. She had taken them to put on Mam's grave but they belonged here in the church, for Tom's poor babe. Their purity, the simplicity of their colours, said something she could not.

She dipped to them both, the two fathers, one upright, abounding with faith; the other bowed with grief.

FOUR

The graveyard was full of squirrels that scattered as she approached. Her hands were in fists, and she loosened and shook them as if to rid herself of Father Leggatt's warning. She went to the hedgerow that ringed the graveyard and cut an armful of hawthorn and cow parsley and dog roses, ignoring their barbs, the suffering of her flesh. Wildflowers were better, had been Mam's favourite. She put them on the grave. Its wood cross was very weathered.

Mam had died an unjust death, a cruel one. Now even her name was fading. But her voice was everywhere, its familiar cadences spouting from the grassy mound and the flowers and the cross. Always she began this way, this same tirade of lament, her catalogue of injuries and injustices. After a time she would settle, as she was beginning to now, her tone calming, her voice a filament of sound coming across the long gap of years. Soon it might be possible to greet her, ask questions. Ask about the poppet.

Martha sat down on the grave. Her head sagged onto her knees. All her zest seemed to drain away, as though through some puncture, some rend in herself. On the black screen of her eyelids the poppet faded into view. As she watched its wax grew vivid, its features stirred and were animate, everything concentrated in its pallid, intense face. Its burnt eyes fixed on her, unlidded, unblinking. She was skewered by its stare. Its lips fluted, parting wider: it was going to speak, tell her something—some message only for her. Her heart pummelled, her every fibre strained, wanting to know. Take care of it, Mam said. Take care *with* it. Still the poppet watched, on and on, impelling Martha with its no-eyes as Mam spoke again. Two choices. Two choices. Saying it over and over—urgent, compelling—even as the sight dulled, dimmed, dissolved into the black.

A warning. A caution. To do with the poppet. The properties of its nature, the consequences of its use. Speechlessly Martha begged Mam to speak again, to explain. But Mam now was going, her words waning, their sense less and less graspable in the rush of the present.

She stood up. All was as before and yet not so. The graveyard was quiet but she sensed a certain commotion in the soil and in the air, these layers dividing the living from the dead. Her face was suddenly damp. She scraped her cheeks and the movement wiped Mam's presence away. For a long moment she stood, stooped over Mam's mound. Alone again. An orphan again. Mam gone abruptly as was her habit, impatient with the living world.

———

Going back down Wish Hill was a trial. Her knees protested, her throat ached. She walked slowly, her conscience unquiet, her thoughts also, jumbling quick and hard against her temples. As if summoned from them, Slip Lane had a waiting figure in it, neat-framed and thin, who fell in step with Martha. In silence they went down to the shore. The tide had gone out a long way and water birds were gathered below the tide-line, pulling prey from the exposed sand. Before them the view unfolded, sunlit and expansive. Martha shielded her eyes and looked out. The village followed the bay's curve. At the southern end was the harbour. Then came the market square, bounded on one side by the Moot Hall and Market Cross, and the Four Daughters alehouse on the other. Then a line of cottages, then Kit's field that he rented out for grazing. At the northern end was the Cleft, the shallow gorge from which the village took its name. Sand martins nested in the bluffs either side and the river ran between them. Twice an hour the flat-bottomed foot-ferry crossed it, carrying goods and livestock and people.

She was Cleftwater born and had lived here all her life, four decades, almost five. Time had not much altered it, the war had passed it by. She knew its every aspect, its tides, its moods, the nature of its soils, where the nightingale nested, where lovers went to tryst, where its bee orchids grew. She thought of every household, touching each one with her mind: prizing all its folk.

Fierce feeling came up in a surge. Cleftwater was home, her place. Her love of it ran through her like the seam of clay in Psalm Cliff. Even in its faults she found perfection. Nothing must change; no harm must come to it.

"I don't quite know what I seen," the woman said suddenly.

Martha started. Her companion was fidgeting with her coif, pulling it over the wine-coloured birthmark that spilled down one cheek. "Last night. At the birth. But I know I seen something strange, maybe terrible. That's all I know."

Martha's heart adjusted, speeding up its beat. Jennet Savory was a plain speaker, not always liked for her bluntness.

"I don't want to think ill of you." Jennet rocked her head from side to side. "I been blocking my mind against my doubts. All day I've been telling myself, no. It cannot be. Not Prissy, gentle soul as she is. Nor Martha, neither. Not our Martha, that has brought so many of God's children safe into this world. So many children and their mams, alive because of you." Her cat's face—lively, triangular, thinly pretty—came around, its glance sidling to Martha. "But then . . . after last night, I can't not wonder." The small eyes were full of questions. Speculation. "I thought I knew you inside out, Martha. You're my friend. I never thought I'd doubt you. But now I'm thinking, maybe I don't. Not so well as I thought. Nor Prissy, neither."

Stop this, Martha signed, scraping the air between them as if to scrub all uncertainty away. *No more of this.* She ran her fingers down her face, miming tears. *I sorrow for you.* Pointing along the street to the Archer house. *For you all.*

Jennet watched, very still. "Aye. Well. 'Twas a bad night. The very worst. My sister had the brunt of it. I think she'll be grievin' forever." On Jennet's face small tears seeped. "You brought me into life, me and Marion, and we've been friends all this time," Jennet wept on, her tears running freely. With her thumbs, Martha smoothed them away. "And I know, I do know it, Martha, we'd have lost her last night if it weren't for you. But you've got so very quiet, even for you. Keeping to yourself, keepin' out of the way. Ever since Kit married and your mistress lost that first little babe. That no one ever saw."

Because it died.

"So you said. And I believed you. I truly did. But last night, after what happened, I got to thinkin! I got to adding up all the misfortunes as have come to you, Martha. Or come around you."

Martha opened her hands wide. *What's your meaning?*

"I mean, the coughing sickness in your part of Cleftwater, that no one's been able to cure, not even you. I mean, Kit's ships that sank. I mean, the Durrikens' hens that've died, one after another. Then Tom's cows with the bloat. And now my sister's babe." She stared past Martha, retreating into some distance. "It's like Cleftwater's got ringed about by badness—by ill luck," she said. "And at its middle is you."

The air between them curdled. Jennet was standing, expectant, with her mouth clamped shut in her customary way. What could Martha say? It was true that Kit's house had been afflicted, but his sunk ships; last autumn's lost babe that had passed unborn from this world to the next; hens, cows, coughing sickness—none of it was within Martha's sway. She lifted her shoulders and made cups of her hands, *I cannot explain it*, then dropped them and pointed to the sky.

"You think it's all God's doing?" Jennet said. Her voice climbed. "That it's His will for us?" She watched as Martha gestured towards the church. "Ach," she said. "I could ask the minister but I'm afeard of what he might say. What he might *do*, now that the witch man's come." Her hands worked at her skirts, twisting them. "I don't know what to pray for. I don't know what to think. Everything's turned. I used to think Cleftwater was a good place—the best place to live. I thought only the best of you Martha, so I did. Until yester eve, when I seen strange things. Un-Godly things."

A flock of gulls shrieked over. Martha watched them pass. The view shimmered; the horizon's azure gleam, the great sweep of smooth water shining like unblemished plate. Above it, thick smoke branched, a strange, grime-coloured ivy growing across the sky.

Look there.

"Jesu," Jennet said. "What is it?" She squinted, steepling her hands into a hood over her eyes. "Is it the fighting? I thought the war was farther away. That's what Tom says." A minute passed. Abruptly she turned to Martha, her face clenched. "Or could it be the Salt Dyke woman? 'Tis said she used her imps to murder her husband."

Martha lost her breath. Sweat crawled like lice in the pits of her body, under her arms and in the curve of her back.

"Maybe today they're burning her," Jennet breathed. "Aye. Maybe it's that. Did you know her? A most pious woman, I believe. A herb-mother like you." A note like dismay in Jennet's voice. "Fallen to the Devil so quick. Pray God she dies as quick."

Martha crossed herself. *May God have mercy on her soul.*

The smoke built and bulked, rising in a soiled-looking column. "People are sayin' of Rebecca what I'm wondering about you," Jennet said. Her eyes had narrowed against the glare. "I'll tell you plain, Martha. I'm afeared that maybe you've got with the Devil. I'm afeared that maybe he's turned you, led you away from goodness." She brought down her gaze. "That's what I'm fearin', Martha."

The words landed like strokes from a lash. How could Jennet think such a thing? How best to soothe her—how to quell suspicion, before it took possession of them both? Martha put up both hands and scissored them—open, closed, open—like flapping jaws.

"Have I talked? No. 'Course I haven't. I'm talking to you

now, aren't I, because you're my friend." Jennet craned her cat's face forwards. "I haven't talked, and I won't, but now I'm askin' you, Martha, and you need to tell me true." Her eyes were very wide, darkly ardent. "What happened last night? 'Cause I can't make sense of it. My sister, she was stuck in her travail, and I said, we need Martha. And you came, and you got the boy born as I knew you would, and when he come out you took him and went a ways off with him, I seen you. Cuddling him tight, like he was your own kin. And then you gave him to Prissy, and she had him for a little while. But then, when she gave the babe to me, he was dead. *Dead*. And with those . . . marks on him, oh, terrible, his poor face. But those marks weren't there when he first come out."

Martha stepped back. She could not persuade her body to stop its tremor. She drummed her eyelids, then pointed at Jennet. *You saw all. All I did.*

"I did see you birth him," said Jennet slowly. "And I did see you holdin' him, aye. But only later, after you held him and then Prissy. So what I'm thinkin' is, that babe got marked, and one of you must have marked him."

Nay, nay! It was already marked. She pulled at her lip, an exaggerated tug, obscuring her nose. *Marked so bad, it couldn't breathe.*

"Maybe so. But then, *why* was it born like that?" Jennet flung out an arm, gesturing to the village. "That's the fourth born this summer with sickness. With marks. So what is it or who is it, that's been cursing our babes?"

How would I know? Her arms were windmilling, propelling away blame. She was desperate to get away, to get home. *Those babes were born sick through no doing of mine.* She made to leave but the younger woman moved in concert, blocking Martha's way.

"Who's to know what life my sister's babe might've had? If you hadn't been there? Or Prissy?"

You speak cruel. You speak false. She gave Jennet a push and stepped past her.

"Do I?" Jennet said to her back. Her voice had got sharper, more urgent. "Maybe I *will* ask Father Leggatt, see what he says. Or the witch man. He would know. He would recognise Satan's work, for sure."

Martha turned. The beach spun with her. Her hands flew up, worked at the air. *You would not. You cannot.*

"I don't want to, Martha. But think on this—think how it looks to me. There's been seven babes born here and in Holleswyck this summer, four of them born wrong. None that lived past a week. You were there at all of 'em. Prissy too. And all those children died."

Indignation, hot as blood, spiralled through her body. She held up her fingers, counting them with quick jabs. *Five. Ten. More. All the births. Many births*—she rapped her chest—*so many births I've been to, and the babes have lived.* Pointing at Jennet. *You as well—birthed by me.*

"That's true, Martha, I do know it. Just please, please, keep tellin' me the truth. Did you curse my sister's babe?"

The worm surged: its bile singed her throat. *I've told you what's true.*

Jennet had started to shudder, her eyes glazing and rolling up, as if they were searching the underside of her skull. Then her knees gave. She buckled over. Martha lunged to catch her but Jennet's weight pulled them both to the shingle. Martha kept hold, trying to keep Jennet upright as she unwound her friend's neckerchief and pushed it between Jennet's jaws. Strange whining noises came from them. Of a sudden her own voice came in a stutter. It was strange to hear it, hoarse and feeble from lack of use. In her mouth her tongue treadled, trying to form useful sounds. What emerged was lowing, was cow-song, *there now, there now*, intended to be soothing. Jennet's spine arched, her head fell back, in the gravel her heels drummed. *Stay with me*, Martha urged in a shapeless keening. She patted Jennet's cheeks, her forehead. *Stay, stay, my friend*. It was an effort to push the sound out, past the blockage of the worm.

Moments passed. Jennet juddered and heaved. After a time her heels slowed, their drumming less violent. She lolled. Martha waited, then prised her friend's mouth open. Jennet was still breathing. She hadn't swallowed her tongue. *Come now, come back now*. Pleading, though her friend was barely conscious. It was not time; not Jennet's time. Not here, in Martha's hold.

If news of the fit reached the witch man, what then?

Impossible. Unallowable. She hauled Jennet up, taking her small weight across her shoulders. The heat was insufferable, an assault. She thought of the Salt Dyke witches, even now being consumed in another heat. Across the street was the Archer house, where Jennet lived with her sister. Tom Archer's cows were in the way and they clustered around Martha's ribs before parting to let them through. On her shoulder Jennet was reviving, the dead weight of her lessening as her soul came back to her body. They shuffled through the yard to the back door; Martha banged on it. Every part of her was in revolt, wanting to get away. On her shoulder Jennet surged, drooling phlegm down the back of Martha's bodice. Light footsteps were coming, arriving at the door. It opened. Liz Godbold stood in the gap.

She is sick, Martha mimed, *with a fit.*

She unhooked Jennet, delivered her to Liz. Against Liz's chest Jennet's head sagged, the birthmark showing vivid against her drained-looking skin, her words coming faint and slantways from the corner of her mouth. "Thank you, Martha." With effort Jennet lifted her head. "I'm afeared for you, Martha. I'm afeared *of* you as well. Is it for you the witch man's come?"

———

Martha reeled away, out through Archer's hen-scraped yard and along Tide Lane. Almost at the harbour she turned again onto the beach, going to the strandline where sea holly grew in spiny blue tangles. Its waxy stems thrust from the stones and came free with a tug. Mam's old cutting knife was in her pouch and with it she cut the sprays into sections, roots, leaves, flowers. Autumn with its harvest of births was a busy time, with new lives coming quick or slow or sometimes only briefly into the world. She would have need of this good herb that had healing in all its parts. Her mind started up, a feverish tallying. Jennet was right: too many had been lost—babes or their mams, sometimes both. The number, the fact of it, made her blink, as if it were pecking at her face.

She stopped cutting. The blue sprays lay heaped at her feet. She gathered them up. Going home the sea was grey and still, striped like a mackerel; the bleached light made a mirror of it that was calming to look at and at the same time she knew to be deceptive. There were faults in the shining surface through which dark things could come. She was nearly level with Knoll

House—Kit's home—when her legs were suddenly disobedient, weakening with each step. Then they folded, forcing her to kneel. Some sudden vision of herself, hunched and repentant as she whipped herself with a scourge.

Stones dug painfully into her skin. She took up a handful of pebbles, grey and brown and plum, counting them out in her palm. Her mind slid, resistant, shying away from the truth. Seeing again and through a stretch of years the babes—not many, boys and a girl—born sick, born frail, blue-lipped, stunted, with no chance of life.

Her lips began to move as they did when she questioned or spoke sternly to herself, as though she were another person. Oh, oh, she would pray for them, extra blessings for the dead babes. Ask Kit to let her visit Prissy in the gaol; protest Prissy's innocence to the judge. To the witch man, if he summoned her.

The stones lay quiet in her palm. They at least would not tell. She let them fall. On the street the cows stood, unconcerned. She went into her own yard and roped the back gate closed. Kit's land, her garden, were safe ground. The sun had burned away the early morning vapour and its blaze was full and severe on the length of line where the washed sheet hung. On the wash-house, where the poppet hid.

FIVE

Thursday

Once in her sleep she flung out an arm to fend off the dream. The movement threw her into day. Not yet dawn, the night just come through blue-violet and close and material, as if lingering in the chamber, reluctant to depart. Through it Mam's voice sounding, a caution of some kind. In the corner a mass of coddling air, forming a figure that she tries to blink away.

Aye, nay, aye, undreamt of for years this sighting of herself as a child—a girl—sore-eyed, thin as a finger in a worn smock. Standing alone and ignored in the seedy tavern, its air felted with odours and sin. Mam at supper; Mam pushing Martha off her lap; Mam at work, straddling the thighs of an "uncle," one of several who visit after dark. Oh, interminable dusks in her cot-bed in the eaves of the attic with the pillow pulled over her head, its sparse straw stuffing not quite muting the grunts and fleshy slappings issuing from Mam's bed. Fitful sleep, stale dawns breaking with the uncle sometimes good-humoured and benign, tossing Martha a spare coin, but more often foul-mouthed and awake, clouting Mam, cuffing Martha. Or more. Or worse. Fingerings, bruisings. A forced entry. Their last morning ushered in by an unremarkable daybreak, Mam already up and dressed, the uncle sprawled and insensible, dead in the bed, his eyes rolled back, his jaw hinged lopsidedly open as though in the night some landslide had occurred and carried off his soul.

The scene like a dream, like this one she is dreaming. Mam sitting motionless in their only chair, defeated. Some essence, a tautness, all gone. Clasping in one fist a doll-shaped stump of wax that she pushes into Martha's palms. Saying, Take it. Saying, Hide it. Use it scarce. Use it well. Only when you've need. But use it.

Saying, 'Tis all we got, this little power, as she folds Martha's fingers carefully over it like it is precious, a thing of grace. Then she gets up and bundles into her shawl her few things, her best wool stockings, the set of brass bowls and scissors, her small stash of coins. Mam's two sides so clear now: one mercenary and pragmatic; the other still capable of fondness. Of a sudden drawing Martha to her, kissing Martha with her scabby lips, fierce kisses, so strange a thing for Mam to do. Saying, God keep you, as she turns at the door. God keep you always. Mind yourself. Hide the doll. The small window gives its mean view, enough to watch Mam fleeing; palm-sized, poppet-sized. Then, gone.

Warmth flees from Martha's clothes. Her lungs hold no breath. The scene presents itself with brutal exactness, the loop of ship's twine hanging from the bedpost, Mam's crucifix dangling from it, the disordered sheets. The uncle is lumpen and crudely dead. The doll is lumpen and crudely made. Someone—Mam?— has thrust a needle through its jaw.

She collapses into Mam's chair and sits for an hour, for ever, wrestling with opposing facts until the lard-faced landlord comes slamming in to re-christen her—doxie's brat, murderer's whelp—before hurling the last of their possessions into the street. Outside she rescues Mam's cedarwood casket which by

some miracle is unbroken. It is not yet dinnertime and she is
not yet eleven, motherless, homeless, the sea vomiting phlegm-
coloured waves, a goading wind at her back, wandering Cleftwater in a kind of stupor, from the beach to the locked church
and on, to the poorhouse. There is nothing, she has nothing
save this mean inheritance: the casket, the poppet; the worm
beginning its work in her throat. Strange gifts.

———

She woke again. Intolerable, oh, unbearable. The memory, the
grief of it fully back: it was *in* her, a spasm like a strained muscle, a wound split freshly open. The poppet was a charm. The
poppet was a weapon. She must not use it. She must not keep
it. These facts or the knowing of them enlarging, tightening in
her mind, until they were fully present in her consciousness,
in the room, stark and inarguable.

Today, this day: she must get up and bring an end to the
poppet—melt it down entirely, pour the wax away.

She sat up and slapped her ears. Mam receded, or her dirge
did. She pulled back the shutter. A first rip of gold in the sky.
The sea like milk. She dressed and picked up her shoes and went
in stocking feet down the narrow stairs. The door to the main
bedchamber was a little ajar. Agnes slept under the canopy of
the marriage bed, covered only by the sheet draped over the
orb of her pregnancy. Her hair was loose and spread over the
bolster. There was a dent in it where Kit's head had been. Martha
stole in and collected the chamber pot. Downstairs the door to
Kit's room was closed and his hound, Matthew, lay across the
threshold. As she went past he lifted his muzzle and she stroked
his head, savouring the softness of his fur.

In the yard she emptied the contents of the pot over the fence onto the midden-heap. Then she went to the wash-house and took the poppet from its hiding place. The hand that held it felt unclean. Bile rose in her throat. In it the worm stirred and its action caused her lips to work, small clicking noises, the beginnings of words like those a minister would speak when addressing God. Let the poppet go. Let it go back to what it had once been: a simple stalk of wax. She went to the kitchen, lit the trivet, put Prissy's pan over the flame. The copper warmed, the air above it wavered. She rested the doll on the pan's base and almost immediately the wax gave, thinning and then beginning to spread, as if in surrender.

From the passageway she heard footsteps. The kitchen curtain moved. Simon, coming in. She put the lid on the pan.

"Mistress wanted chicken for today's dinner. Do we have one? I'll pluck it for you, if you want."

She stared at him, blank. The commotion in her head was huge. Then she summoned herself, went to the pantry, took the bird from its hook. *Pluck it outside*, she told him, indicating the back door.

He nodded. "I'll do that." She heard the back door close and a minute later his tuneful whistling started up. From the pan she picked out the poppet. It was warm and tacky in places but she knew that it was still potent. She put it in her pocket together with some coins from the purse that Prissy kept hidden among the cloths and old linen in the storeroom. She went out by the front door and turned right for Kit's field, following the track that ran parallel to the house down to the shore.

The beach was smooth and empty, inviolate. A shifting pearl-coloured mist hung an arm's width above it. Her confusion was waning, making space for a rise in her spirits, subtle adjustments of an inner barometer. All things at peace. The village at her beck this morning, in this best hour in this best of places—the shore with its constancy, its reassurance of water and stone. She had only to wait, to be open and waiting, and the Lord or Mam would lift her. She mouthed a prayer, asking for confirmation. After some seconds it came, a small rising sensation in the muscles of her chest. At the water's edge she cupped the poppet in her palm. Truly there was no honourable use for it. Reviving it had been a mistake, born out of panic. Let it go to the waves. Let God take it—this error, this sin— in exchange for Prissy. She would surrender it gladly if her friend were spared. She held the poppet by its yellow head and drew back her arm. Small, mild waves lapped and fell back, lapped and fell back; they were her only witnesses. She flung. The poppet arched into the curtain of haze. She heard it pierce the still water. Already it would be sinking to its sandy bed where only the currents would find it.

O God wash me thoroughly from mine iniquity, and cleanse me from my sin. She was free of the poppet, and no harm done. Let there be no further harm.

The sun was clear of the horizon and stronger now. She lifted her face to its cleansing heat and felt relief, the colour returning to her soul. There was a bit of time before Mistress Agnes got up. Martha would walk, pick some plants. Always she had need of plants. Her clogs were full of tiny brown stones that jabbed as she walked, but she was free and Prissy was not and her martyr's shoes were the right penance. She went south along the beach towards the harbour, scanning the shingle for sea kale, nipping the new leaves with her thumbnail. The fishing fleet was out and she could just see the last brown sails rounding the Holleswyck sandbar. Its bell-buoy tolled the warning, over and over. At the harbour she watched the tide turning, dropping away from the barnacled steps that led to the harbour wall. It would be pleasant to walk here later, to bathe her feet in the calm green water, after a day's work had been done. The sundial in the market square showed it was half past six and she stood for a few moments to watch its slice of shadow grow.

She turned for home. The village was coming awake and the air carried morning smells, salted fish and baking bread, and from John Sparham's cottage the yeasty scent of brewing ale. Five or six yards along the beach Liz Godbold and her oldest son were opening up their fish stall, Liz's litter of small black-and-tan terriers skirling at her heels. Martha bought two eels, smoked to the colour of leather and strung together through their gills on a length of twine. The transaction was quick and silent; Liz's look slid, evading Martha's. Hesketh's forge had started up, filling the air with din, the ring of a hammer on pliant metal.

At the garden gate she was struck by the notion of repair. How some things were beyond correction. How others could be mended or made good.

SIX

Home. The mist was all gone and the washed sheet hung limp on the line. Under it were the hogs, sprawled full length on a patch of almost grassless ground. When they saw her they got up and came complaining. She had kept back a bowl of cabbage and turnip parings, and she went to the kitchen and threw the scraps down. While they ate she scratched around the ears of the piebald hog, the bigger of the two and her favourite. He grunted and lifted his snout to grin at her. He had a big grizzled patch over one side of his head. Sometimes he would grin at her from the grubby white side and sometimes from the other. He was marked for the table come All Hallows, when the baby was due. She must curb her fondness for him.

She glanced up at the window of the main bedchamber. Mistress Agnes was still abed, growing big with the babe. Mistress hoped for a boy, Kit also. Agnes was the widow of a Salt Dyke alderman, privileged, used to having her way. Kit married her in spring last year and very quickly mistress was with child, though she'd lost that first one, a tiny boy. In the aftermath Agnes had been a trial, a test of loyalty, pettish and harsh, demanding every attention. She, Martha—Kit's one-time nurse-maid and for years his fondest companion—must daily attend to every whim of his proud, indulged wife. Most of her silent rancour was gone now; she had been disciplined, worked hard to grub it out of herself, like a rotten tuber.

Kit's dog, Matthew, had come out looking for water, and she went to the well and pumped, petting him while he lapped. On the line the sheet flapped. She ought to take it down. A cough came without warning, so sudden that she took hold of the washing line to steady herself. The rope lurched when she did. After the first wave there was a break. Her throat felt raw. She opened it to suck in air but the breath set off another bout as fierce as the first.

Then it stopped. When she opened her eyes she saw what she had put on the linen. Small clots, red as berries. She had marked it, the way she herself was marked. It would have to be washed again. Slowly she unpegged it. All summer the worm had grown and all summer she had kept away the knowledge of it, from Kit as well as herself. She felt worn down by it. She was *being* worn down by it. The dog was watching her with his head cocked, as if he had known all along. For a long time she stared at the clots and then her world around them— the house, the village. Her physick garden: a life's work. In her chest her heart toiled. In her head she could hear a prayer sounding. May God grant me healing. May God grant me this autumn, to greet Kit's babe and hold it close.

———

The kitchen was a blizzard of feathers. Simon was on the kitchen stool holding the half-plucked chicken over a sack.

She flapped at him. *Out! Out!*

He grinned. "Don't fret, Martha." He looked at the mess. "I'll sweep up after. I come in 'cause it's too hot to be outside."

She caught up a handful of feathers. *Keep these.*

"I will."

She watched him work and then took two cups from the shelf and poured them both some cider. They had pressed it together, she and Prissy. Every mouthful a reproach.

Where's master?

"In his room. Been in there all morning." Simon looked pointedly at the cider jug. "He'll likely welcome some of that. He went upstairs to see my lady, and then he come back down and shut himself behind his door." He nodded at her. "I dursn't go in. But you can. He's always pleased to see you."

There was a gold hair stuck to his tunic. One of Prissy's. She picked it off. Simon saw it also, and when she made to put it on the fire he stopped her and coiled the hair into a ring and put it in his pocket. "To bring her home," he said. She nodded. Tears pricked. She filled another cup with cider and was about to take it to Kit when Agnes called from upstairs. Simon stopped plucking.

Take this one to master. Martha took down a fourth cup, filled it for Agnes. Partway up the stairs she remembered the chamber pot, most likely what mistress wanted. She went back and fetched it. The stairs were steep and narrow and she went slowly lest she spill the drink. At the door she had to juggle the cup and pot before knocking. The room was in twilight, the shutters still drawn.

"Drink in one hand and the pot in the other?" Agnes pulled a face. "You mean to be helpful Martha, but truly . . ."

Comely mistress, always so ready to find fault. Martha put

the pot discreetly under the bed and the cider on the rosewood table, one of Kit's wedding gifts for Agnes. The top had an in-laid pattern of flowers that Kit said were carved of bone. The cup scarcely touched the pattern before Agnes seized it and drank. Martha went to the shutters and opened them. Daylight poured in.

"It's too bright, Martha!"

Pardon, mistress. She adjusted the shutters so that mistress's face was in shade. Agnes's cheek was marked from the bolster, where the linen sheet had creased. She fell back against it with a sigh.

"The babe lies badly today. It crushes my guts."

May I look? Martha lifted the coverlet. Straight away she could see the swelling, of mistress's hands and ankles. The orb of the babe looked uneven. The top of it was sunken and the lower portion bulged. It seemed to have dropped overnight, like a full moon about to set. She looked to Agnes for permission, then ran her hands over it. Here was a foot. Here an elbow. The babe was very big.

She stood and pulled up the sheet. The room had an odour, an intimate, sickroom smell. Mistress needed to bathe. *You would feel better if . . .* She made washing motions.

"If you are quick with it, Martha, and not too rough with your cloth."

She went down to the kitchen and took the big kettle from its hook, filling a basin with warm water that she brought up-stairs. Agnes got slowly out of bed and stood over the pot, cradling her belly.

"It's so heavy. It lies on my hips."

Agnes crouched. The contents of the pisspot were bright yellow and frothy. Martha helped mistress take off her nightshift, sopped the cloth, worked it over the pale freckled skin of Agnes's arms, soaped her pits and wiped them clean. Agnes's breath was sour and Martha kept her head lowered. She washed down mistress's spine, its knobs, the flat bones at the back of her hips, careful not to press too hard, that the cloth be not too hot or harsh. Even so, Agnes recoiled from her every touch. Gently she prised mistress's legs open, working the cloth upwards from the knees. The groin bulged. The babe's head was down—well down. She rocked back on her heels while she reckoned, counting the weeks and days. The babe was due in late October—more than a month away. But this morning's evidence was unmistakable, plainly visible between mistress's thighs.

"Why do you peer like that? Is all well? Is there something wrong with the babe?"

Nay, mistress. She spread her fingers into fans, trying to quell Agnes's distress. *There's nothing wrong.*

A truth of sorts. She bid Agnes sit while she went to the cabinet and took out fresh linens, a clean shift for mistress, a fresh sheet and cover for the bolster. Agnes had embroidered them herself, a pattern of plaited vines that made the letters A and C. Agnes and Christopher: twined. Martha helped Agnes back into the grand bed, cupping mistress's feet so that Agnes need not lift them, then plumped the bolster behind her back. All this Agnes let her do in silence. There were seldom any thanks. When Martha drew up the sheet Agnes kicked it away.

"Can't you see I'm too hot?" A noisy sigh. "Ask my husband to come with a book. I would have him read to me."

Mistress, his door is closed. He is busy with some work.

"It is a small thing he can do," Agnes said, suddenly peevish, "for his wife, who is heavy with his child. Heavy in body, and today, heavy in heart." Her head dropped as though its weight were too much for her neck. Tears squeezed onto her lashes. "Oh, I know full well, Martha, that I complain too much. It's only that the babe lies so heavy. And there are pains—not all the time, they come and go—but they're sometimes so fierce."

Where?

"Here—under the babe, and across it. Like this." Agnes made small clenching movements with her hands. "What are these pains? Is the babe coming?"

She hesitated. Agnes saw it, was immediately vexed. Red flamed up her neck. "What, Martha? Is there something wrong? There *is* something wrong—"

No, mistress. She composed her mouth into a smile, folded her hands atop each other and pillowed them against her cheek. *The babe is peaceful.* Scribed the babe's bulk on the air. *But he is big.* Pointing at the cradle, standing at the ready beside the large bedroom window. *And so he may come soon.*

Agnes's face altered. When she spoke again her tone was softer. "I would be glad if that were so. If my son came soon. I have wondered how I will bear to carry him for another month." Her eyes flicked, her expression hunted-looking. Finally she looked at Martha. "We'll need extra hands once he is here. We need Prissy back. Or if not her, then some other woman to help." She waved at the door. "Tell all this to Kit. Go now, and tell him that the babe is near, and that he must, he *must*, get Prissy back." She stopped, caught her breath. Her hands flew to her stomach. "Here it is again."

Martha saw the mounded sheet pucker. Agnes whitened. "The babe—this pain—it drives me from my wits." Pretty, peevish mistress, frightened now. "Wait, Martha. Send my husband up. I'll tell him myself. I forget you are a country nurse. I forget you are dumb."

SEVEN

What did it matter, that Agnes thought so little of her? Kit was loyal; she had his love. Downstairs his door was still closed. She knocked, softly at first and then more loudly, stopping when he called out "Away." He sounded tense, unlike himself. She went through the kitchen to the cool store. Simon had swept up. The naked chicken was on a plate. She jointed it, put it to stew in the largest of Prissy's pans. She had in mind to make a pottage with barley and some garden chard. It grew at the sunniest end of the garden, a bright stripe of green.

She picked enough to fill the creel. The sun beat on her head. Her hands picked, her mind worked. Somehow she had grown old with no kin but the plants. The best part of her life she'd given for Kit: his own mother had died not long after birthing him; over time Martha had taken a mother's place. Her devotion to him lay just under the surface, a sinew of love. Because of it she'd taken no husband, forgone children, denied herself fleshly pleasures in the steady progression of her life. All these sacrifices of her own choice; she had made them freely. Until Agnes came, she had not regretted them.

Maybe the babe's arrival would claim the last of Kit's attention, drive Martha further from his mind. Or maybe it would affirm something, strengthen family ties. Agnes would determine which. Mistress Agnes of the two faces: with Kit she was charming and spoony; with others she was haughty and demanding, a difficult woman to like. For a span of seconds Martha saw herself as Agnes must: an ageing servant in a faded green gown, her hair beginning to lose its colour, her skin its lustre, her girth slackening and filling out, chapped hands like skinned spiders crawling over the plants. She stopped. Chewed the inside of her cheeks. These hands that mistress thought so lacking: they were honest hands; had served tirelessly for forty-seven years. All her skill was boned into them.

———

She spent the morning in the kitchen making bread. Mistress was fretful, calling demands and complaints down the stairs. She was hungry but when Martha took up a bowl of stew she took only four spoonfuls before declaring she had room for no more. Later Kit brought up a chair and sat by the bed. From downstairs Martha could hear them talking, Agnes's tone high like a child's, Kit's gentle responses. The kitchen's warmth was a trial. Martha washed the pots, ladled a small bowl of pottage for herself, and supped it sitting on the garden bench. When she'd finished she put the bowl under the bench and went to the wash-house, glancing at the rafter where the poppet had been. It was a relief, to have it gone. She filled the tub and rinsed and rinsed the birthing sheet but the new stains were resistant—lodged in the weave. She hung it again on the line. The heat would bake it dry.

From the pump she drew up a bucket of water and took it to the stretch of earth where her herbs grew, greeting each plant with her fingers. Her battered tin watering cup hung from a nail in the wall, and again and again she filled it, dousing the roots of the plants. They leaned towards her as she worked. In each one there was a gift and a purpose that was of God but also of the earth. Something of it passed to her as she touched. Parsley that made a woman's milk flow. Sage with its furred tongues that could make it stop. She stepped farther in. In the middle were the taller herbs, grown for the sicknesses that came every winter to the village. She knelt. The plants swayed, a confusion of scents and colours. To be among them was to lose herself, to enter another country. Colour surrounded her, an ocean of yellow, flower heads like burst suns, ranks of green pillars, their stems stout with sap. To see Kit's babe born and perhaps, God willing, to live and watch the child grow— this was all her hope.

She reached for a spire of foxglove, fingering its stippled pink caps. The poison plants had seeded themselves at the back of the bed. Foxglove, hemlock, monkshood. They throve on nothing, on poor soil, in meagre light. Dangerous plants. Necessary plants, that she had never quite brought herself to root out. She thought of all the taken women—the ones already dead, those waiting to die. They would be glad of such plants, of their numbing poison. Pray God they would never be needed.

She waded out of the bed. The afternoon's purpose was suddenly clear. She went inside, knocked at Kit's study door although it was open. Kit got up, came to her. Behind him Agnes sat in the high-backed mahogany carver chair, her limbs relaxed, her face soft.

Martha saw she had interrupted something, the beginnings of a love act, perhaps. *I beg pardon, master, mistress, if I've—*

Kit laughed. "You haven't disturbed us, Martha." He motioned her in, went to his table, and sat down. In November he would turn thirty. By then he would be a father. Marriage had completed him, brought him fully into manhood. Agnes had made a gentleman of him. Pale lemon light came through the big window, lighting his hair and the long plait of his lovelock, its pearl glistening at the tip.

She held both palms out like shallow cups, her sign for wanting to talk.

I worry for Prissy. That she hungers. There is bread, ale, she could have. I would take some to her. May I do this?

Agnes looked at Kit. "What is she saying?"

"She is anxious for Prissy. She asks if she may take food to the gaol, for Prissy."

Agnes's face creased. "I think . . . not," she said slowly. "It would not be proper. It would reflect badly on us, on this household, to be seen to aid a witch."

Kit breathed in slowly. "Sweetheart, Prissy is no witch. She's been taken in error. And the gaol's a dreadful place. They've got all manner of women, not just from here but from Holleswyck and Sandgrave too, all crammed in the dark and dirt, living off the most meagre rations. Prissy will be suffering. Some decent food will boost her spirits while she waits." He sighed. "I hear, oh, all manner of things about her supposed crimes, from slight rumours to the wildest accusations I struggle to believe."

"What crimes?"

"Well. That she gave bad grain to some of the Irish who were begging here in the spring and that some of their elders took sick, and one of them died." Kit's brow furrowed. "And

also that she killed, or had a hand in killing, the Archer babe."
He looked at Martha. "How is this rumour come about? You
were at that birth with her, weren't you?"

Aye. We birthed the babe together.

"What happened?" Agnes said.

The babe came, but barely alive. Martha pinched her nose
and mouth closed. *Born like this. He couldn't breathe.*

"What does she mean?"

"I think she is saying that the child was born with some
affliction," Kit said. "Not able to breathe. Is that it, Martha?"

Aye.

"It was born like that?"

It was.

"You could not save it? With all your skill?"

She could feel the worm sawing at her throat. *I did what
I could.* Her hands moved slowly, as if reluctant. *I tried. There
was little . . . that could have saved him.* This much at least
was true. She steepled her fingers. *I have prayed for him, for
his mother too.*

"Mistress Archer lives?"

*Aye. For now. She is very weak. God willing, she will pull
through.*

"That's good. That's heartening," Kit said. "Pray God she'll
recover." He was distracted, sifting through his desk's clutter,
the mess of maps and bills and letters scribed in strange scripts,
some of them stained red from the light coming through Kit's
prized glass goblet. Its rim was patterned, an etched garland
of mother pelicans pecking at their breasts.

"—speak with Master Makepeace," Kit was saying. "Martha

may be able to help Prissy's case." Again he looked at Agnes. "Prissy needs someone to speak up—speak *for* her—make the witchfinder know the truth."

"Then you go, Christopher. You go, and speak to him, tell him of Prissy's innocence and bring the girl home. Martha will stay here with me."

"Sweetheart, in the matter of the Archer babe, what Martha knows is crucial. It could save Prissy's life. So she must go, and I must go with her. It is a matter of common sense."

"It makes no such sense. There is much to do here, and Martha has already been out today." A pout; mistress's hazel eyes glinted. "You give her too much licence, husband. I know of no other household that allows its servants the freedoms Martha has. And as she constantly reminds us, we are short-handed. Her place is here, aiding me and doing her work."

"Agnes. I wish her to come with me. We'll not be long, an hour at most. If we are able to get Prissy freed and bring her home, you may count it as an hour well spent—"

"You over-estimate your influence," Agnes said, cutting Kit off. "I cannot see that Master Makepeace will consider your testimony, even less the prating of a serving woman—especially one that cannot talk."

Kit's chair scraped the floor. He stood. "Agnes," he said, his tone an accusation. "We will go, and go now; find Master Makepeace and acquaint him with the facts." He looked at Martha. "Gather what you need."

EIGHT

They went together down Tide Lane. Kit walked in silence, with long, scissoring strides that she struggled to match lest she spill the ewer of ale. He noticed and slowed down.

Kit said, "I am sorry that your mistress spoke to you as she did. She is not well today. She didn't intend . . . what she said."

'Tis nothing, master. Her hands made brushing motions, unconvincing even to her.

"I hope . . ." Kit began again. He broke stride, came to a stop. He was sweating. A puny breeze came off the ocean, rifling his hair. "Agnes can be sharp, I know it, especially when she's vexed. But Martha, please don't take her words to heart. She never meant . . . She never means to hurt." His eyes were full, seeking hers. For once she couldn't do what he asked: reassure him; comfort herself.

She managed a nod. *We should make haste.*

"Yes," he said, crestfallen.

They walked again, more quickly. They passed the run of familiar houses, Spalding, Durriken, Farrow, Archer. Limp nets and washing being bleached on sagging lines. Cats and goats and dogs and chickens inert in meagre patches of shade. Then Piss Alley with its forceful stink. Opposite was the faded black needle of the watch-tower, empty now that the fishing fleet was anchored for the day. The road was quiet. Their shoes scuffed. Her stockings chafed. They went through the market, a stretch of road filled with stalls and handcarts and trestle tables, strangely empty of buyers. The fishmonger, the alewife, the cooper, the undertaker, the smith; she knew them all, Kit too, but none of them gave any greeting. She glanced at Kit, saw his discomfort. Knew this to be a starting symptom, this turning away of once friendly faces, this sliding away of eyes.

Ahead was the Moot Hall, its half-timbered walls stark against the bald blue sky. Cleftwater's landmark, not a large building but an imposing one, built centuries ago when there had been more land between the village and the sea. Its upper floor housed the Great Hall, where all Cleftwater's important business was transacted—disputes heard, accounts settled, justice dispensed. In front of it a crowd was clustered, watching intently. Kit and Martha skirted the edge of it, arrived at the entrance to the Hall. Kit conferred with a guard who stood aside to let him pass.

"When you've seen Prissy, wait for me in the street." She nodded. Already her pulse was speeding up. The Moot Hall had a double staircase, one flight leading up to the Great Hall's oak-panelled chamber, the other down to the gaol. She went down it. The steps were few but steep. Moss grew at the mouth of the short tunnel that went into the gaol. Martin Strong was on watch.

"Martha? What brings you here?" He was startled, overturned his stool as he got up. Another village lad birthed by her, grown up now, a man, fine-featured except for his jaw that was large and over-long, like a mule's.

"You're wantin' Prissy?"

Aye. She looked past him into the gaol's depths. In her girl-hood it had been a stables and the old stalls remained, some with their halter rings still set into the brick. Last winter, when Kit's money troubles made prison conceivable, she'd come down to gauge the state of the gaol. Then, the floor was churned mud and its air frigid. Now, the place was stifling, its air rank and circling with flies. She could make out the soil bucket in the middle of the tramped earth floor. She breathed through her sleeve to hinder the worst of the stench. The gaol was full. Every stall held a prone shape—featureless in the dusk—sitting, lying, collapsed.

"She's not here," Martin said. "They took her a while ago, across the road to the Four Daughters. There's that many women, they're using some rooms in the alehouse. For walking 'em, I'm told." His wore a stunned expression, as if he had been hit. "More of 'em coming in each day. I dunno where they all come from. I dunno where to put 'em." On his neck was a mark like a ragged red star, still angry-looking, the last of a boil that on Tuesday she had lanced and poulticed. Without thinking she came close to look at it. He jerked his neck away. "How can it be that the Devil's brides were among us all this time? Living here, doing their bad work?"

She put a hand to her forehead, rubbed at her brow. *I am as amazed as you.* Then she remembered the parcel and opened it to show him the bread.

"For Prissy?" He hesitated. "She's not allowed it, Martha. I dursn't give it her. I dursn't make it worse for her. The women, they're only to have gaol rations. Such as they are."

She nodded. *Have it yourself.*

"That's all right. I don't need it," he said firmly. She fingered the wrapped loaf, wondering whether to wait.

"Best not to wait," he said, reading her thoughts. "They're walking the women for a long time—all through last night, all through today. So I'd say, Prissy won't be back for a while." He regarded her. "That's what they do to 'em, Martha. To all the women. Young, old, sick: it makes no difference."

She shook her head, incredulous. Behind Martin the gaol's gloom had begun to seethe. The shapes were moving: stirring, sitting up, beginning to strain at their tethers. They were shades, spirits; they were women she knew.

"—pray they go gentle on Prissy," Martin was saying softly. "But likely not."

Eyes gleamed at her from the murk. The women: dirty, tangle-haired. Gape-mouthed, damaged-looking. A low keening was starting up, soft pleas and cries, the noise something she had heard before, recent, a stamp on her mind.

"Best if you go now," Martin said again, mildly urgent. He eyed the bread. "Best take that home."

The women wanted what she had. Bread, drink. Sustenance. The keening intensified, battened her conscience. Martin was urging her to go, away, home, where it was safe. Nay, nay: she would not. It would be wrong to go. She went past him and in. Her eyes adjusted. Old Ellen Warne, here. Hannah Holland, a dairy lass of maybe sixteen years, here. Three women from Sandgrave she knew by sight though not by name ranged along one wall. Ma Southern in the far corner, lying in her own filth. She could feel some courage hardening in her. She broke the bread, dipped each piece in ale, bent to push it into the reaching hands. How quickly the loaf reduced, was almost gone. The last piece she kept back. She got up, went to Martin.

Give this to Prissy.

"I told you. I can't do that, Martha."

Yes, you can. She prised his sweating hand from his dagger pommel and smoothed out the fingers, placed it on his chest.

"What's that mean?" His eyes widened.

She meant for him to search his conscience, find the necessary courage. But his face only clouded. "I dunno what you're saying. What I know is, the gaol's near full. There's as many witches as gulls. That's how it seems. It's got hard to know what's right to do." He jerked his head to the street. "It's got so that everyone's afeared. Even me, Martha."

Anger, a bolt of it in her breast. She could feel herself expanding with its force. Her own history was here with its broken bones, its snapped sinews, Mam's barbarous ending, the whole bitter jag of the past that was now shoving her into the future. She struck, harder than she meant, at Martin's chest.

"What?" he said, stepping back.

Do it. For Prissy. For any of them. Just . . . take it.

He took it. She left him standing in the gaol's dimness, out of reach of the sun. Went up to the street, into the heat that wrapped the village like a shroud. She pushed past the bailiffs, crossed the road to the alehouse. She would go in, find Prissy, take her to Kit. Two more bailiffs stood at the alehouse door. Already the anger was thinning, draining out through the faults in her soul. Robert Bullard barred her, asked her business. When she told him he grunted and sent her back out.

She stood uncertainly in the middle of the road. Twenty

paces away was the Market Cross with its thatched roof, the only other prospect of shade. It was rammed with spectators. She scanned them. No sign of Kit. The Moot Hall clock struck a quarter hour, then the half. She thought of Prissy, the gaoled women; quick-darting thoughts that fell over themselves. Then, Agnes. Free Agnes, big with child. She went back to the Moot Hall stairs, signed to Ned Bullard—Robert's brother—who knew her and knew what she asked. He took her up. The Hall door was ajar and she peered through the gap: a cluster of folk, men and women, Liz Godbold among them, queueing for an audience with the witch-hunter.

Who are they all?

"Tale-tellers," Ned said bluntly.

Kit was near the back. Ned went to him, tapped his shoulder, pointed to where Martha stood. Kit looked tense, on the cusp of anger. His fingers wrote: *Go home.*

NINE

She went back by the shore, hoping for a breeze. The tide was out and she walked below the kelp line where there was sand. Her steps left a line of clear prints. They worried her, they were a sign, evidence of her freedom, her trip to the gaol. Shafts of afternoon light fingered the houses, staining them yellow. How was it possible that Cleftwater had got so afflicted? Which households, which lives would be touched by the hunt?

She had these thoughts, then made herself dismiss them. Where they led she didn't want to follow. Approaching the house she found herself reluctant to go in, to the chores, to Agnes. She lingered for a few minutes watching the waves. They came in steadily, grey-green scallops rimmed with froth. The water was clear, inviting. She cupped her hands, brought the coolness to her forehead. A rogue wave came and then another, and she stepped back but not quickly enough. Water filled one of her clogs. She bent to empty it. At her foot was the poppet: unscathed.

She looked wildly around, trying to take stock. All else was in order, the shale, the dunes, the stand of pink valerian, the greying carcass of the wrecked boat. How could this be? She was certain, she had been sure of her throw. She thought through it again. Felt again her arm's lift, the poppet's slight clamminess between her fingers, its sound as it entered the water.

Her breathing was ragged. The poppet's eyeless gaze drew everything towards it. She could not decide: its reappearance—was it good or no? Why had it returned to her? Had Mam returned it to her? She kicked some wet sand over it, stepped away, half turned for home; rethought and came back. Impossible to leave it here, where other hands might find it, might use its powers for ill. Or worse: some other woman falsely accused of owning it. She picked it up through the stuff of her skirt, put it in her hip pouch. The thought came that the poppet was hers alone, was bound to her forever.

The prospect set her legs moving. There was half an hour before she would be missed at home. She went north, walking fast along the road that led to the Cleft. The poppet jogged in her hip pouch. A gleaming image of its waxy grin veered into her mind and she tamped it down. The shoreline curved and then bent inland. Where it angled was the mouth of the Cleft. She left the beach and went up the narrow street that ran parallel to the river. On both sides the houses were built close to, listing at all angles. Cleft-dwellers were a different sort—fisherfolk mostly, people of shade—shady livings, shady dealings. As if God's light seldom touched them. Simon was from here, his church was here; St. Hilda's, dour and cheerless, built against the flank of Psalm Cliff. At its crest the sand martins flocked. Their gabble carried, clear across the gulch.

She walked on, up into the Cleft. The afternoon light was sheer but the river was slow-moving and dark, almost black. Centuries ago a masonry bridge had joined the two cathedral-high banks; its foundations still stood and were always draped with drying nets. She went up the steps onto the abutment. On clear days the view was limitless, unimpeded across an expanse of sea stretching to Salt Dyke. She gripped the remains of a parapet with one hand and with the other felt for her pouch. It opened like a shout. Inside the poppet seemed to cower. She took it out: this last gift of Mam's that she could no longer endure. Not so much the doll itself but her dread of it; its legacy.

The tide was arriving in sluggish braids of current. Good. Let it wash the damned doll upstream where it would be caught in the reed beds, find a grave in the silt. Martha let it go. It fell but not far—caught by its legs in a crease of netting. She heard herself let out a bleat. It was cursed. *She* was cursed. She reached down. The net was stiff and crusted with salt that stung as it worked itself into the cracks in the skin of her palms. From Psalm Cliff the ferry was coming, pushing across the current. An array of figures sat or stood on it; church folk, coming back from evening prayers; a party of drinkers, coming for small beer at the Eel's Boot, the tavern on the nearside jetty. The drinkers had seen her. One of them saluted, a mock greeting. His companions' crude laughter glanced off the cliff and the hard water. She had got the poppet free of the net but she could not be free of it, not yet. Nor could she be caught with it. She pushed the poppet up her sleeve and retraced her steps. Over the Cleft the sky was a pale, leached blue. She needed somewhere dark for the burial. On the muddy bank at the foot of the jetty a small brindled dog with a scarred pelt nosed at the slurry pooled there—puke and rotting food and worse—and she was suddenly glad of it, this filthy place where people would not look.

With the tide fully in, the mudbank would be covered. Just now it was riddled with holes. Easy enough to find a resting place for the poppet. The mud was as much slime as clay. She crouched and dug in the black sludge. Every hole caved in and sealed itself, as if to resist any further blemish. The ferry had docked, the churchgoers disembarking, going off to their houses or the tavern. Up behind her a man hollered and whistled and the dog left off its rooting and ran away.

"Who's that there?"

She shrank down, trying to disappear herself but the man came on, squinting at her, determined to search her out.

"Martha? Martha Hallybread? Long time since you graced us on this side of the village."

Mogg Basford. A Welshman, come a long way east. Tall and rangy, though his skin had the Cleft-dweller's bloodless cast. In church he led the choir, chose the psalms and hymns, sang them in his resonant bass voice. She could feel his eyes on her, the light-blue bore of his look. She stood up. Beside him his dog crouched, rubbing its muzzle against his shin. The sky leaned, the mud sucked.

How be you, Mogg? she gestured.

He stood at the top of the bank and produced a cough, fleshy and wet.

"D'you hear it? That's how it goes with me." He pouted, looked past her. "It come early this year. The cough. Brung on with the heat." He hawked between his feet.

I will bring you—

"Ach, that's nice, Martha, but don't waste your herbs on me. Gin, now. That's my physick." His grin was lopsided, falling off his chin. "What are you looking for?" His dog followed as he lurched down the bank. "What have you lost?"

I, I dropped . . . She made a ring with her fingers for him to see. *A coin. No matter. I can't find it.*

"Aye, well. 'Tis a graveyard, the Cleft. Christ only knows what's been lost to it over the years."

Sweat stroked his cheeks, ran into his beard. The ferryman had come back to his vessel with a tankard of beer that he swigged as he watched them.

"It's a hot day, Martha. Will you take a drink with me?"

I thank you, but I must—

"Ah, come now." Mogg jerked his head at the Eel. "We don't have to go in. We can sit at mine. Just a cup. I owe it you. For all the care you took of my Judith before she passed. She would've wanted it, to say thank you. I'm sure your fine master and mistress won't grudge you one drink, eh? A sit-down for Martha and a tipple of good cheer." His rat-coloured beard broke open as he smiled. "A gin? A cider, then. Aye, that's your tipple. Come on. Take a cup of cider with a friend."

He seized her hand and led her up the bank to his cottage. There was a bench out front and he tried to make her sit, kicking away the creels and an eel trap to make room. She sat. She would humour him for a few minutes, and then she would go. Mogg went inside. The Cleft was very still and gave back the different sounds, the sand martins' clamour and the slurred merriment from the alehouse. Mogg was returning with a jug and two chipped beakers.

She got up. *I must be away, Mogg. I'm needed at home.*

"Aw now," he started to say before the cough overtook him.

She could hear the ragged working of his lungs, the rasp in his chest.

She indicated her pouch. *You must let me herb you. Let me tend—*

He shook his head. "I thank ye, but there's nothing'll touch what I got. No physick to bring my Judith back. Not even those weeds of yours, Martha." She knew what was coming, had heard this petition many times before. She backed away but Mogg caught her hand again. She tried to extract it from his grasp but he only increased his grip. In his face was ardour mixed with something else. A shrewdness. A slyness.

"It's a lonely life, Martha. Being a widow-man." He was studying her, too close. "I'm guessin' you got some idea of it, always being alone yourself. Except that you got family of a kind, living with the folk you do. But when you're like me, when you've had someone and then lost 'em and you still got your life ahead. Days of it. Empty days, maybe." He coughed some more. "Could well be I got the same sickness Judith got. That same rumble, in here. If I have, that's all right, I'm content for it to do its work." He looked out over the water, to St. Hilda's church and the graveyard above it, where his dead wife lay in the ground. "I don't know as I want too much more life. Maybe the Lord will call me soon. When He does I'll be glad enough to answer."

In her sleeve the poppet was softening, relaxing against her skin.

"Unless the Lord sends me some comfort," Mogg went on. "Someone to hold. To keep close. To share life with, while I still got it." He put calloused fingers to her chin and turned her face towards him. "Eh, Martha?" His eyes were cloudy, like boiled gooseberries. "Two people who've known each other as long as we have. We're not so young as we were but I reckon we still got time, eh? Whatever you want you can have. We can match for good or we can match just at night, if you get my meaning. You tell me which. Just know that I'd be willing—more than willing. I'd take your herbs then, Martha. If we were matched. 'Cause then I'd have reason to take them, so I would."

He'd been handsome once. He was smiling, warmed by his own daydream which was taking on colour and realness as he spoke. "Think on it. You'd have a man by your side. Keep you company in summer, keep you warm in winter." His eyes swivelled, raked over her. "Someone to protect you, keep you close in bad times like these when all is turned to rumour, to harm. When lonesome women can't feel safe."

I thank you. Gesturing, but not at him, with her other hand. *For your . . . kind words.* She tried again to free her trapped hand. *I must get home.*

"Let me walk you."

Not just now, Mogg.

"Ah Martha, why so hasty? Don't grudge me a few more minutes of your company." He was suddenly grave. "You know Cleftwater's not so safe as it was. We got witches among us. You mustn't go about alone. Besides, it would bring me some cheer to walk with you. So's folk know our Martha's not to be harmed."

She let out an exasperated breath. Then pointed up the muddy lane to where the cottages thinned and the gulley narrowed, a place favoured by shitters and whores, both. People went there to relieve themselves in all the different ways. A hope, fleeting, crossed his face. Then he knew what she meant. "I'll wait for you."

God love him, the sad old lubber. He should look elsewhere

for a new wife. She leaned into the bank and pissed over a fern. The sound of it was lost in the steady churr of crickets on the top field. Heat came off the earth. But no: it was coming from her, from her body, her over-heated mind. Even her piss was hot, etching the soil. She took the poppet from her sleeve and regarded it sourly, holding its head in a pinch. This witching doll that she'd tried so hard to get rid of: some part of her wanted its power to be true. Her grip softened. Maybe she could use it this once. Use it here, now. Maybe then Mogg would retreat with his unwanted advances.

Down the lane he waited, peering at her business. She wished again and with fervour that he would leave her alone and knew he would not. She had two choices: to go home by way of the open streets with Mogg in misguided high spirits at her hip, or slip away now up Cart Scour—a narrow track worn into the bank. There was light enough to see the way. She stowed the poppet in her pouch. Cart Scour was steep and always dank, and she grasped at plants as she climbed, ferns and long coils of vetch, their purple flowers going over now and turning to seed.

On the slope of the High Street she stopped to catch her breath. A view of the sea and the late day's light on it, brassy and burnt-looking. Home—Knoll House—was not so far and all downhill, and her lungs quieted as she went. The High Street was broad and well-lit, punctuated on each side by the entrances to the Scours, a lattice of sunless alleys so narrow a child might barely pass through them. The left-hand ones led to the river and the Cleft; the ones on her right sloped down to Kit's field. People—fisherfolk—eked hard livings here, in cramped, mean houses. Scour mothers were thin and exhausted, too often called to the Lord before their time. Their children were ravenous and sick. It was not uncommon for Martha to be fetched to some ailing fishwife, summoned for her charity as much as her skill with herbs. She was conscious of them now, watchfully clustered at the tops of their lanes. Beacon Scour. Dutchie's Scour. The next was Shitter's Scour: she could hear the grunted work of the feral pigs and dogs that liked to lurk there, browsing the mounds of dung. And here was Mogg emerging from it with his bent-kneed gait: even on land he was always at sea. She felt his mood, the strength of it, just as she saw his expression. The sunset had got into him, into his skin and hair. Oh, fool woman to have come this way.

"Why did you leave me, Martha?"

I need to get home. She made to go around him.

"Home, aye, and I said I'd walk you." He stepped in front of her, forcing her to a stop. "Not good enough for you, is that it?"

She shook her head, thrusting out her crossed hands. *I never said—I would never say that.*

It was true and she meant it, but he was determined to take offence. Bad language streamed from his mouth, insults like wanton and shameless and scut. Jezebel, jade. She stood with her head down and her hands clasped—a martyr's pose—thinking of his wife and children, dead of his temper as much as disease. He raged on. Witch. He was calling her a witch. Her thoughts sped up, careening from dead Judith to Prissy, from the stargazer babe to the poppet. Why hadn't she used it when she could? Mogg's words were slowing, his tirade burning out.

"—true enough. People think well of you. *I* think well of you." He blew out his cheeks and was briefly silent. His look was high, then suddenly penitent. "Think you might've taken me wrong, Martha. Or maybe I got ahead of myself. Aye, maybe I did. I was right glad to see you, 'cause you always lift my spirits. I thought as maybe we could spend some time together. But I didn't mean to fright you. If I did I'm sorry." He took off his hat and doffed it. His breeches were coming untied at the fly. "You're a good woman." Another lopsided smile. "We're neither of us beauties but I'll say this of you, Martha: you're comely enough for me. I mean it truly. And maybe it'll get so's you find me the same way." His eyes sought hers. "Give me a bit of cause for hope, eh?"

It was necessary to humour him, though what she really wanted was to shove him away. He crooked his arm, which she patted and gave back. Friends again, for now. She walked faster, lengthening her step. For a few paces Mogg kept up and then fell a little behind, walking in her wake. He talked on, words streaming from him like chaff in the wind. More compliments, or so he thought them; praise of her dependable looks, her Godliness, her healing hands. He chuckled, delighted with his wooing. The laugh turned to a cough. He started to hack. She searched in her pouch for something to give him and found only sow thistle.

"Tha's why I need you, Martha. You got herbs and a good heart." He wiped his mouth and grinned. Her very nearness was a spur. Of a sudden he was jubilant, seizing her, then capering them down the street like a groom. His dog caught his change of spirits, sprinting around them in circles. "Look at us, eh? Stepping out together. You holding that weed like a bride's posy." His jerkin stank of the fish he gutted, and she craned her head away. He was drunk on some vision of an unattainable future. He danced them on, past the doctor's house and the grocer's

and the chandlery. They were almost back at the tavern. In its
porch two men loitered.

"See here, friends," Mogg called, "see here my Martha, who's
bringing cheer to an honest man and given him reason to be
gay." He halted, put his lips to her ear. "And here's our little
party—now, don't be like that, Martha."

"She don't look so gay," said one of the men, the shorter
one, coming closer, to leer at her from a gap of inches. She
could see the salt in his eyelashes and coarse hair, on his lips
which were cracked open in a grin. Herry Gowler: fisherman,
wastrel, one of Cleftwater's gaolers. His companion was barely
a lad, scraggy with a nose like the butt end of a capon and ears
set at seeming right-angles to his head.

"Why now, 'tis our very own Martha Hallybread. *She* is
Mogg's darling," Herry crowed. His breath was sour with drink.

Mogg pulled her close. "That's my wish, gentlemen. She's
not said aye but she's not said nay either, so I've cause to hope.
Now, sirs, I pray you, show this good lady some respect."

"Is it true, Martha, what Mogg says? That there's to be a
weddin'?" Herry said. A slow grin. "Have you told Master Kit?
Has he given you his blessing? Or is it," he said, glancing at his
companion and back at her, "that you've put a spell on Mogg?"
His look was sly. "Master Kit marries, his loyalty has gone elsewhere. So now you're for bagging Mogg. Is that it, Martha?"

They thought her toothless, inconsequential in her dull
clothes, a model of mute forbearance, a gurning crone who
could be baited without consequence. She kept her face steady,
squeezing the sow thistle until its barbs bit her palm, willing
Mogg to put an end to his game. He said nothing. His grin was
wide, a provocation. The coals of her annoyance burst into

flame. She felt a meanness, the need to pay him out. She gave him a boiling grin before shoving him in the chest. *Leave off.* She held her ring finger to his face while her other hand removed a phantom wedding ring and tossed it to the gutter. *Not you. Never you.* Stepped back, then violently slapped her mouth. *Cease your mocking.* She could sense the rage spurting in him like water from a burst pump. *Speak no more to me.*

Mogg assessed her, stoat-eyed. "Well now. She wants no more of our company, lads, that's plain." He gave her an exaggerated bow. "It was a jest, Martha, just a bit of a game. But you take it as you see fit." He tore the sow thistle from her hand. "I'll bid you and your weeds good evening, you dry old maid. Maybe these other young sirs will be more to your liking." He looked at Herry. "Or maybe they're of a mind to catch themselves a witch."

He whistled for the dog and they went down Brine Scour and were gone. She clasped her hands to steady them. Haste, she must make haste. From the corner of her eye she could see Herry and his jug-eared friend exchanging smirks. When she set off again they followed, hanging back at first. The street's tilt and indifferent people only emboldened them, their taunts and quips getting louder and bolder as they darted about her, like herding dogs. "Be mine, Martha. Say yes to me. Marry *me*."

Dutchie's Scour. Cran Scour. She was almost at the foot of the hill where the High Street curved and opened out and became Tide Lane, running the length of the beach. Grope Scour was on her right, the last one. She turned into its shade. Uncertain light came from some of the houses, wan in the Scours' wrong dusk that was blotting out all hope of safety. At the top it was scarcely a shoulder's width across, though it widened as it sloped. Its cobbles ran with filth. She went rapidly down, passing shadows—listless, incurious women loitering in lightless doorways, a child prodding a wooden toy boat through a pool of muck. Every face was jaded, pinched with want. The lads were still following, silent in the alley's dead air, determined to prevent her escape. She began to run. The Scour dog-legged, darkened under a mass of branches, sloped down even more steeply before giving onto a flight of steps. As she came to the top of them there was a surge of clothing—bodies parting, a metallic chink. A shape brushed past and went quickly uphill and disappeared. A second shape crouched in an archway, pissing from under bunched petticoats. Martha halted. The woman started and dropped her skirts.

"What are you doin' here?" Jennet stood up, in the same movement pocketing a coin. Her cheeks were very flushed. She laughed a little, stroked down her hair. "Martha Hallybread. You surprised me. You're the last person I thought I'd see here." She straightened her bodice. "Thought you were a tart just now. Or a thief." She read Martha's face. Her gaze flicked up the Scour to where Herry and Jug Ears stood, poised at the top of the steps.

"Aahhh. I see. Good evening to you, gentle sirs. What brings you to Grope Scour? A party, is it? A bit of merry-making?"

Herry glowered, his chapped lips pinched shut. A big tabby cat emerged from a bush and made to twine itself around his legs. He booted it away and came heavily down the steps.

"Quick temper in a man," Jennet said, not budging, "shames him soon enough."

"Fuck that. Fuck you, if it come to it," Herry said, advancing.

"Now *there's* a proposition." Jennet turned to Martha. "Amazin', isn't it, what come out the mouths of these choirboys when they've sung themselves hoarse in church." She looked at Herry. "Why don't you go off and wet yourselves in the Eel?"

"Shut your mouth, you poxy bitch," Herry said.

"Shut yours, Herry Gowler." Jennet linked arms with Martha. "We got no dealings with you."

"Then what's your business here?" Jug Ears said.

Jennet spun around. "What's yours, friend? There's only one kind of man who come to Grope Scour, and that's one who has to pay for his pleasure." She looked them up and down. "What a pair. What entire *specimens*. Look at them looking at you, Martha. See Master Ralph here like a randy pest-catcher with his tongue hanging out." She came up a step. "Do you never leave off, gentlemen? You go to church and pray for your soul and then you come out and make arses of yourself all over again. It must be tiring, being so two-faced." She looked back at Martha. "Herry is that, wouldn't you say?"

Aye, Martha confirmed, inscribing a pair of buttocks on the air. *An arse always has two sides.*

"D'you see that, Herry?" Jennet crowed. "That's Cleftwater's finest midwife describing you. A proper arse, she says, with a hole in it for letting out wind."

"So help me, Jennet Savory, shut your gob or I'll shut it for you." Herry lunged and caught hold of Jennet, catching her jaw between his fingers. "You'll go off quietly, Mistress Savory, if you know what's good for you. Our business is with Martha."

"Is that so? Well. It'll have to keep, for Martha's away home with me."

"She's not," Herry said. "She's coming with us." He pushed his face into Jennet's. "She's got some unfinished business with Mogg Basford—an apology she owes for slighting him, the old hag."

"I see," Jennet said. "That's as should be, then. For 'tis not right at all, insulting one so fine as Mogg Basford." She shook off Herry's grip. "Master Mogg Basford! A man so gentlemanly he's sent his two pet ferrets to do his own errand." She shoved Herry up one step, then another. Martha watched, marvelling at Jennet's boldness, wishing she had some herself. "Let me ask you this, sirs: if Martha's such a hag, why is Mogg always pestering her? 'Cause she's forever telling him no." Jennet shoved again. "You're simple, Herry, and because of that, I'll tell you plain." She put her hands to her cheeks and dragged them down, exposing the pink innards of her eye sockets. "You want a hag? Here's one." She put up two fingers in a fork. "Fuck off and look to yourselves, the pair of you. And leave us women who've done you no wrong alone."

She turned her hand palm out and raised the fork in a crude salute. Horn hand. Hag hand. Ralph's jaw hinged open; he gasped like a landed flounder. Herry threw up an arm, turning his head as if ducking a blow.

"Jesu, Jennet—"

"Jesu to you, Herry Gowler. I'll tell you again, and you tell Mogg: keep away, keep right away. From Martha. And from me."

———

The Scour led to Kit's field, a sloping square of green that they crossed on the diagonal. After the gloom of the alley Martha was temporarily blinded by the unfettered light. Her hands tremored with after-shock and she clasped her sleeves lest the poppet slide out. The sole of one shoe had come loose and flapped as she walked. Cows, gulls, a hedge sparrow's liquid piping. They came to the cowpond and saw Tom Archer on the far side, filling a bucket. Without conferring they waited behind the stand of sedge that fringed their side of the water.

Martha held up both cupped hands in a V. *Why did you help me?*

"Why did I help? Why wouldn't I?" Jennet said, bluntly. "Yesterday you helped me. Today I help you. That's Godly. That's friendship." She grinned at Martha. "So called."

Thank you. Oh, I thank you. She kissed her fingertips and tapped them to Jennet's neck. *My Samaritan. My friend.*

"Anyways," Jennet continued, patting Martha's fingers, "I got no time for Herry Gowler, pox-faced meddler that he is. He wants putting in his place, so he does."

Maybe, aye, But you should not have horn-handed him.

"Ach, I'm not scared of Herry. I don't pay him much heed. He's all wind—full of his Bible-speak that he's picked up in church. I tell you this, Martha, there's more wisdom to be found in one of Father Leggatt's farts."

Their laughter welled, her own a gusty wheezing that she'd not heard for a long time.

"Shall we go?"

Aye, so. We're both needed at home.

As they went past the cowpond the father swan rose out of the reeds with his great wings spread wide, hissing at them.

"How are you managing? Without Prissy?"

Well enough. She sighed. She was very tired. *There's much to do.*

Jennet slowed, giving Martha an earnest look. "What's to happen with Prissy? When will they let her come home?"

Martha shook her head. *I don't know.* She raised her hands and clasped them, shaping a prayer. *Soon, God willing.*

"God willing. Or the witch man. Depending."

She looked at Jennet sidelong; the slanting sloe eye, her cheekbone, the wine-coloured bloom by her jaw. Everything about her was sharp, chiselled-looking, even the rim of her birthmark.

Why were you at the Scours?

Jennet kept her eyes ahead. "That's between me and the Lord, old friend. Let's just say I was returning a favour." She walked on, another twenty paces. "And you? What were you doing over there?"

The lie came easily, tripped off her fingers. *Running an errand.* She thought some more. *Taking herbs to a sick man.*

"What kind of sick?"

Heartsick.

"Is that so?"

She couldn't read Jennet's face.

"What herbs cure a sick heart?"

But they were at Kit's gate. *I'll tell you another day.* In the yard the pump wheezed and gushed. She heard the slop of the bucket and Simon's weighted tread as he took the water inside. Even from here she could sense Agnes's annoyance, as though it seeped from the house. Already she was inventing excuses, the reasons for her lateness, her dust-coated skirts. Jennet nodded at her, aye, aye, a knowing look.

"That's a good thing about you, Martha. You keep secrets."

She grinned. *Who better than me?*

Jennet caught hold of her, pulled her into a bony embrace. "I'll say nothing if you say nothing—not you about me, nor me of you. For now at least. That's us evens, old friend."

TEN

Simon had over-fed the kitchen fire and used up all the kindling. She sent him out to chop more. The house was stifling, tight with Agnes's displeasure. Martha brushed down her dress, downed a cup of cider. Time to face mistress. She went softly along the passage and found Kit's study door ajar. Agnes was still in the high-backed chair. Before her Kit sat on the footstool. From the doorway she watched them. They made a fine couple: handsome Kit, not tall but well-proportioned, with his strong features and shock of thick dark hair; plump, comely Agnes, sidling away from Kit's touch with coy, girlish movements. On her face all the signs of vexation—a creased brow, a rosy flush. On Kit's, infatuation.

"—all day he has kicked me in the ribs," mistress was saying. She passed a hand over the curve of her belly.

"Then let me bring Martha. She will know. She has good herbs."

"She has already looked."

"That was this morning. Let her look at you again. She may know of something, some remedy that will settle you tonight." Kit got up from the firestool and put it under Agnes's feet.

"I cannot," Agnes said plaintively, restless against the hard wood, "get comfortable. The babe lies so low. Martha says it may come soon because it is already so big. Sometimes a babe will come early, when there is no room left in the mother." She turned her face to Kit. "His size is healthy . . . but how will I birth him?"

"With Martha's skill—"

"Martha! The same Martha who is not here! She is a rustic—a herb-woman, nothing more. She is no physician. Her knowledge is lore. Her herbs comfort but they can't cure. You know as well as I that the only cure is mother's labour. And if the babe survives and I don't, how will you fare? You'll be a widower with a fine son and no wife to bring him up." She pushed Kit's caress away. "But no, I'm being foolish. With Martha as his nurse our son will not lack. He will doubtless prosper. You will see to it. The blessed Martha will see to it, of this I have no doubt. And then, in due course, when the mourning is done, when the prayers for my soul are all said and a stone of fine marble set in the ground at my dead head, you will find another wife, and she will doubtless delight you, as once I did."

"Sweetheart, no, no. Don't speak so. Don't think so. What you say will not pass. I promise you only the best of care, when your time comes. If it would help you to have Dr. Quinnell here, then I will arrange—"

"I ask only this, husband: in years to come, on the date of our son's nativity or my death, think of me. Think briefly of your Agnes, and wish me well, wherever I am. Then I give you leave to go back to your pleasant life, enjoy our child and your new young wife and of course the company of Martha, your ever-loyal Martha, whose skill was not enough to save my life."

Agnes stopped abruptly, as if overtaken by rancour. In the

doorway Martha drew back and into herself, condensing to her most meagre form.

"Agnes. My love, my only love. You are out of humour today. The babe lies badly, you are uncomfortable, your thoughts are out of right order—"

"Husband! Stop! I'll not be patronised. Don't dismiss what I say. I speak true. Suppose the babe does come early. What then? We have two servants only, one of them a lad, the other old. The third is still in the gaol."

"Agnes, you must not vex yourself. I have spoken to the bailiffs; God willing, Prissy will be home soon. And why this questioning of Martha? Who has never been anything but loyal, and a good helpmeet to us both. Why do you doubt her?"

Agnes made a dismissive sound. "Christopher: she is mute, but you are blind. You do not, will not, see her faults. Her loyalty to you eclipses everything, as does yours to her. You don't see how her reputation is clouding, falling into shade. Only two nights ago she was at the birth of the Archer babe; that child died, one of several lost this year despite Martha's skill. Or maybe because of it: no one knows save God and Martha. It pains you to hear it, husband, as much as it pains me to say it, to speak the truth. And I know what you will say—that these events are not linked, that the babes were lost, as babes sometimes are. Perhaps that is the truth of it. But if you love me, then hear me. I am afraid of relying on Martha, to have only her tend me when my time comes. I would have any other midwife—Liz Godbold is experienced and skilled. Even Jennet Savory has some skill, I'm told. Or Prissy, who please God will be home soon. She has some experience; she will know what to do."

"Sweetheart, Prissy was also at the Archer birth, with

Martha. They delivered the babe together. If you accuse one, you accuse the other."

"I don't mean—I'm simply saying . . ." Agnes shifted in the chair. "I'm saying I don't want Martha at the birth of our child. You must bring some other midwife and bid Martha to stay away."

The words were like a slap. Her mouth made a noise; she covered it, gasped the rest into her hands. Kit's knee cracked as he stood. He took in a long breath. "You forget, wife, that Martha has spared nothing—will spare nothing—to see our child safely born. She lives for the babe's arrival, to be present at his birth. How can I bar her? Forbid her presence? I don't know how I'd tell her. Or the reason why. What you ask is too much."

"I think not, husband. Do this for me. I know your regard for Martha. She's been your nurse, your housekeeper, I think also your friend. But she is gone past the peak of her skill. The day comes, if it is not here already, when she should give up her herballing. Perhaps it is time for her to retire, to go to the almshouse and live quietly. What I ask is fair: only that another midwife aids me at the birth."

"What you ask is very much, indeed," Kit said, unwontedly sharp.

———

She had heard enough. She trod away on the balls of her feet; empty, hollow. Subtracted. In the pot over the kitchen hearth were the two eels, steeping in the liquor they'd been boiled in. Two sleeping serpents. She lifted them out and they broke apart, into uneven portions.

She put a small helping aside for Simon and laid out the

rest on two plates. Then spooned over some white vinegar and the garnishings from the pot, slices of ginger, segments of an orange. As an after-thought added bay leaves taken from the dried spray in the pantry. Boiled eels were one of Prissy's special dishes; no doubt Agnes would find her own effort wanting. She picked up the platters, a handful of cutlery, loaded them clumsily onto a tray, clumped loudly along the passage. Coming again to Kit's door she could hear them, words being exchanged in heated flurries, Agnes by turns plaintive and demanding, Kit's perplexed responses. She knocked. They continued. They hadn't heard her or their quarrel was too fierce.

"I have shown my loyalty in more than wifely ways, Christopher. I have cleared your debts. I have helped rebuild your reputation and tried to make a good life for us here, in this place, which you know full well suits me ill—" Agnes broke off.

"What's wrong?"

"Nothing. The babe moved." A pause. "Feel his foot here. Feel how he kicks."

"He has grown, even in the last few days."

"He has got too big for his little mother." Mistress let out a short, high laugh. "He agrees with me. He kicks to remind you of your duty. Of where your affections should lie. You are a married man now. Which means your first loyalty is to me."

Martha was suddenly weary, as if she'd aged a century over the course of the day. She knocked again and this time they stopped. Footsteps came to the door. Kit: her rueful master. She handed over the tray, nodded good evening, closed the door.

Simon was outside on the bench, playing a tune on his jaw harp. She offered him the portion of eel.

Have you eaten?

"I'll have more if it's going." He gave her a quizzical look. "Don't you want it?"

Nay.

"You're not hungry?"

She shook her head.

He hesitated, took the dish, patted the empty space beside him. "Sit with me."

I can't, lad. I've more to do.

The sky was colouring with long smears of flame. This day, this cursed day, nearly at an end. She crossed the yard to the wash-house, took out the poppet. It fit neatly in her palm. Misshapen, ill-aspected, Mam's last gift. She put it on its rafter. She could feel the approach of the old grief, the dark wing of Mam's goneness, folding her in its lightless pit.

ELEVEN

Friday

Mid-morning, and Jennet came to the house.

"My sister's still bleeding. She fevers, she calls for her babe. When she's not doin' that she's weeping forever, hours on end. I tried all I know, Martha. Nothing's helped. Will you come look at her? She's past what I can do for her."

Not now. Gesturing to the bleached sky in which the sun climbed. *I'll come later.*

"She'll be dead later." Jennet's eyes sought Martha's, looking at and through her. "And that'll be another life lost, a babe and its mother from our house in a week. One more burden for your conscience, Martha."

I can't come yet. She mimed the bulge of Agnes's babe.

"Agnes's babe? What's wrong with it?"

It's big.

"What's wrong with big?"

She shook her head. *Nothing.* Tapping her eyes. *But I can't leave mistress. I must stay and watch.*

"If it's watching you want, I can do that. I'll stay and watch your mistress. You go see if you can find what ails my sister. Then you come back and tell me what she needs." In Jennet's face some reckoning was taking place, a debt being totted up. "I think you can do this for me, Martha. After all that's happened. Things I've done for you. Things I've *not* done."

———

At the Archer's door she knocked and without pausing went straight in. This house was so much smaller than Kit's, its contents—battered furniture, worn knot-rug, the thin mattress on which Marion lay—shabby and tired-looking. The kitchen table was a clutter of used dishes, piled washing, and an eel trap. Tom was by the fireplace, bent over his wife, who was barely awake in a truckle bed drawn up to the fire. On the hearth the blood-soaked birthing pallet was in stacked-up pieces, ready for burning.

How does she?

"Bad," Tom said. He glanced at Marion, then at Martha, anguished. "I should be workin'. I got a cow with the bloat. But I daren't go." He looked past her. "Where's Jennet?"

At mine.

He nodded. "I beg you, Martha, do your best. God's taken our son and that's grief enough. But I can't lose Marion as well. I just . . . can't."

She went to the bed. When she lifted the coverlet the smell at once assailed her, corrupt and wrong. This mattress too was ruined, was caked with blood. Marion was very sick. Martha knelt, lifted the patient's smock. Out of habit she chafed her hands to warm them before putting them to Marion's belly. Gently Martha pressed and searched. Marion cried out, but hoarsely—a moth's scream. She was sweating and ill-favoured, her eyes opened now but looking upwards to some prospect only she could see. Martha took hold of Marion's hand and turned it palm up, wishing she had Mam's gift. Mam could see into the future; she could take a palm and study it and tell whether a body would marry, how many children; how long a person would live. The palm of this woman here in the truckle bed: the lines on her hand were long but feathered; the life-line itself was broken. Death was coming, she could sense its approach, hear it in Marion's laboured breath, feel it in the too-fast tick of the woman's pulse.

She kept hold of the hand and closed her eyes and breathed out, in. After some moments she had cleared a space, a gap in herself. Then she began calling. Mam was far off, a long way. She could feel herself thinning, making more room. She kept calling. Sundry thoughts seeped in—how long for Marion, how long must she sit?—and she pushed them away. The fingers holding Marion's cramped and then tingled. Keep calling. Keep breathing. The tingling intensified. Mam was coming, arriving in gentle, vaporous smudges. Martha's mind was suddenly lit: with a knowing that pushed up in her, demanding to be used. In Marion's womb the caul and the afterbirth remained, breeding their contagion. The image faded, replaced by another. The necessary plants presented themselves, each haloed in their own curious light. Vervain. Rue. Mugwort: plenty of it in the hedgerows surrounding Kit's field.

Thanks to Mam. Thanks be to God. She might save a life and in the saving of it redeem her own. That was the potential, the gift of this day.

She brought Marion's hand to her lips and kissed it. Saw the grooves in the skin below the little finger: two faint lines for two possible children. She tucked the hand below the coverlet and drew it over Marion and got up. Tom was watching, expectant.

On her way past she tried to reassure him, but her hands balked. What were the signs for "save," for "soul" or "death"? She had no shapes for them.

———

So well she knew the field, its every tump and hollow. Mugwort grew in abundance in the hedgerows and in the wasteland by the Scours. She would bring some to Jennet, tell her to boil it to a mash and then make a poultice that could be bound onto Marion's stomach. The mash would drive out the sick flesh and the fever, both.

The field was empty except for the cows, the one with bloat penned in the far corner in a patch of shade. Its cry was persistent. A thin dirt track went up beside Kit's house with other tracks branching off it, going across to the Cleft. She went up to the top of the field where there was a big clump of the wort. It was nearly noon or just past it. A small breeze came off the sea, not enough to be cooling. The sun was fierce. She worked fast, cutting an armful. When she turned for home there were three men and a dog blocking the path. The sun was in her eyes and its sheer light hid their faces.

The shortest one spoke. "All night I been in the gaol," Herry said. "Keeping watch. On the witches, including your friend Prissy. Another two brought in yesterday. More due in today, I'm told. All kinds. Young, old." His eyebrows went up. "Who'd a thought it, Martha? That we got so many witches in our little nowhere-place. But that's Cleftwater: full of surprises. Two churches, two alehouses, and more witches than can fit in the gaol. That's why Ralph here is come all the way from Sandgrave— to help guard 'em—there's that many."

The sun seared her scalp. "Hot day, eh, Martha? I tell you, it's even hotter in the Great Hall. They got the fire built right up in there, on purpose. Make the women sweat. They're taking 'em out of the gaol one by one and bringing them up to the witch man. He talks to 'em, asks 'em questions, hours on end. What they been up to. What imps they got. What witchings they done. He's thorough, very patient. He's not swayed by no one. Not the witches, that's for sure, though they do cry and beg, make like they don't know what he's on about. That's how your Prissy was, when she saw him. All blotch-faced and weepy. Specially after your master Kit'd been in, trying to wheedle Prissy free." His eyes were hard on her, watching her watch him. "But Master Makepeace, he's not for moving. He's got a job to do and by God he'll do it, and I say thank Jesu Christ for men like him who'll rid us of these bitches and their Devil's work."

His ferret's face, its darting eyes, his mocking voice. She brandished the mugwort at him, a vigorous movement meant to sweep his accusations away. *Go your ways, Herry Gowler. All of you. Get away.*

"Why does she flap her arms about," Ralph asked, "like a scarecrow in a gale?"

"That's her way of talking," Herry said. "She got no voice. Or she chooses not to use it. No one quite knows which." He grabbed the sheaf of weeds. "Either way, she's a puzzle, ain't you, Martha." He pulled her closer. "I'll tell you plain: he's inspired me, has Master Makepeace. In these wicked times he is a truly God-fearing man. It's got me to thinkin', it truly has. Specially after what happened yesterday with you and Jennet. That sign she made."

Not again. To contradict them would enflame them more.

The sick cow brayed, clots of desperate sound. The stripe of her shadow lay on the ground and she saw its tremor.

"Mogg and I, we got talking," Herry said, companionably. He motioned behind him. "You might know how Mogg loves his Bible. And on the matter of witches, it says this: Suffer not—"

"—a witch to live," Mogg said, thrusting out his worn book so forcefully that Herry had to move aside. "That's what it says, directly. On the matter of witches. 'Thou shalt not suffer a witch to live,'" he intoned, in his most sonorous tenor. In the air between them he made the sign of the Cross. Herry made to take the Bible. Mogg reached it away. "Who are we to buck what's writ in the Good Book?" He opened it to show her. "See these? Ancient words, Godly words, writ down by wise men, that have stood the test."

What test? Her brain whispered, her mind worked. She raised her hands. *Yester eve you would ring my finger. Today you would wring my neck?*

"I dunno all you're saying," Herry said quickly, "but I do know as Jennet Savory cursed us, or tried to. Gave out a hex with that, those, horns she made. I seen it before, I know what it does, that curse. And not an hour after, my skin started itching and hasn't stopped, like it's being bitten by a thousand mites— like some demon's trying to pick it into pieces. Ralph here says he's got the same. And Mogg says as his dog's been like cursed, doing strange things—stealing food right off the plate, the beer out of his ale can. And look you, see how her belly swells. All her paps are showing, her teats stick out. She wasn't like that, before. Not 'til Jennet put on her hex."

"What's riled us," Ralph said, "is how many witches are still

free. The gaol's near full up and yet the witchfinder says there's
likely more to be found."

"Are you one of 'em?" Herry broke in. "Mistress, look at me
when I'm talking. I've got questions for you—plenty of them."
His voice was blurred with drink. "What kind of woman turns
away from a man so righteous as Mogg Basford? Eh? Answer
me that. No, wait," he said, lifting a finger to silence her. "I'll
answer it for you: it's one that don't want to be found out, who
don't want to get too close to a Godly man, lest she get too close
to the Lord. Like yourself. Like your Jennet friend. And why
would that be?" he asked, not really asking. "Why would a lady
so coy and virtuous-seeming not want to be seen by God? I'll tell
you. The answer is, she wants to keep to her own doings. She
wants to go freely about her witch's business. Specially at night,
when even beasts are afeard to be out." He came unsteadily
towards her, stopping some paces away to peer, as though she
were a fairground freak. His eyes flickered; some crude logic
being worked. "I'll tell you somethin' else. I seen what you done
to Mogg's dog here. You've witched it. I can see it, in its eyes.
Can't take them off you. It watches you like it's waiting for your
bidding." His face creased. "It's not natural, the way her paps
stick out. I don't like it."

"Is that what you've done, Martha?" Mogg said. "Witched
my dog? Made it your creature? So it'll suckle your imps?"

Sneering Herry with his eyebrows lofted up, Mogg with his
yellow teeth and drooping beard, like a dead animal pasted to
his chin. Donkeys, both.

The dog, she motioned slowly, *is a bitch.* They backed away
as she gestured.

"What's she sayin'?" Ralph asked.

"Somethin' about the dog," Herry said, needlessly. His sneer faded.

She caught hold of the dog, indicated the swollen teats, the pink mound of its sex. *She is with pup.*

"With pup?" Mogg said.

"Whose pups? A dog's? Or the Devil's?" Ralph said to Mogg and Herry, beginning to catch on. "We saw last eventide how she goes about, free to do as she likes. How is that? How is she not needed at home?" He looked at her. "Or does the Devil need you more?"

But he wasn't asking. The ground was thinning beneath her feet or her feet were growing light, preparing to flee. Mogg was old, Ralph was slow; she might give them the slip. That left Herry. Maybe she could out-run him. She shoved him in the chest and he staggered back and she ran past him down the track. Mogg's dog loped alongside. The field stretched out in all directions, a dimensionless expanse. Her lungs sped up, pumping with a strange rasp as if the worm had riddled them with holes. If she could get home to safety: the afternoon was narrowing to this single aim. She veered abruptly left onto one of the tracks that went across, then realised her mistake. The Scours were too far and in the wrong direction, away from help. She turned around, broke into a run. If she could reach the street. If she could get to her own back gate. She had lost both clogs and the ground bit her feet. Every pebble had malice in it, was conspiring with the weeds to trip her. She stumbled, almost righted herself, then fell.

The men arrived, surrounded her, pulled her upright, and began to march her back the way she'd come. She resisted, dragging her feet, trying to find purchase on the rough ground.

"She proves herself a witch," Ralph said. "Why else would she run away?"

"Why else would she witch my Jess?" Mogg said. The dog hung back, watching him with strange yellow eyes. Mogg whistled it to heel. "Come, Jessamy, come, girl." The bitch came but reluctantly, creeping to Mogg with her belly scraping the long grass. "What have you done to her?" he asked Martha, panicked now. "Undo it—undo whatever spell you put on her. Take it off! Take it off, you hag!"

The afternoon wavered. There was no Jennet to aid her now. *I'm no witch*, she wrote, scrabbling at the air.

"She's hexing you, Mogg. She's hexing the pups. You'll have to drown 'em. Drown your Jess, if it come to it."

"I'd sooner drown Martha," Mogg spat.

The idea ignited. They seized her, bound her wrists with the dog's rope, hauled her through the fringe of reeds into the shallows of the cowpond. The three swans who lived on it retreated, hissing protests. Mud rose like smoke through the churned water. They dragged her in farther, up to her knees, to her thighs. She was terrified of falling. The water licked, readying itself to swallow. From the reeds the male swan reared up, priest-like with wings outstretched. Where the pond floor dipped they stopped to argue, unable to agree what should be done. Herry and Ralph wanted to swim her: if she floated she was a witch, if she sank she was mortal. Mogg was less sure, wanting his dog's curse lifted first. Her heart was flapping half in her mouth, half out of it. The day had divorced her; all its outcomes were calamitous. While they batted the yea and nay of their argument between them she cast around for sources of help. All along the beach folk were working, landing catches, mending nets and boats. Help was not far off but she could neither beckon nor call for it—not Kit, not Simon. Not Jennet, not the poppet, useless on its rafter.

Ralph lost patience, took her by the hair, and dunked. Her face went in. She choked, opened her eyes. A ways off the swans paddled, serene and aloof. Ralph hauled her up and Herry's face loomed, asking again if she was a witch. Water streamed from her nose. Herry was accusing her, foul things that had never been true although he said them like they were. She watched his lips moving, pulled another lungful of breath from the sky. The bloated cow groaned, bemoaning her fate. Ralph pushed her down again. Her lips kissed the water. Countless tiny skimming creatures moved freely over its surface, barely denting its skin. Was it deep enough to try her, to discover if she was a witch? Was she a witch? They wanted the water to tell. Again Ralph pushed her under. This time he kept her there. Her mouth filled, her lungs emptied. Then a prayer came, *Father of all, I pray to you for mercy*, and she choked it into the flood. The pond's tarnished green: it was her life's dusk. All its battle and clamour were fading, going out with her last breath. Grey grains of sightlessness swam towards her. Death was here, she could feel herself succumbing, folding into its chill.

Then the rope went slack.

She thrust up her head, broached the surface, heard the singing cow. The light was a curtain. A figure came through it. It was coming to the pond. She got to her feet, staggered to the shallows, and keeled over. Water filled her nose. Get up. Get up. The poppet came on with its limping gait, right to where she was. She peered: the air around it puckered, seemingly charged. Now it was leaning over, its hands—living hands!—dragging

her from Hell or that place she'd reached that was halfway to
it, back into the living world. Part of her fought it, wanted to
finish, to make an end, but her lungs were busying themselves,
rushing in air. Still the poppet held her: drew her to her knees,
to a stand.

"How do you, Martha?" Its voice was earthy, deep as a man's.
She spat, gargled. She'd bitten her lip. Blood moved down her
throat. "Lean on me," it urged. Gulls shrieked, the cow bawled,
making a dry music in her head. What was unfolding? A miracle? A conjuring? Her body had the rigours—an uncontrollable
quaking—as if trying to shuck off what had happened, the hurt
to her body as well as the deeper injury to her soul. Yet how
dear and cared-for she felt, walking beside the poppet with this
new wonder in her heart. Could it be—was it possible—that
the poppet could save as well as destroy?

Her hands shook and she clasped them, taking hold. Side
on, the poppet looked very like Simon. The wet cleared from
her eyes. It *was* Simon. He untied the dog rope and her hands
flew up and began to signal, frantic as fleeing birds.

Thank you, I thank you—

"Ach," he said hurriedly, "I done what any Christian would."
Abruptly he turned and shouted across the field. "Shame on
you, Mogg Basford. Shame on you, Herry Gowler, to set on
Martha, who harms no one and does naught but good in our
village." He spat. "I got no time for them, wastrels that they
are." He put an arm around her waist. "Can you walk?" She
nodded. "Lean on me," he urged. Her legs wobbled, uncertain
as a newborn foal's.

"I was coming to get you anyways," he said. His breathing
was as ragged as hers. "I went to Marion's, I thought that's where

you was. Her fever's that bad, I said her a prayer. Then I come home and who do I find but the gaolers, come for Jennet." He gave her a stricken look. "They've taken her, Martha. Like they took Prissy. Hauled her away in ropes. They're sayin' Jennet's a witch."

TWELVE

*S*he stood in the glare of the downstairs windows, waiting for the trembling to stop. So frail she felt, a near-drowned sac of tissue and bone, as she went unsteadily to the yard bench to sit. Simon worked the shrieking pump, filled and brought her watering cup, dabbed at her mouth with his shirt. He meant well but his fussing was too much and after a time she sent him to check on the mistress. Her body shook; her thoughts were disordered, running in all directions. Jennet, Jennet: what would happen to her? The hogs came to nose at her skirts, then went away to lie in the shade of the garden wall. The sun blazed, a gleaming disc in the chalky sky. What would have happened if Simon had not come? Why had she seen him as the poppet?

She got up. Her skirts were almost dry. In the wash-house she felt along the various beams. Which one? She couldn't remember, had lost the proper use of her wits. When at last she found the poppet she stared at it as though for the first time, turning it over and over in her palm—this stump of wax that only yesterday she'd tried to throw away—its two faces alternating, one mute, one about to speak. She half-dreaded and half-hoped it might blink or move or give her some sign. Her ears, her head, were full of the sound of waves, their approach, their retreat, rhythmic as breathing. Just as they'd sounded decades ago, when as a foundling she'd gone searching for Mam, holding the poppet like an unlit candle, as if it could show the way. And maybe this was true, for had it not by some strange grace guided her from the Scours to the market square, on a certain day in a certain year, to the hiring fair? Where she'd been picked out by Kit's mother to be his nurse-maid, and gone with her, and cared for her infant son? And in this way, had helped her find a home?

Perhaps time had cleansed it. Perhaps after all the poppet had some capacity for goodness, for healing. Perhaps it was for her, Martha, to discover its gifts and use them. In this way, she could keep it. *Use it scarce, but use it.* The thought came that there was still some time, today, to bring herbs to Marion. She folded the poppet into its linen wrapper and stowed it in her pouch. In the field she walked fast, holding her cuttings knife blade out. The memory of the morning's events followed her like a stray dog. When she came to the heap of dropped mugwort it was too much. She sat heavily down, staring at the ground. She took a stem of mugwort and studied the gold froth of its flowers; trying to reclaim herself, to salve the wounded parts, though a despair ran through the anger. She remembered Marion and mouthed a prayer for the two sisters, Marion and Jennet, while she looked out at the steady, muscular motion of the sea. Felt again the familiar sense that at any moment—this moment— a door in the world might open and Mam step through it and show her what to do.

Though she knew what to do. She stood and took fresh cuttings. She retraced her steps. The sea, the horizon, its clouds and birds, all moved exactly as they ought, in their given order. Liz Godbold answered the Archer's door and she pushed the herbs into Liz's startled grasp. *Boil them. Have Marion drink them.*

Going home she kept her hand on the pouch. Felt the poppet, moving as she moved; the stirrings of its love.

———————

In the yard the stained sheet flapped. From the upstairs window there was rapping: Agnes, beckoning for her help. *Come here. Come now.* Was the babe coming? Pray God, not today. She went to the kitchen, filled the ale jug, snatched up some cloths. Took the stairs two at a time and was halfway up when Kit called her to come down.

"Martha," he said. "I am sorry to interrupt. I need your help."

I was going to mistress—she calls for me.

Not yet, he shaped back.

He brought her to his study, opened the door, stood aside to let her go in. A visitor stood in the bay window, turning to face her as she entered. A gentleman, of an age with Kit but thinner and beginning to stoop, his bloodless face earnest, the skin taut over prominent bones, the cheeks holding cups of shadow. She advanced as far as the rug and stopped. Kit's dog got up from the hearth and stood close, fanning his tail. He was old now, though she could remember him as a pup. She let her fingers rest on his head, finding comfort in the nap of his fur. Kit had closed the door and stood beside her.

"Martha, this is Master Makepeace, the witchfinder. He is a Godly man, very well versed in the ways of witches and their evil, and much skilled at finding them." Kit was squeezing her arm, wanting her to look at him. His face, too, was pale. "You will know about the witches that were lately found in

Salt Dyke. They were discovered by Master Makepeace." He stopped, pressed again. "Now he is come to Cleftwater. He is here because of certain . . . rumours—claims, even, that we have witches here."

Her heart had sped up; now it raced. She wet her lips. The hound rested solid against her thigh. His heat came through her gown. She was embarrassed by the state of it, the stain of pondweed on the cloth.

"Master Makepeace is greatly concerned. Already there are a number of suspected witches in the gaol. Master Makepeace believes there are more to be found." Sweat sheened Kit's face. His fingers were like pincers. "Perhaps even a coven among us."

"Almost certainly," said Makepeace, "there is a coven." His eyes were wide and strangely lit: windows, inviting her to look in. From Kit's table he picked up a book and opened it, leafing to a page that he smoothed with the heel of his hand. "Can she read?"

"A little, yes. I have taught her," said Kit.

Master Makepeace raised the opened book. "In these pages I keep a list—the names of those known to be witches, or thought to be involved with the Devil. I pray you, mistress, to look at the names writ here." His tone was reasonable and pleasant. "You must tell me if you see one you know."

His writing was cramped but ornamented. The names scrolled in a column down the page. Elizabeth Bradwell. Cecily Hockett. Jane Crispe. Helen Leach. Little charcoal-coloured sparks sprayed behind her eyes. With her fists she scrubbed at them.

"She looks, but she does not speak."

"She cannot," Kit said. "She has a sickness in her throat that hinders her from talking."

Martha looked again at the page, read carefully all the way to its foot. Her name was not there. Exhaustion washed through her, mixed with relief.

The witch man turned the page.

The list went on. The names grew more familiar; women from the villages around Cleftwater. Sarah Hating. Meggs Lacey. Katherine Greenliefe. Dorothy Hare, the baker's wife. The witch man saw where she looked and with his long finger—its clean, unblemished nail—underlined Dorothy Hare's name.

"I'm told she boiled eggs in a pail of water, to make Jed Phillips's boat go down, and shortly after Phillips's boat did sink and two men drowned. Also that she keeps five imps in her linen chest, that she feeds and cossets, and then sends out to do harm."

Martha knew both families, had helped birth their children. A protest formed on her palate; her throat flexed, but nothing came.

"She knows them?" he asked Kit.

"Yes. They are families of these parts. She—we—have known them a long time."

The witch man exhaled, a breath with a rasp in it. "Look at me," he said. She looked—blinked—at his pallid brilliance, the glare that seemed to radiate from him, glancing off the pages of his book.

"What has caused this affliction of her voice?" he asked Kit. His gaze was on her, very severe. She felt exposed in it.

"I don't know. She was my nurse-maid, I have known her all my life and never heard her speak." Kit's expression was fixed, masking uncertainty. "As I told you, I vouch for her entirely. She is a true Christian, very God-fearing, much respected in the village. She treats her affliction as a gift."

"Meaning?"

"Meaning that she accepts it, and goes about her bidding with good grace and no idle talk."

The witch man made a sound, a small grunt of acknowledgement. He wielded the book once more. "Which of these names do you know?" he said again, but too loudly, as if she were a dullard, or hard of hearing. She stared where he pointed, at the looping nooses of the letters, the scrolling nut-brown of the ink, here light, here dense where the pen had faltered, leaving clots of juice.

Priscilla Persore. Cook.

Jennet Savory. Spinster.

Was her name here? It couldn't be. It must be: that was why she was being tested in this way. She was like Agnes, harbouring a bulging secret, only hers must never be born. The house was unquiet, her heart tripping over its own beat. On the page the witch man's script was contorting, rearranging itself in a blur. She wiped her eyes with her sleeve and instantly regretted it, this traitorous gesture of unease. Then forced herself to keep reading, looking for the shapes that spelled her name. Towards the bottom of this page there were a cluster of names she knew or thought she did: Hannah, Ellen—

The witch man lowered the book. "You know these women?"

Her hands were useless; bags of bone and skin. Slowly she nodded. *Aye.*

"And do you know *why* their names come to be writ in my book?"

Nay.

"No? But you must do, mistress—?"

"Her name is Martha."

"Mistress Martha. They are friends of yours, I'm told. You

must know quite well why these women have their names writ here."

The room was too warm and the sea suddenly quiet. Even the birds were hushed. She looked from the witch man to Kit, seeking guidance, finding none. Only a barely perceptible shake of Kit's head, easily missed had she not known him so well.

The witch man gestured again to his book with its great weight of names. "Look again. Look carefully. Surely you have some knowledge of what dread deeds they have done? What Devilish acts?"

She shook her head. *I know of none.*

"I believe," he said—unyielding, unsatisfied—"that you do." His eyes skimmed, appraising. Her skin crawled. The moment yawned, an infinity. "Doubtless I need not remind you, mistress, that it is your Christian duty to tell what you know." The man was slight but a choler came from him, a vast, pursuing rage. In the well of her lungs the worm stirred, threatening to bring on the cough. She put a fist to her mouth to stifle it, not daring to look away.

Kit cleared his throat. "Martha. Because of the quantity— the sheer number of witches—Master Makepeace seeks our assistance. He and I have come to . . . an arrangement." He hesitated, weighing the moment. "Master Makepeace seeks virtuous and upstanding women, those with skills like yours, for this Holy Work. Skills in—"

"—examining the accused," said Makepeace. "For suspicious marks, especially paps or teats left on their bodies where a witch has joined with the Devil, or where imps have suckled." He stroked the book. "Such marks—Devil's marks—are oft found on witches."

A moment passed. Kit said, "I, I . . . have told Master Make-peace about you, your skills and your work. That you are famil-iar with women's bodies. I have vouched that you know well what marks of the skin are right and usual, and those that are not. So we have agreed: you will go with Master Makepeace, to help examine the witches."

She looked at him, astounded. "I have assured Master Makepeace that, as a Christian woman and an honest one, you may be depended on to do this work," Kit went on. He looked in this moment somehow smaller—a boy playing at being a man. Then he reached for her palms, opening them out flat, like pages. *I am sorry*, he wrote, *to ask this of you.*

Skin to skin: he was being so public with their private script—their personal dialect of shapes and writing, known only to themselves. She felt a needling panic, followed by re-sentment. *I fear for Prissy*, his finger spelled; it was damp, and his eyes were unblinking. She read their plea. *Do all you can for her*, he scribed. *Then both come safe home.*

Apprehension had gone through her like a poison in the blood. In her throat the worm clenched, balling up her protest. She was careful to look obedient, though underneath was a brewing anger. Oh, oh, it was hard, impossible to contemplate, that Kit would barter her loyalty in this way. She let out a breath and drew in another she hoped would calm the heat and race of her thoughts. If I do this. Do what is asked; do it quick but true. So that Prissy is spared the worst.

So that Prissy was spared: this same Prissy—friend, near enough to kin—who was in the gaol in Martha's stead.

Both men waited. The world had contracted, to just this room with its lance of sunlight; to this moment; to this request.

She looked at the witchfinder and found that she was trembling. *I will do what you ask.*

To Kit she signed: *I will need my herbs. In case Prissy lacks.* From the corner of her eye she saw the witch man watching, knew that he misread.

"What are these gestures that she makes?" he asked.

"She talks with her hands," said Kit. "Because she has no voice."

"I see. And what does she say?"

"That she accepts this task willingly, for love of God," Kit said firmly. For a moment he faced the witch man, his jaw pushed out, his face flushed. She could see a belligerence passing between them. "Martha is my valued servant. She is not in full health. She must bring her medicaments, which she needs." Kit increased his voice. "I ask that you take care of her, have regard to her strength."

Again he took her hands between his, which were smooth but over-warm and clammy, and pressed and pressed his gratitude into her palms.

———

No time for second thoughts. She ran upstairs, changed her shift and put on her second-best gown and jacket, tied on a fresh kerchief and coif. A red-faced Agnes met her in the passageway and began a complaint, but Martha threw up her hands and backed away. Outside the hogs watched as she bent to the pump, dousing her face and hands to rinse them of the pond's taint. She could not control events but she might temper them: divert the witch man's attentions; allay the women's suffering, find nothing but innocence on their bodies.

Or she might do some damage. To the witch man's book. To the man himself, if it came to it.

Her head and neck were drenched and still she felt unclean. She crossed to the plant bed and stepped in, cutting quickly, different sprays for bruises and cuts, for exhaustion, for her cough. She paused, wiped her forehead with her cutting hand. Her cough threatened, came again. She spat its bloom into her handkerchief; thought how it had worsened, how she had need of a second crop. She bent again to the herbs. Foxglove, poison parsley. Plants that could dull a life or stop it short, slow or quickly. Her own, or another's. If needed. If it came to it. Bending caused the worm to strain in her throat, but how else was she to cull? Water filmed her eyes and she wiped it impatiently away. It was too much, what Kit had done. His Judas kiss, the gulls' racket, the lowing of the still-sick cow: they were disordered, they had rent the fabric of her world. Out of it came Mam's voice, Take heart, sweetheart, my true girl, my own—

She looked up.

—Poppet.

Her heart calmed. She went out of the garden not minding where she put her feet, only that the ground felt firmer. On the garden bench she emptied her pouch and put the poppet at the bottom and covered it over with the herbs. Bringing it was a risk but she had need of it now, the reassurance of its potential.

In the house Agnes stood at the top of the stairs, Simon at the bottom, Kit by the front door. He opened it. Martha went out first. The witch man bridled, withdrawing himself so that his clothes did not touch hers. At the street she turned and looked back. The door gaped open like a wound. Kit stood in it, stricken-faced. She lifted a hand in farewell. Godspeed, he wrote back.

The witch man walked in the manner of his being, quick and deliberate, with one shoulder thrust somewhat forward as though he were pushing against the world. They went down the whole length of Swallow Street. At the crossroads he turned left. He was taking the most public route into the centre of the village. Maybe he wanted them to be witnessed. Mid-afternoon with the sun over the street and the witch man's shadow slanting across it. She must walk not just at his heel but into his shade, into the negative of him. Somewhere near, a small child cried. The sound reminded her of the stargazer babe. The child cried again. She looked around and saw, a dozen yards away, Liz Godbold jogging her youngest child on her hip. Their eyes met. Liz looked accusing before she turned away.

Going past the Market Cross she saw why all was so quiet: the village had left off its ordinary business to wait expectantly before the Moot Hall. Ranged along the townside wall a line of boys stood or knelt on the shoulders of the taller men, peering through the Hall's lancet windows. Merchants and traders were clustered in watchful knots, their wares—loaves and pies and fly-flecked sides of meat—hastily packed away in anticipation of the day's more sombre business: this weighing up of women, on scales she suspected were already tipped. Even the dogs were silent, nosing at the edges of the crowd. Nan Dolan stood on the stoop of the Four Daughters, ewer in hand. Master Makepeace nodded to her.

"Here is where you will search," he told Martha. "You will work for Mistress Knill, my search-woman. The accused will be brought one by one. You will search; what you find must be told to Mistress Knill. When you are not needed you will stay in the gaol," he said, heavily. "Watching the witches. You must listen to them, to all they say—their secrets, accounts of witch deeds, their vows to Satan, the names of their imps. Do you understand?"

Aye. Nay: the world's old logic had been annulled and a new logic was taking its place. They crossed the street. Martha scanned the growing crowd. Today all looks were wary. Master Makepeace called out, "Make way, make way." Every head turned, the crush of bodies parted. Unease came from it, as corporeal as a smell. They passed through and came to the foot of the Moot Hall's double stairs. She wondered where the witch man would send her—up to the Hall or down to the gaol. He began to climb, signalling for Martha to follow. The crowd's murmur built as she went. Someone called her name.

"What brings you here, Martha Hallybread?" A grinning Mogg Basford. "Will you know your sisters for witches? Will you help rid us of them? D'you vow it?"

She hesitated. The crowd went silent, tense faces blurring as she stared. Oh aye, she would vow it—if only she could vow it! But she was falsely here, on false pretences, riven to the point of collapse; feeling that her outer self might shear off like a landslip from Psalm Cliff, leaving her true intent exposed. From below, Mogg watched, his companions also, waiting for her answer. At last she ducked her head. Let people, let Mogg, read her as they would.

She took the last of the stairs. Her hip pouch drummed and she steadied it, felt again the poppet's small mass against her thigh, which was, with all her other reliable bones, walking her into catastrophe.

PART TWO

BLACK BILE

THIRTEEN

Friday afternoon

The Great Hall seethed with movement and unease. Many men had come and were arriving still. Behind Martha the door swung repeatedly open, each time admitting more. Before her, some twenty paces, was the dais. It ran the width of the Hall and culminated in the fireplace, and on it the ceremonial table and fine chairs had been set up for the magistrate and jurors. Constable Napier and the mayor stood with Master Makepeace, flanked by the two clerics—Father Leggatt and Minister Deben of St. Hilda's Church—all in earnest conference. From time to time they glanced over to the witches.

The women were corralled against the rear wall. Martha counted seven, of all ages and stations. Hannah Holland was the youngest, ancient Ma Southern the oldest. No one knew her true age but she was deaf and half-lame and destitute, a hedge-pauper who eked an existence from church alms and begging. She stood, crutchless, trembling and confused-looking, propped against the wall on one side and Ellen Warne on the other. Ellen was from Holleswyck, a fishwife. The Durriken sisters, near neighbours of Kit's, stood nearby, furtively holding hands. Prissy was next to them, distracted, coifless and with her hair all hanging down. Her dress that had been fresh on two days ago was now much begrimed, its yellow cloth dulled. A few paces away was Jennet, white-faced under bruising. One of her eyes was swollen almost shut.

To Martha's left the Cleftwater banner of blue and red and gold hung from its pole. It must have been unfurled especially. In its shadow a knot of women stood, all midwives. Liz Godbold; Sue Ruddock and Kate Weeting from the Scours, also midwives, both war widows, disliked for their begging, their relentless wheedling for bread and meat and milk. But Godly enough—they sometimes came to All Saints to worship. Once or twice she had called on them for wet-nursing. What had brought them here? She thought to stand with them and began to weave through the crowd of bodies; was stopped by a hand on her shoulder. The hand was clean-skinned and cared-for, belonged to a full-figured woman, older but handsome, her complexion wholesome and clear.

"Are you the Hallybread woman?"

She dipped her head. *I am.*

"You are the servant of Christopher Crozier?"

I am.

The woman regarded her. "I am Frances Knill, principal search-woman. Master Makepeace will have spoken of me."

She bowed her head. *Aye, madam, he has.*

"He tells me that you're to join us as a searcher." She made an airy gesture to where the other midwives stood. Her eyes were lustrous and blue, so bright they looked painted. They fastened on Martha. "I hear that you are skilled. And that you are mute."

Martha made a sawing gesture across her throat. *Alas, 'tis so, madam.*

A tight smile. "No matter. Doubtless we will come to

understand each other. For now I have need of your eyes more than your voice."

She took Martha's elbow, a signal for them to walk. They went at a deliberate pace towards the banner, Mistress Knill guiding Martha like a groom escorting a bride. "The Lord calls us to this work. But in answering that call we must make sacrifices." Martha, walking with her head down, took in the woman's fine kid shoes, the extra flesh about her ankles, the rich black stuff of her gown. Evidence of Mistress Knill's sacrifices was not so apparent. "Such as," Mistress Knill continued, "the comfort of family and friends." She slowed. "I wonder, Mistress Hallybread, whether you will be able to set aside your loyalties to your household. To your fellow servant Priscilla, and your friends." A glance to where the accused women stood. "This work is a privilege—an honour. To do it you must forget all friendships, all ties." Her expression shifted. "Especially kin ties."

Easy for someone like you, Martha thought. Easier to do when there's coin involved, warm from the hand of the witch man.

"And yet, at the same time you must remember everything, no matter how small," the search-mistress went on. They were passing a knot of aldermen, conspicuous in their wine-coloured robes, who glanced at them—through them—apparently without seeing. "The Devil is artful; but there is art in what we search-women do. And there is grace in it also." Mistress Knill stopped, let go of Martha. Light from the stained-glass window fell on her, brightening her countenance, setting her faded hair ablaze. When she spoke again it was through the rainbow of glassy colour, like some messenger angel. "Remember this above all else: we are handmaids of the Lord. We convict the body in order to save the soul." The painted eyes, the pointed gaze: pinning Martha where she stood. "We search-women are your kindred now." Mistress Knill smiled. "Can you be trusted? Can we count upon you to commit all your soul to this task?"

Best now to empty her face, to place one palm on her breast and drop a curtsey. *Aye, madam, you may.* Let the woman think her compliant, that her silence meant consent. In her mouth her tongue treadled: witch man's strumpet.

"Good." A brilliant smile: the strumpet, showing a full mouth of teeth. "We understand each other."

On the dais the knot of men broke apart. The jurors took their seats; Master Makepeace and the constable stepped down off the platform, also the gaolers, who ranged out in a line facing the assembly. Above them a short square gentleman with a red complexion took his seat in the largest of the high-backed chairs: the magistrate, by the name of Bacon. Martha's spirits rose a little. Judge Bacon was known to be lenient. Perhaps he would be so today and bail the women or even let them go. Despite the crush of bodies she felt suddenly exposed. Where now was her right place? She couldn't stay where she was; she must make some move. She looked at Prissy and Jennet, beaten-looking in their prisoners' corner. She wavered, debating. To stand with the search-women was to take position with them, to commit to their cause. Then she remembered her promise to Kit, and went to stand by Liz.

Ma Southern was called first, led up to a makeshift dock of two benches angled together in a V. Her thin hands, like bundles of kindling, were tied in front of her with the same rope that circled her waist. The constable read out her crimes. The list was long and petty, mostly bad ends to old quarrels.

The neighbours' chickens and pigs made sick; a new chimney caused to fall down. Ma Southern's face furrowed. Master Bacon asked whether she understood. It was clear she did not, for she craned forwards and swung her good ear one way, then another like a hound listening for its master.

"Do. You. Understand?" the judge called, but Ma Southern could neither hear nor grasp the consequences of not hearing. She was trembling so much that her good leg threatened to give way. Martha took some involuntary steps forwards, caught Mistress Knill's reproving glance, stepped back. Best for now to bide her time. If—when—it came to the searching, she might better aid the old woman.

Master Makepeace approached the dais. "Master Judge, Master Jurors, I have fresh evidence that I would present to this court," he said.

"Do so," said Master Bacon.

The witch man bowed and stepped back, to pace up and down before the dais, his little barbered beard wagging as he spoke. Ma Southern was an idler, a burden to the parish who caused mischief wherever she went. Her sins were many, her crimes likewise, chief of which were her cursing of the Brookes family; the children had sickened with winter fever and all three had died. His evidence was all story, a patchwork of gossip and rumour. Martha waited for the rest—what all Cleftwater knew. True, the children had perished, last autumn, yes, when sweating fever had gripped the village and taken many other lives. What Master Makepeace did not tell was how the children had for years persecuted the old woman, baiting her, filching her bread, hiding her crutch.

"How do you answer, madam?" asked Master Bacon. The

Hall was expectant. Ma Southern was silent, casting bewildered glances. Where she looked, people ducked or dodged or turned aside as though her glance was poison.

"See how she dissembles," said Master Makepeace, moving carefully towards her, his face full of distaste. "She feigns to neither see nor hear, though she knows full well her part in these crimes. And were we to let her go—to follow her home and spy on her at night—we would see the truth. How she is joyful when her imps come. How she suckles them, and then sends them to do her bad bidding." He turned to the assembly. "It is common for such women to pretend. To lie, even on the Bible."

"But if she cannot hear what charges are against her," Father Leggatt asked, "how is she to plead?"

A smattering of ayes followed his question. The witch man's glance quashed them. "You will find that it matters little whether she understands or no. Spend an hour with her: she will deny the charges. She will evade, she will lie. This is true of all witches. What comes from their mouths may be false, or a distraction, sent by Satan to confuse God-fearing men—the honest men of this court." Another volley of muttered ayes, louder than before. "Give me a day and a night with them and then, oh, *then* I will show you their true natures." He stepped closer to the judgement bench. "Your Honour, I will speak plain. When pressed, these witches will tell all. Of their marriages to the Devil. Of their vows to him, and of the black magic the Devil himself has taught them." He turned to face the crowd. His gaze roamed, meeting the eyes of the men, and in meeting them, seemed to strengthen. "And well I may say that I have witnessed—oh, such sights, that are too frightful to speak of here, when a witch, in her desperation, has called on her master for his Devilish help." He shook his head. "Such sights cannot be forgotten. They cannot be unseen." He turned again to the magistrate. "I speak of what I have seen with my own eyes, sir. And from my skill in finding witches, wherefore this village has summoned me."

"What do you propose, Master Makepeace?" a juror asked.

The witch man drew himself up. "Permit my women to search her. By examining her body we will find whether or not she bears the Devil's marks. By which I mean, sir, those sundry blotches—teats and little blemishes of raised or coloured skin— got by those who have suckled imps." He held up his hands to quell the cries of alarm from all around the Hall. "And in the same way, by watching the witches through the night, we may see how the Devil comes to them in all his forms—in the likeness of dogs or mice, spiders, snakes, or as some hellish, un-natural creature—a goat or pig, married with the hind-quarters of a polecat or worse," he said more loudly, so that his voice carried over the wash of anxious murmur. "By these methods, of searching and watching, the true natures of these women can be known. When they confess, then you may try them, and know your judgement to be sound." He bowed to the bench. His expression as he came upright was stern. "Other courts have used such methods and found them to be true."

Master Bacon pulled out his kerchief and scrubbed at his forehead as if to wipe away doubt. "Let Elizabeth Southern be watched for three nights. Let all her talk and her actions be noted." He stowed the kerchief and took up his pen. "If during this time there is seen anything untoward, then it must be re-corded, and brought to the court." He gave Makepeace a severe look. "But if, after three days, there is nothing—neither evil sights nor strange talk—then this, too, must be told to the court, and she must be let go." He banged down his wooden hammer. "Who is next?"

Ma Southern was led away. Martha scanned the company, the wary faces. What was happening, what sober business was occurring here? Among this company of fault-finders—good Christian men who would sooner quote scripture than cast a beggar-woman a crust of stale bread. The air was a fug, hot and getting hotter, filled with the rising reek of the pisspots in the gaol below. Martha wedged her spine against the wall, felt the dig of its stone in her back. An hour went by as Hannah and then Ellen were brought before the bench. Then it was the turn of the Durriken sisters, Joan first and then Rose, though they were accused of the same crimes.

The clock tolled again, mourning another hour. Martha was thirsty, longing to sit down. Fatigue dragged at her like a weight. Prissy's name was called. She came haltingly to the bench. Already she looked thinner, dark circles under her large brown eyes, her hair tangled, like used hemp. In spite of the gaol's reek she was still comely, drawing eyes towards her. Minister Deben read out the charges, which were met with gasps. She was accused of many crimes; not only the Archer babe's death but of cursing the mother, who was even now, Minister Deben told the court, ravaged by some unnatural contagion and fighting for her life.

Would no one speak for her? 'The charges against you are serious," Judge Bacon told Prissy. "The most serious of all. What have you to say to them?"

Prissy's mouth bunched and opened; a tear etched a trail

down her cheek. She was glassy-eyed with panic. "I . . . I say my prayers, sir. I go to church. I serve the Lord, I serve my master and mistress. I done none of this, none of what he says I done," she said, indicating the witchfinder with a glance. "Why would I? I wish no harm to anyone—least of all Marion Archer, who is my friend."

The judge was silent, regarding her. Then he picked up his pen and wrote on a paper. "You also will be searched and walked, Mistress Persore." He leaned a little over the table. "'Tis my hope you will use this time to examine your deeds and your conscience," he said, more gently. "If you have sinned, confess it and humble yourself before God. Let Him be your guide."

His hammer banged again. The gaoler Gil Hesketh tugged at Prissy's tether and began to lead her away. Prissy followed, leaving a wake of dread: crossed breasts, muttered prayers. She reached the Hall door just as Kit came through it. Prissy gazed at Kit, then around the chamber. Her eyes found Martha's, stared so piercingly that she was thankful when Prissy looked away. Kit made to go to her. Gil prevented him. Prissy stumbled and put out her hands. On her wrists a pair of red rings showed; raw skin, from where the rope had gouged.

They should be mine. The rope, the gouges. Martha could feel the guilt working, chafing her conscience. *Now, now: it was time to act.* She opened her lips and wet them. For one reckless moment she thought to go up to the bench and declare herself, relieve herself of this burden. She turned to Liz, who leaned a little towards her, her coif almost touching Martha's, as if to receive a confidence. Martha raised her hands. In her craw the worm uncoiled, her voice strained, its sinews cracked. Nothing: neither sounds nor words. The Hall door swung closed. The moment was gone, sweeping Prissy with it, and the mayor was calling another name.

Jennet. Who came to the bench holding her trussed hands before her, as in prayer. Master Bacon read out the charges. There were so many, a shocking number. That Mistress Savory kept an imp—a toad in a box—that she had for five summers or more let loose in Cleftwater, bidding it to spread the coughing sickness to every house in the village. That she had encountered a pedlar on the road to Sandgrave and cursed him, causing his donkey to fit; its owner was still lame from being trampled by it. That she gave bad ale to some Sandgrave beggars; when they confronted her she had fallen backwards to the ground where she had wantonly writhed and tumbled and called upon the Devil. Whereupon the oldest beggar—harmless, guiltless—had died of fright.

"What clearer evidence," proclaimed Makepeace, "need there be? The woman is a witch, and brazenly so. Only yesterday Mistress Savory encountered one of Cleftwater's gaolers—Master Herry Gowler, a God-fearing man—on his way home from evening church. And this gentleman did try, without regard to his own safety, to escort her out of the village, receiving for his pains the curse of the horned hand from this bold witch." Exhalations, gasps. Master Makepeace wheeled around to the judge's bench. "There is more," he warned, "and it is worse." He checked himself. "But perhaps it will be too much for this court."

"If you have evidence," the judge said, "then we must hear it."

The witch man listed them off, a litany of untimely deaths—some lingering, some short and brutal—at Jennet's hand. Muted cries and muttered prayers came from every quarter of the packed chamber, which seemed as the witch man spoke to contract, the light patching Jennet with glare and shadow, picking out the livid blotch on her cheek. She glowered. She swayed. Her guards snapped to, pulling her binds taut.

"Jennet Savory, the charges against you are many. They are severe. Do you hear them?"

"Oh aye, I hear 'em."

"You are charged with the deaths—murders—of many citizens of these parts. What say you to these charges?"

"I say they be false. People speak wrong, to say I done such things. I didn't do 'em. Nor even thought 'em. I never done harm and I never would harm anyone in Cleftwater, not man nor woman nor child. Nor any beast. Why would I wish harm on folk I live with?"

She glared at Judge Bacon, stiff-necked, defiant. Martha saw how he returned Jennet's look, a lingering one. In it was some history—encounters in the shifting summer dark, gasps issuing into the thick of the evening, a coin changing hands. Jennet transferred her gaze to the witch man.

"Your claims are false," she spat. "I'll not grace 'em with an answer."

A breeze had got in that filtered about the chamber, riffling the charge sheets. The judge clamped his hand on them. From the street outside came the toll of a handbell, then roars and jeers. Martha looked at Liz: another woman, being brought to gaol?

"False tales," Jennet said again. "Told by false people." She tugged urgently at her tether. Her eyes were wild and widening; her head jerked up and back. The guards backed away and tightened the rope. Jennet fought it. "Ask them, ask *them*," she shrilled. The rope surged as she thrust her hands at where Liz and Martha stood. "I saw what they done when my little nephew was born. Born marked so bad, he'd scarce drawn breath before they'd taken him from his mother. And then he was dead. *She* was there," Jennet shrieked, "and *her* as well. One of them's done evil, I know it, I swear. Make 'em tell it." Jennet's face was flushed, an unnatural red. "Think not ill of me, think no evil of me, who'd never harm my own kin. I am true. I done no harm."

She ranted. Words sprayed from her in a stream. With her sleeve, Martha wiped her face. She closed her eyes and straight away an image of the poppet bloomed, a perfect likeness. It gazed at her, mournful and accusing, wanting her to confess: that *she* was unnatural, a false friend to Prissy, a sinner worse than Jennet. Suffer her not; suffer not a witch to live. Martha clutched for her pouch, found the doll's slight bulk. Around it the air seemed to swarm. She mashed at it. Stop. Make this stop.

Jennet fixed her black eyes on the judge. "All Cleftwater's cursed," she told him. Her speech had grown sing-song and faint, as if she were retreating into a distance. "Cursed when we were cursed. Us women." She looked at the witchfinder. "You come like a flame to a candle," she said, raising one finger to point, "and set Cleftwater afire." She stopped. Her mouth fell open, as if emptying itself of its contents—of all Jennet. Then her knees buckled and she went down, landing sideways on her ribs. Her eyes rolled. Martha felt the fit coming as though it belonged to her. Jennet's spine arched: her own clenched in tandem, pulling her head sharply back.

The crowd bellowed, one man's panic setting off another's, alarm spawning alarm. Martha could feel Jennet's breath, the lungs pumping shallowly and too fast as if worked by bellows belonging to a demon. Jennet's heels drummed the floorboards, a frantic jig that set Martha's feet in motion. She rocked where she stood. Heads turned, looks were cast in her direction, the witch man's among them. She received them all like blows. What Jennet had implied—her unfinished accusation—the crowd was completing, filling in with suspicion. Oh, Martha, what have you done? What have you left undone?

On her hip the pouch swung and even as she felt the poppet through the leather the frenzy passed, as though the doll had somehow quelled it or sent it spiralling upwards, to the roof-beams where a host of painted angels, blue and red and gold, looked mildly on. She brought down her head. Jennet lay with the rope twisted around her. The guards had dropped it and fled to the far wall. Jennet's drumming heels slowed and then stopped. She lay gasping like a netted fish. Her bodice lacings had come partly undone and her breasts threatened to spill out.

A minute passed. The witch man walked to where she lay. So narrow a man, thinly built, his frame fitting easily within the shaft of mottled sun filtering through the west window, picking out his collar, the gilded cross on his neck. He leaned over Jennet, not too far. Contempt swarmed in his face.

"Does she live?" Master Bacon asked.

Master Makepeace prodded Jennet with the toe of one boot. His top lip curled. "She lives." He looked around for the guards. "Get her up," he told the Bullards. "Move her, I say," he said, clapping his hands for emphasis. Ned Bullard came and took Jennet by the shoulders. Gingerly he levered her up.

The judge said, "Open the door. The lady needs air, and we need cooler heads."

"You see first-hand how it is," Makepeace said to the whole

assembly, his face bright, his tone high and expansive. "You see how the Devil possesses those of her ilk. Makes toys of them, causes them to blather and lie."

"Perhaps," said Master Bacon drily. He had pulled off his wig and his hair stuck up like boar's bristle. "But she is well known for these fainting fits. This was not the first. Aside from them her record is blameless."

Jennet coughed, gagged, vomited a string of drool down her bodice. Father Leggatt went and crouched beside her with his hand on her back. "For pity's sake," he said. "Can she not have a drink?" No one moved. He looked around, his face full of appeal. "Friends. We *know* these women. We have lived with them, beside them, as our sisters, our wives, our friends. Until this week we thought them our own." He looked at Makepeace. "Jennet Savory is of age with me, I have known her all my life. I cannot believe what you say of her—these, these accusations you make."

"Hold, hold," a voice protested. Mogg Basford pushed his way to the foot of the dais, to plant himself before the judge. "Will you not ask whether the witch says true?"

"Whether what is true?" queried Master Bacon.

"What the witch said, before she fainted," Mogg waved to where Martha stood, "about the women there."

"We should pay no heed to the ranting of a woman in her sickness," Father Leggatt said.

"But I do heed," Mogg insisted. "She was very clear. Pointing to Martha Hallybread there."

"She pointed at all the search-women," said Master Bacon. "She singled none out. Besides, I do not judge that a woman's talk, when she is taken sick to fainting, can be thought accurate or true." His cheeks shone with two scarlet patches as though they'd been slapped. "Mistress Savory will be searched and watched, like the others. In this way we will arrive at the truth. What she says will be written down and brought before me in three days' time."

"Three days? Do you wish these Devil's bitches to prosper? Three days is ample time for 'em to do their work—to summon their imps against us."

"Mogg speaks true," said the mayor. "We should act now to stop them."

A salvo of ayes rippled around the Hall. The mood was souring, turning mutinous. Martha could see the change taking place, reading it in the shocked faces. A rescinding of goodwill; a cancelling of doubt. Already she and Liz were being stared at. They were corrupt. They were leprous, needing to be cast out. She shrank against the wall. Over the swell of disquiet Father Leggatt was calling for peace, pleading for calm, for reflection on the wisdom of St. Thaddeus. Let him without sin. Cast something: a stone; a die. Now the mayor was on the dais, shouting over the minister's words.

"—time for prayer has passed," he bellowed. "St. Matthew also tells us: 'If thine eye offend thee, pluck it out.' By like wisdom, when a surgeon is called to treat a rotten leg, does he let the whole body sicken in hope of curing the limb? He does not. He cuts out the bad to preserve the good, and no one thinks ill of his reasoning." His voice climbed. "So we should act, in this matter of witches. While they live they'll spread their contagion. Delay will cost us dear. You have only to look," he shouted over the crowd's roar of agreement, "at Mistress Savory. She is young, yes, but that stain on her cheek is doubtless the Devil's brand. So I say: let her hang, with her sisters, this day."

"Without a trial you cannot know," the priest retorted, moving to shield Jennet's body with his own, "that the women are guilty of what you say."

"Until they are dead," the mayor said, rounding on him, "you cannot be sure that Cleftwater is free from evil. Is it some Popish notion, some chancy article of your faith, that you speak up for these witches? Why plead for charity when they have shown us none?"

"Because these women, that you are so keen to condemn," the clergyman said hotly, "are no more witches than I am."

A pause: immediate, stunned, as if all air had been sucked from the chamber. The priest had made an error, Martha knew at once. He stood scarlet-faced and with his jaw working; the countenance of a saviour, or of a martyr. Then, as shock hardened into riot, he was surrounded and hauled by his cassock to the judgement table. Over the din—claim and counter-claim, Master Makepeace's loud insinuations—the gavel banged and banged. Judge Bacon was shouting, "Order, order," but it was going, almost gone. The All Saints bell began to sound and a fraction later the Moot Hall clock took up its tolling. Four o'clock on a winter Friday: the chimes were announcing a season of blame. A time to get, and a time to lose; a time to love, and a time to hate.

There was a falling sensation, as if her life's scaffolding was giving way. Martha stood in a stupor, trying to still the spin of her conscience, the riot of inner voices. All the accused had been taken away. Father Leggatt was gone—roped and led roughly out—with Jennet dragged behind him. The jurors dispersed, Master Makepeace went. The Hall emptied, its door swinging repeatedly open, letting in the outside world where the gulls went on with their screaming. Martha came back to herself, found that her hand still rested on the poppet. She let go of it. Where had Liz gone? Where was Kit? A scant ten paces away Mistress Knill stood, her eyes studying the pouch. How much had she seen?

"Tell me, Mistress Hallybread. What do you keep in your little bag?"

Be careful. Martha loosened the pouch fastening and pulled out a sprig of mallow. With her other hand she touched two fingers to her mouth and chest.

For my cough.

"For your cough?"

Aye.

A faint smile. "So many herbs, for a cough?"

Indeed, madam. She collected herself, remembered the kerchief. She took it out and held it up, bloody side out, to Mistress Knill. The thing had its own magic, or its stains did, for the search-mistress took a step back.

"The evil of witches is contagious, Mistress Hallybread. It spreads as quickly as the pox. Take care that you don't catch it. Vigilance: keen eyes are what is needed. Keep yours on the women. Ignore nothing. Report everything. No sign is too small." She turned for the door, turned back. "You should know that, just as you will watch the women, I will be watching you."

FOURTEEN

Friday evening

The search-room was a bedroom on the top floor of the alehouse, a chaos of blunt hatchets and bald brooms, battered pans heaped with old cutlery, cracked pisspots still crusted with filth, punctured buckets and piles of worn-out linen. The windows were curtained with old sheets roughly tacked to the frames. By the chimney was a sagging four-poster bed with one leg propped up on a brick. A small jabbing fire burned in the grate. At the end of the room a pair of men held a woman by her elbows, walking her between them but with such rapid strides that she was almost running. Her hair had worked loose from its cap and tumbled messily down her back. As the search-women came in, her panted lament stopped abruptly. The walkers turned, wheeling around their captive. Prissy hung from their grip.

"Come sit," Mistress Knill said, not unkindly, arranging a chair and a stool to face each other.

The floorboards creaked at their approach. Prissy fell like so much shed clothing onto the stool.

"You would make matters much easier, Mistress Persore, if you would tell us the truth, and unburden yourself."

In the pause Prissy's gaze travelled from one search-woman

to the other, coming to rest on Martha. "No? Nothing to say?" said the search-mistress.

Weary Prissy with her stunned expression, her martyr's air. Three days in captivity had marked her already; her cheeks hollowed, her eyes dimmed. "I pray you pardon, mistress. I don't know . . . what would you have me tell you?" She clasped her hands, then released them.

"No, Mistress Persore. You mayn't quiz *us*. It is we who ask the questions, and you who must answer them. I ask you again: what have you to tell us?"

The room was very close or its heat seemed to be closing in. Prissy clung to the sides of her stool with bitten fingers. "These last days I been walked and walked, and all this time I been rackin' my brains for what I done wrong." Again she looked at Mistress Knill. "I'm telling the truth, mistress. But no one'll hear it."

Mistress Knill nodded, steepled her fingers, placed them to her lips. She stood and dismissed the men. "Undress her," she told Martha.

———

Unlacings. Unhookings. Lifting off Prissy's bodice and blouse; a fixity of gazes. They worked in silence until Prissy was stripped. On display now her shapely arms and thighs, the outline of her ample bosom that she tried in vain to cover with crossed arms. At a signal from the search-mistress, Sue shaved her sex of its gold feathers. Then began the searching of all Prissy's body from the head down: her scalp, the back of her neck, the pits of her arms. Martha must steel herself to look, her fingers to prod the folds of Prissy's buttocks, the cleft between her legs. Then Sue lifted Prissy's breasts in turn, weighing their poundage like a butcher. Under the left were flaps of brownish skin—a cluster of them like fleshy mushrooms. Some of them were pink. Others were pale and strained-looking, a nail's length or longer. Sue paused her searching.

"What are these?" Mistress Knill said, peering at Prissy's torso. "Priscilla. Tell me. What do you say about these marks?"

Prissy looked down, craning her head to see what incriminated her. She fingered in her armpit and under her breast. "These? These are old, mistress. I don't know how I come by them."

"Do you not? You have forgotten? Or you think to deny the truth?"

"I . . . I . . . neither, mistress, I—"

"What have you *done*, Prissy?" Sue cried. "Have you promised yourself to the Devil? I always thought you a gentle soul, and harmless, who wanted only to please by making good ale and bread for her master and mistress." On the stool Prissy shook. Her terror seemed to infect Sue. "Look you, friends. See how she's given me her shaking." She held out her arms that tremored violently as if they were fighting the very air. "What are you doing to me, Prissy?"

"Calm yourself, Mistress Ruddock. I warned you both that witches deceive; it is their very nature. Our task now is to expose her, get her to confess her Devil's pact." Mistress Knill looked again at Prissy's marks. "Many times I have seen marks such as these on the pelts of witches." From the belt circling her waist she unhooked a tool—five slender inches of steel ending in a point. "My lancet," she said, holding it out for them all to see, "is immune to evil, indifferent to a witch's tales. It knows only what it finds at its tip." Gently the search-mistress applied it to her thumb. Martha saw how the point was tarnished, a rusty pink; under it the flesh dipped, as if in submission. "It will enlighten us," Mistress Knill went on. "It will show us the truth."

On the stool Prissy cowered, looking from Sue to Martha, regarding her with white eyes.

"Stand up," the search-mistress said.

Slowly Prissy rose. Expertly Mistress Knill applied the lancet, needling with a surgeon's care. Prissy grimaced and flinched. "Martha?" she said, in a half-whisper, her face screwed up with terror. "Tell them, I pray you, tell them how I done no harm to no one—"

Martha stepped closer to Prissy and took her arms, angling them back so that the young woman's hands were behind her—out of sight of Mistress Knill. Courage, courage: her fingers scrawled; a frantic message, and a dangerous one. Prissy fell silent. Had she understood? Impossible to know. Over the younger woman's shoulder Martha watched the working of the lancet, relentless, remorseless, scoring crimson daisy chains on Prissy's skin.

At last Mistress Knill straightened. "See here," she said, waving her instrument at the tags of skin, now reddened and wounded-looking. "See how these excrescences are insensible to the lancet? They do not bleed, even though they are pricked. And this long one here, that has a little hole in it? Unless I am mistaken—and I think not—this is a teat from which an imp has lately suckled." She thrust her face at Prissy, her gaze at full bore. "Is that not so, Mistress Persore? Tell us. Tell me of your imps."

"I . . . I have none, mistress."

"No? Then how is it that you have these teats?"

"I don't know, mistress. I only know I've had 'em since I was a maid."

"We were all maids once," Mistress Knill said smoothly. "It's plain that you are not one. You know full well," she said, underscoring her words with the pricking-tool, "what these marks are. Confess now, how they got there." A pause, while she studied Prissy. "Must I call Master Makepeace? He is a discerning man, experienced in the ways of witches. He will question you much less kindly than I do now. I have only to tell him of this teat, and *this* one, so strained from where your imp has freshly sucked. He will know you for what you are."

"But I'm nothing, mistress, nothin' but a village girl, like Sue says. Ask Martha. She'll tell you. Won't you, Martha?"

In Martha's gorge the worm surged so forcibly that she lurched, letting go of Prissy and almost over-balancing the stool. On her own skin gooseflesh sprang up as if already pricked.

"Tell 'em as I got nothin', not even lies," Prissy said.

Lovely Prissy with her liquid brown eyes, guileless as a child's. Small tears oozed from them as she stared about her, at Martha, the licking fire, the red-tipped lancet, Mistress Knill's expectant face. The stool rattled softly under her trembling.

"Foolish girl. Foolish Devil's darling. It profits you nothing to pretend." Mistress Knill knelt, bringing her face up close. "Tell us the truth, so that we may help you," she said, more gently. "What has your master, Satan, promised you? Only good things, I'm sure. A place in his bed, and fine clothes, and sweet things to eat? And no doubt he has pledged, oh, that no ill luck will come to you—that he will aid you in your distress. But where is he now?" Prissy went very still. "Has he shielded you thus far? Has he spared you from the gaol? No. He has wholly used you—his print on you is plain to see. He has taken what he wanted; now he deserts you." She sighed. "I have heard this story countless times. Listen to me now, Priscilla. I say: repent. Give up your imps—send them away to where they came from. Renounce whatever compact you have made with Satan; confess the truth and save your immortal soul."

"I cry you mercy, mistresses. If you know what I done then tell it me. So that I can confess it, and own it, and ask for God's forgiveness. But I cannot think of what I done—no crime I know, and I swear, no witching."

Mistress Knill let out a soft hiss of exasperation. From outside the room came scuffling footsteps, raised voices, a woman's shrieked protest cut off by a slammed door. Martha thought she recognised its tone—Rose Durriken or her sister. The cry came again, sharper, more panicked. Moments later someone rapped at their own door. Mistress Knill opened it. Liz Godbold stood with Kate Weeting, a fishwife from one of the tiny, light-starved cottages on the far side of the Cleft. The three women conferred in low voices. Thaddeus Spalding, the village undertaker, was behind them, staring intently into the room, where Prissy was still naked. Martha saw how Thaddeus's eyes glazed, how the cloth stirred at his crotch. She crossed to Prissy, standing squarely to screen her from view. Prissy's breasts could be hidden, but the teats—were they truly that, these little mushroom-coloured stubs of skin?—had declared themselves, whether Prissy owned them or no. Such marks were common enough; but oh, how life had turned about, when blemishes were judged to be evil.

A ribbon of sweat ran down Prissy's temple and Martha

put her sleeve to it, wishing her own distress could be as easily wiped away. The Lord will fight for you, and you have only to be silent: so Father Leggatt had preached, only this last Sunday. Holy silence. Consenting silence. Or this wicked silence, of which she was culpable; Martha the mute, the sham, the sinner. She could feel her guilt enlarging, a kind of soul-swelling, like a bruise.

She picked up Prissy's discarded shift and dropped it over the girl's head.

"Let's be havin' you," Thaddeus said, approaching.

Mistress Knill was stowing her lancet, preparing to leave. "Mistress Ruddock. Mistress Hallybread. I'm needed elsewhere. Master Spalding will stay here with you and I will send up Master Hesketh to help. Between you, you must watch her and keep her walking." To Thaddeus she said, "She must not rest. Do not let her sleep. She may have a sip of ale from time to time, but nothing else—no meat. Watch for anything, any act or sign. She will plead with you, and you must harden your ears. When she tires: that is when her imps are like to come, or she will call to them. They will be hungry, they will want to suck. Once they've fed she will no doubt bid them go to work. Note all you see. Learn their names, what she tells them to do. Keep your ears and eyes open, but doubt all she says. Send for me if you need to." A last look at Prissy, collapsed on the too-small stool. "It will go better for you, madam, if you confess quickly to what we can all see."

"I can't lie, mistress, for that's a sin. Yet Master Makepeace says my silence is also a sin." Prissy raised her child's eyes, looking at them each in turn. "What should I do?"

"What you do is tell the truth," Sue intoned.

"What you do is walk," Thaddeus said, raising Prissy to a stand. "Walkin's simple."

Martha put two fingers to Prissy's chin and tilted up her face, arranging her own so that the dismay wouldn't show. *Be comforted. Be steady,* her hands wrote quickly, though she looked at Prissy with a loving gaze. *I will do all I can.*

"What are you tellin' her?" Sue asked sharply.

Martha shook her head and crossed herself, then made washing motions with her hands.

The walkers made an unholy three as they went to and fro: the penniless Scour-wife, fishbone thin in her patched dress; the lustful undertaker, desire bulging in his breeches; between them, the hapless cook, who would not confess her familiars.

———

A witch may work her ill deeds fast but confess slow. This was how to tire her. Walk about, thirty paces. Turn around. Pace again, another thirty steps. Do this thirty times. Then another, and another. See the day fade into evening.

At suppertime came a change of watchers—Ned and Robert Bullard replacing Thaddeus Spalding. They would walk Prissy overnight. In the ale room Nan Dolan had set out a simple supper of boiled cod, day-old bread with butter, a dish of sea peas and another of turnip greens dripping with vinegar. Plain fare for plain women. Martha sat at table beside Sue Ruddock, hungry, queasy, trying to ignore the tread of feet over their heads. She took some tentative bites of bread, chewed, and gave up. *I need air.*

"I'm that weary, I can hardly eat myself," Sue said. "But we've earned our supper, eh, Martha?"

For an instant she felt a smudge of affinity, a faint sense of being one part of a process. Then it passed and she remembered what it was that linked them—this work they both did.

———

The evening was like the pressure of a hand, moon-dark and close. Coming out of the alehouse front door she caught sight of two men leading another prisoner back to the gaol. Dismay leapt in her like a shout. She crossed the street. At the top of the gaol steps she met Constable Napier coming up.

"Martha. What brings you over here?"

She dipped her head, told him with her hands that she'd been sent for news of confessions, though she knew he wouldn't understand. He regarded her suspiciously, as if deciphering her lie. At last he stood back. "On you go, then."

Martin sat by the gaol's locked gate with his chin sagged onto his chest. She shook him and straightaway he got up, rubbing his hands over his face and neck, over the burst boil's star.

I'm here to see Prissy.

"What?"

Prissy.

"Oh." He pointed with his chin. "They've taken her upstairs to see the judge. They're up there now."

She could feel anxiety being passed between them. *What for?*

"Nothing I know, Martha. All I can say is the witch man's up there too."

From the dimness beyond the gate came moaning. Martin

picked up the lantern. A figure like a dropped ragdoll lay prone in the filthy rushes.

Who's that?

"Ma Southern," Martin said flatly. His face creased. "They walked her wi'out stopping all around the Hall for three nights and a day. She's had only sips of water. If she's alive in the morning . . ." His voice trailed away. He peered through the grille. "She's done for." In the sickly light Martha could see how very tired he was himself.

Let me go to her? Martin hesitated, then unlocked the gate.

The prisoners lay or sat, ranged about the walls. Prissy was not here nor Rose Durriken, but Jennet and Ellen lay nearby, collapsed next to Ma Southern. Against the far wall Joan Durriken sat, dishevelled and folded over. Next to her Hannah Holland was tied up in a stall, lolling in her tether.

A lantern hung from the tie beam and by it Martha could see the various states of dismay and dejection, the signs of interrogation, clothing half undone, bare skin showing rope burns as well as bruises and welts, the lancet's tell-tale traces—tiny red blisters, like a pox where it had pricked. Martha's heart shook, as if in revolt; her body registering every wound like an injury to itself. She went to where Ma Southern lay. How many steps, how many miles had she been forced to walk in the last three days? Too many. Too many for this old woman, lame as she was. Her feet were bleeding and swollen—monstrous feet, like those of a hag. Now even her injuries would convict her.

Martha undid her pouch, feeling around the poppet for the herbs. She took them out and spread them on the floor in the arc of lantern-light. Yarrow, thyme, sage. She rolled them between her fingers and straightaway they released their healing scent. Her hands took over, knowing even in exhaustion what to do. She tore a strip of linen off the old woman's shift and bound the herbs to the damaged feet. This small assistance— this made-up last rite of dismay and torn linen: it was not enough but it was all she could offer, the best she could do. Ma Southern's breath whistled, faint through her slack mouth.

Martha left her and went to Ellen, almost tripping over the soil bucket. Ellen lay right beside it, too close to its contents, its terrible stench. Martha sat heavily down. The world seemed aslant, in disarray. She herself had played a part in disordering it. There was a duty to help right it. Carefully she made a cushion of her petticoats, then lifted Ellen's head and arranged it on her lap. The woman was dead asleep, her dirty face closed up. Martha stroked the greying hair. After a time her own eyes shuttered down. The tide was coming in, she could hear it, the hiss of its approach. The sea-surge and the smell of sweat and the low basic hum of the guards merged and wove together. She could feel herself thinning, slipping through some gap in herself, drifting through the long darkness over fields and reed beds, cliffs, staithes, arriving at a place that was familiar—dreamt or real—some landing-place of her soul.

It was dim but not lightless where she was. She loitered, anxious to be gone, lacking strength to pull herself away. Far off a small shape composed itself, limned by some tarnished glow. The figure advanced, and then was upon her. The poppet: in living detail, its wax vividly translucent, its nostrils breathing, its lips plumped and curving into a kind of smile. Light ran in its veins. Martha heard herself gasp and wrenched her eyes away. Felt in her palm a soft heft forming; looked down and found the poppet curled there, the bud of its thumb in its open mouth, watching her with calm white eyes. A babe, it was Kit's babe, with Agnes's slightly hooked nose. She could only watch, pinned in the moment. After a time or an eternity the wax billowed, folding in, opening out. In her hand a figure crouched, like Mam in all her ruined beauty, shaking her head from side to side, now smiling, now viewing Martha with a sorrowful gaze. *Two choices. Twice missed, twice rueful. Your choices.* Mam's entreaty sounding, bell-like through the doll.

Then the figure split, forming into two. That in turn split again and doubled—pairs of figures, one leading the other— a mother and child? a master and servant?—that multiplied again and again, becoming a host of poppets, too many to be counted. All of them damaged, all of them regarding her. Then they melted, condensing, merging into a single poppet that called her name in a multitude of voices, even as it dimmed and turned and limped away.

———

She surfaced with a jolt. A hammering in her pulse. The lantern leaking oily smoke like a bad thought. She forced herself fully awake. The gaol, she was in the middle of it, on the floor. By the slops bucket, its smell almost touchable. Ellen's head still cradled on her thighs, which were aching now. Guards one side of the gate, women on the other.

She felt her pouch. The poppet was there in its cocoon of herbs. A visitation or a dream: which? She scrubbed her eyes, chafed her arms, feeling out her edges. Despite the night's heat she felt chilled and somehow exposed. A painful truth had been revealed: of the fissures in her conscience—her own divided nature—its capacity to heal or harm. Overhead the

Moot Hall clock began to toll, marking the end of first watch. Three of the clock, that fault-line in the night's passage, when good and evil forces rose from slumber to resume their various labours.

Soft primitive noises came from Ellen's open mouth. Her lips had cracked open with thirst. Martha eased herself to stand and waved at the gaolers. They were sitting beyond the gate around the fire cradle, its embers like a glowing eye. They hadn't seen her, were too busy passing the ale jug between them. She went to the gate and rattled it. Judah Godbold—Liz's son—glanced over. She mimed: *Something to drink.* Judah regarded her, then got up and brought across the bucket. He filled a cup for her and passed it through the grille. The water was unclean, filmed with dirt and bits of rush. Balm. She drank half.

More?

He hesitated. "What?"

She waved the cup behind her. *More water. For the others.*

Judah glanced behind him. "What's she saying, Ned?"

"I think she means for them all to have something to drink." Ned looked at Herry. "What did Master Makepeace say?"

"He said nothing about drink," Herry said, comfortably.

"But he didn't say they couldn't."

"He didn't say they could."

Ned hesitated. "A few sips, only. He needn't know unless you tell him, Herry."

"Well guessed, my friend. I will be tellin' him." Herry jerked his head at the women. "They can wait. Ignore them."

Too late. Joan Durriken had seen the cup and sat up and begged to drink. Her complaint woke the others. Their hoarse refrain built.

"How can you deny 'em?" Judah protested. "They've bin here for hours with nothing. All they want is a sip."

"And then a cup, and then the bucketful," Herry said. "They want it, right enough, so they can suckle their demons." He took the cup, swigged, hawked the contents through the gate, splattering Martha's skirts. Through the iron lattice she glared at him. She'd known his mother, dead some years, but Herry had been the apple of her eye, cherubic as he passed around the collection plate. The women were on their feet now—those strong enough to stand. Anger was rising on both sides of the gate. Jennet rattled it.

"Give us that," she told Herry. "We're not proved guilty yet, you witch man's scab."

Herry's expression altered: some new calculation printing itself on his face. He picked up the bucket, raised it to shoulder height, began to pour out the contents, the liquid silver streaming onto the dirt. "Here's water for you, you Devil's sots," he taunted. "Get your imps to fetch it, if you thirst."

Behind him the gaol steps were filling with boots. Four pairs: one lustrous and new-looking. Master Makepeace, with Constable Napier and two guards. The witch man came up to the gate. He paused, his eyes tracing the outlines of dishevelled figures, of uncovered heads and bosoms. "They may drink," he said, at last. "A half-cup each. This one too." He meant Prissy, collapsed between her captors. He motioned for Herry to unlock the gate. Half walking, half dragged, Prissy came in. When she was let go she fell straight to the floor and lay utterly still.

Like a corpse. Martha crouched. A current of sick feeling went through her that she fought hard to keep down. Judah brought the bucket. There was very little water in it—a knuckle's worth, that he poured into the cup. Martha roused Prissy, tried to tip small mouthfuls in. The liquid dribbled into the dirt. Martha knelt and lifted Prissy's head onto her lap and tried again, ladling the water past the girl's parched lips with her fingers. Pray God Prissy would recover quickly: once she'd been let go—in the morning perhaps, when the men realised the girl was blameless, an innocent with nothing more sinister than burnt porridge or undercooked bread to confess. Maybe she, too, would be let go, having done her share of searching. She pictured their homecoming, Prissy once more in the kitchen, herself among the herbs. The house light and eased of burdens, its cheer revived.

Prissy stayed blank. As she smoothed back strands of sweat-damped gold hair Martha became aware that she herself was being watched. She glanced up. The witch man and the constable were studying her with serious faces. Noting her care of Prissy, suspecting her of fellow feeling. She thought for a moment, then resumed her stroking, slow, deliberate, feeling over Prissy's scalp, behind her ears, the sides of her neck, her chest. Inspecting what she found. Making a show of it: this mock searching. Let them think her watchful. Let them think her diligent.

"What do you find on her?" Constable Napier called. "Is she marked?" The uneven lantern-light made a monster of him, his features contorted, his silhouette grotesque.

Aye, she shaped, *but no more than you or I.*

He didn't know her language. "What's she saying?" he asked Judah.

"I can't rightly tell. The Persore wench has been searched already, but what they found I don't know."

"Has she talked?"

Gil Hesketh grunted. "Aye. She has."

"What has she said?"

"Enough," Gil said.

The men moved away. Martha watched them converse. They were too far off to make out what was said. What had Prissy said? Been forced to say? Gil was still talking, very earnest; the witch man impassive, the constable responding with incredulous looks and small shakes of his head.

When the men left she followed them at a careful distance up the steps. The witch man glanced around and saw her and motioned for the others to be silent. On the street they nodded to her before parting, Master Makepeace back to the alehouse, the others for home. Judah Godbold lived at the foot of the Scours and without a word to her he set off along the beach. She trailed behind. Maybe he would talk. Maybe she might pry some useful fact—

"I can't tell you nothin'," he said abruptly, wheeling around. "So there's no use you even askin'." He looked exhausted. "I'm away to my bed. You should do the same."

————

Judah's boat was with several others that were pulled above the tideline and turned on their sides against the weather, a cluster of bulky wooden forms showing definite in the darkness. Martha lowered herself to the shingle and propped her back against its planking. The sea breathed. From somewhere—Psalm Cliff or Top Field—the plaintive call of a pheasant. A sense of Mam and countless people before her who had watched and waited and read the sea and the stars and the movements of the moon, trying to discern their meaning.

As she was now. Of the constellations she knew—Kit had taught her—she could see the Plough and the belt of stars of the Hunter and, faintly, the girdle of the Chained Lady. Silently she laughed to herself. Even stars could be trapped. The bay curved north and south and the shore was outlined in both directions by village lights, thumbprints of flickering amber. Here she had stood just three nights ago with Prissy, washing her hands in the brine. Carefully washing her hands of the Archer babe; of the tragedy of his birth.

The sea was silk and the sky clear with a slender moon, and in its lustre her cowardice was no longer deniable. It should be her, Martha, in the gaol, her body being searched, her pretences with her clothing stripped off; her essence exposed.

She breathed in deeply. Gorse and dry grass and salt. Pure scents. Wholesome scents. The pump of her lungs and the beat of her heart felt definite and useful in her chest. If she, Martha, took Prissy's place there would be an end to torn loyalties; an end to searchings—of bodies and her conscience. She would be able to live with herself again—for what life she had left.

The decision felt almost physical, an appreciable lifting in her blood.

FIFTEEN

Saturday morning

S omeone shook her awake. "Martha. *Martha.*" Sue shook her
again. "Shift yourself. We've to go to the alehouse. Mistress
Knill wants us."

Daybreak, just. Martha lay for a moment taking in the
details of the beach. An intact morning, the sea still and tin-
coloured, framing Sue's sombre face. It was an effort to come
back into herself, to re-enter her body, to make it stand. She had
slept the last few hours of the night propped against the boat,
and now she was chilled and stiff. She followed Sue along the
street and went through the alehouse yard, past the stable and
along the flagged path to the scrubby patch of ground that was
Nan Dolan's unlovely vegetable patch. Behind a tall clump of
mulleins she lifted her skirts to piss. The heat hammered, above
and around, and the sky was scumbled with cloud every shade
of grey. She had been a search-woman for less than a day and
already she was thick-headed with confusion. The facts glared but
she struggled to assemble them, to put them in their right order.
How was it, that she was here? Shuttling between the gaol and
the alehouse—poles of suffering and ease—in her stale clothes?

Because the witch hunt had requisitioned her. Because Kit
had, with the best of intentions, bartered her. Last night's resolve

to take Prissy's place seemed void now, as if drained out through the cracks in her conscience. In its place was an ache of resentment, of foreboding. There was too much risk, too much that could miscarry. As it had for Mam, who had after years come back to Cleftwater, to redeem herself in her daughter's eyes at least; whose return had culminated in a savage death.

No. Never. Not for her that course. In the water-butt by the stables she was startled by her reflection, wild hair escaping from her coif, eyes staring from the intricate lines of her face. She looked like a witch. Was she one? She was suddenly and briefly elated, then just as suddenly dismayed. In her head a new argument started up, a hubbub of dissenting voices. She could go to the constable, make a show of revealing the poppet. Feign to have found it in Kit's house, or near it. That much at least was true. Then seed the suggestion that a stranger had left it—to bring misfortune on Kit, maybe. Last year's storm took lives as well as his ships; not everyone wished Kit's house well. Through the leather of the pouch her fingers found the poppet. The lump of it; its small mass. She cupped it in one hand. Like holding the littlest life, the tiniest babe. Kit's babe. A rush of feeling went through her. Aye, aye. The pattern of history was abruptly clear. Mam had surrendered herself to secure Martha's freedom, leaving the poppet in her place. She, Martha, might do the same: hand over the poppet, and in surrendering it, buy freedom for Prissy and herself. So that they might return home and help Agnes birth Kit's child, and live to see it grow.

She found Mistress Knill at breakfast with the others, Sue and Liz and Kate. Mistress Knill looked very well, calm and tidied, her hair neat under a snowy coif. She bade Martha sit and so she did, slumping down next to Kate on the bench. Liz passed her the bread. Martha broke off a piece. It was freshly baked, warm and fragrant. She chewed for a long time, savouring it before swallowing. Besides the beer there were some small wizening apples and a plate with a wedge of pale cheese, waxy as the doll. Her hunger was sharp but she could not bring herself to eat the cheese. She took an apple instead.

"I'm told you visited the gaol last evening, Martha," Mistress Knill said. "Did you see anything? Hear anything? From the prisoners?"

The apple's sourness scoured her mouth. She had eaten too fast and the food balled in her craw, lodged there with the worm, with all those things that mustn't be said.

Nothing, mistress.

She drank a long draught of small beer. The alehouse was filling with noises, unfamiliar oddments of sound. The boards of the ceiling creaked and groaned. Already the walkers were at work; the next witch being put through her paces. Where they ate was at the back of the tavern, and as she put down her cup she saw Master Makepeace waiting on the back porch. Mistress Knill got up and went to him and they greeted each other with warmth, like brother and sister. They went outside, walking slowly, conversing with their heads inclined together. The subdued light picked out their colours, the witch man's spade-like beard that moved up and down as he talked, the night black of Mistress Knill's gown. They walked to the end of the path and paused. Mistress Knill glanced briefly over her shoulder at the watching search-women, who bent again to their meal.

"I hear there's more folk being brought in today," Sue said.

"More?" Kate said. "Who can they be?"

Sue shrugged. "We'll find out soon enough." She took the ale jug and re-filled Kate's cup and then her own. "I'd hoped we'd be finished today, get back home to our families, but no." She ran a hand over her forehead, pushing back stray hairs. "There are so many to search."

"Do you doubt this work?" Liz Godbold said, looking at them all with her poacher's face. Her slack jowls hung down like wattles, quivering as she chewed. "D'you doubt the need of it? Your part in it?"

Kate lowered her knife. "Sue and me, we're not for doubting, Liz. I'm as pledged to this work as you. But I got children at home and so has Sue, and she got a husband away fighting. When we said we'd help we told 'em, we can't be away for too long—"

"Hush," Sue said urgently. "They're comin' back."

From lowered eyes Martha watched the pair returning, two black carrion birds. She thought she heard Father Leggatt's name. Her lungs halted and her belly jack-knifed. No. Surely not the priest. Christ's own messenger, here in Cleftwater. She put down the apple. She wanted her cup, something to spit into. The others were supping with their heads down. She felt for the pouch, opened it, touched the shape of the poppet nestling there. The thought of using it drove away the sickness and made her feel alive, uplifted.

The witch man stood at the top of the table, put his palms together, and slightly bowed his head. Mistress Knill copied him. Martha glanced uncertainly at the others. Liz had stopped eating and put down her bread and cheese, and after a moment they all did the same, sitting silent and expectant. A moment passed. Then another.

Then the witch man's eyes opened. His gaze found its focus, arriving as if from far away. "Mistress Knill tells me of your dedication," the witch man said. "That you have been unwavering in your work. I thank you for your efforts. With me, you are helping to purge Cleftwater of a sickness—a cancer, a plague, a most grievous contagion. Though I've been here but four days, I find that Satan's brides are rife in this village, as they are in every part of this county. They never cease to scheme against us. They must be halted and cast out, so that your village can be whole again and return to health in God's eyes." He folded one hand over the other. "God suffers the Devil many times to do much hurt; that is a mystery, and not for us to question. What we can know is that Satan stands ever prepared. Being of long standing—above six thousand years—he is a skilled and subtle tempter: no one is immune from his reach. When he covenants with a witch to depart from God and become his own darling he does so with her blood, and promises to shield her, and save her from downfall. But as fast as he tricks, he betrays. His victim thinks to save herself with silence or denial or by force of her own stubborn will. She may even—at his persuading—offer herself of her own accord to be searched and tried, believing that her Devil master will deliver her. But he does not, and he will not, as these wretches soon discover." His expression was pinched and grave but Martha could see his pride poking through it. "You will likely witness all these deceits today. You will be called on to search friends and neighbours who you know well—who you thought beyond the Devil's reach." He made a quick, sweeping gesture, as if he were cutting something. "All these friendships, these loyalties, these affections—they must be doubted, they must be set aside, to do this work. Believe nothing. Examine everything."

Slowly and deliberately he looked at each of them in turn. "Will you do this? Will each of you give us your word, to make your searches thorough?" His gaze was stern. When each woman had nodded agreement he clasped his hands once more. "'Let your light shine before men, that they may see your good deeds and praise your Father in heaven.' These are the Apostle Matthew's words. Remember them as you go about your work today." He glanced at Mistress Knill: his lips curled, more grimace than grin. "I will leave you to your search-mistress." Then he slipped his narrowness through the doorway and was gone.

Martha was paired with Sue again. They followed the search-mistress upstairs. On this floor there were two search-rooms, each one with a captive. On the landing Mistress Knill told them to wait until she summoned them. She unlocked the door of the right-hand room and let herself in.

The alehouse had not cooled much overnight and the air of the upper floor was stale. Martha went to the small casement window and tried the catch. It was stuck closed. The view was halved by the panes of glass. One had a flaw in it that made the scene warp. Three people were crossing the street, a prisoner and two gaolers. They came on, walking into the fault. They were briefly monstrous and then they were through and whole again: a limping Father Leggatt, being led down Tide Lane towards the Cleft.

A sharp throb of misgiving below her breastbone. Where

were they taking him? As if he'd heard her thoughts he looked up. His face altered—a stricken look—and he gave a wan wave. She checked herself, and the urge to step back. Nay, aye: she must support him, she must stay this course. Carefully she nodded to him, brought the fingertips of both hands together and kissed them. *Fear thou not; for I am with thee: be not dismayed; for I am thy God.* He would understand this sign that was meant to buoy them both. Perhaps he would fare better than the others, given his faith. His certainty, not just in God but in salvation. That was what he'd preached.

She could feel her conscience beginning to sway again, its needle starting to lurch. In the salt-smeared glass her reflection signalled, caught her own attention. At her hip was a pouch with a poppet in it. Useless, until she used it.

She glanced around. Sue was sitting with her back turned at the top of the stairs. Martha surveyed the window. Its frame was damp around the hinges. She picked at the rotting wood until a splinter the length of her little finger came free, which she tested against the inside of her wrist; imagined it piercing the poppet's skin. Downstairs the inn door opened, admitting tramping feet and voices. Gaolers, coming in. In the same moment a voice called for her and Sue. No time to grapple with it, for Mistress Knill was summoning them to the search.

———

"Bring more light," the search-mistress said.

Martha lit a rushlight from the wall sconce and went slowly to the table where Jennet lay clothed only in her shift. Her head hung over the table edge on an angle that exposed the bones of her throat. How slight she was, how pale.

"Bring that closer," said Mistress Knill. She had folded Jennet's shift up to her hips; now she pushed the young woman's knees apart. Martha lowered the rush. The stuttering light showed Jennet's privy parts, the flesh in a shaven nest of hair. Martha looked away. Wrong to see this, Jennet's modesty, so ruthlessly displayed.

"See here," said Mistress Knill, reaching for the rushlight and bringing it right down, almost to the skin. Jennet cursed, then mewed with fright. "Look closely," said Mistress Knill, "and tell me what you see."

"You see nothing," Jennet barked, "but what all us women got."

Martha forced herself to look. The folds of Jennet's privates were dull pink and secret. Mistress Knill ran the blunt end of the lancet over them, lifting the cunny-lips. Martha saw their defect at once. The lips were large and sagging, like miniature udders. On the table Jennet fought, trying to pull her knees closed. It was an effort not to help her. Mistress Knill was waiting, her face alight, her eyebrows arched.

What answer should she make? The cunny-lips were ugly, aye, but not a sin. God had made them this way.

"What say you?" the search-mistress said, pointing with the lancet. "D'you not think her lips large?" She looked at Sue, who nodded.

"Aye, mistress, they are."

"What say you, Martha?"

She rocked her head, making a show of considering, trying to win more time. *Maybe. Maybe.* Her fingers sketched her doubt, the many privy parts she had seen, the many cunny-lips.

Some longer, some scarcely formed—such imperfections were the very nature of nature.

"Yes, yes," Mistress Knill said, impatient. "You have tended many women, and seen their privates, and what should be correct in them, and what is not. I ask about *this* woman. Look you. These are not the parts of an honest woman. These are the lips of one who has been pleasured by the Devil, are they not?"

Martha's thoughts were blazing in her head. Careful now, go carefully, for Jennet's sake and for her own. One wrong word could damn her friend, but with silence she might damn them both. On the table Jennet winced and jerked; she was trying to sit up, to lift her head.

"I got no imps," she said. Her voice was hoarse, coming from her stretched throat. "I swear it. I'll swear it on the Bible if you want. I'm no witch. I got no imps."

"Then how is it," said Mistress Knill, "that your lips have got so large? These are no virgin's lips. Who has used them?"

"Nothing. I've opened my purse to nothing—"

"But it has been opened. These are the lips of one who has known the Devil, and suckled his imps."

"No, mistress, no! None of that!"

"You lie. The proof is plain to see," said Mistress Knill, waving the lancet. She leaned over Jennet. "Think of what you face—your body on the gallows, your soul in Hell. Tell us the truth while you still can."

"I got none to tell," Jennet spat, straining away from the lancet. The cords of her neck bulged. "'Cause I'm no witch."

A pause. In the shifting light Mistress Knill seemed to change shape, enlarging with conviction. "Sit up, then," she said, coldly furious. Carefully she stowed away the lancet. Jennet pulled herself up, tugged down her shift. Her eyes sought Martha's, arriving full of complaint. She couldn't return Jennet's look. She felt a draining sensation inside. What help could she give? What help was it possible to give?

The fire exploded. Huge flames flared, roaring up the chimney, expelling volleys of sparks that skittered across the floorboards. Martha ran to stamp them out. There were too many. Sue joined her. The fire vomited again. They stamped harder, circling around the spitting hearth more and more urgently. The sparks were obstinate, refusing to die. Mistress Knill seized a balding broom to swipe with. It caught fire, its head flaming until Sue doused it with the contents of the pisspot. Jennet watched white-faced from the table with her bare feet drawn up for safety. After a time all the danger was stamped out. The room's light was unnerving, complicated with smoke.

"You try to work the fire against us," Mistress Knill told Jennet. "But you are only damning yourself with this display of your craft."

"I do no such thing," Jennet insisted. "For I got no craft." She swung her legs from the table and stood up. Her bunched shift dropped and with it came blood, a sudden crimson gout, that puddled on the floor. Jennet gasped and clapped her hands to her groin. Through her splayed fingers her shift speckled. "I've got the curse early," she said, and looked at Mistress Knill. "You done that. You pricked me so it would come."

The search-woman made a small noise of disgust. "You forget, Jennet Savory, that I have seen all—every witching antic. None of your tricks surprise me. None will save you. So I bid you: clean yourself."

Jennet's pale eyes fastened on Martha's. They were frightened but their expression held a plea nonetheless—a wordless appeal for help. Martha blinked, slowly, the subtlest indication of assent. The smell of suspicion seemed to follow her as she sorted through the room's debris, the confusion of baskets and crates, the derelict bed. She tore a piece of moth-eaten damask from its once fine drapes. On the edge of her vision she saw a lump move, detach itself from the bed-frame— a solid knot of moving black. She froze. The thing ran, its spindle legs pumping. It was running towards Jennet, towards Sue and Mistress Knill, who had not yet seen it. On Martha's neck the fine hairs stood to attention. Instinctively she reached for her pouch. The creature reached the margin of the blood, probing at it with raised front legs. Mistress Knill screamed, a long curdling sound. The creature darted, skimming over Jennet's foot. It found Jennet's dropped blue dress, a fold in its cloth, and went in.

Her pulse thundered but her mind was the opposite, skittering madly, like a startled deer. She felt hard at the edges but untethered inside. The room, their reason, had been overtaken by this terror that would only breed unless it was lit away. She picked up the rushlight she'd dropped, went to the fire, relit it, gave it to Sue, pushing it into her hands. Then lit another rush, then another. What was it that they'd seen?

Spider? she shaped, in a large loose movement, trying to convince Mistress Knill. Trying to convince herself. Her head swam; the room rocked. Her hand when she opened the pouch was an old woman's hand, blotched and veined and trembling. She pulled out the wad of herbs and thumbed carefully through it until she found a sprig of sage, blessed herb of protection, that she lit and waved over the dress. Its smoke was reassuring, a steadying, Godly scent.

After all, the room was old and full of webs; the alehouse thatch was thick with them. Besides, it was September, when spiders were more bold.

Mistress Knill expelled a huff of breath, twisted to look at Jennet. "That was your imp."

"I got no such thing," Jennet said.

"But you do. All three of us saw it."

"'Tis but a mouse or a spider, that's all. This room's likely full of 'em. You can't say as it's mine."

"Oh, but I can! You stirred up the fire, so that it would come. And come it did, and sup your blood, and now it is waiting in your gown." Gingerly she came to Jennet, skirting the blood. "Lies will not save you." She scanned Jennet's face. Her own was bright. "The truth will out. Come now, tell me. What is its name?"

"How would I know, mistress? It's a spider. If it has a name you'll have to guess it, 'cause I don't know it."

"Don't toy with me, girl. The proof of your wickedness is plain to see—it is everywhere in this room. You are lost—you must know that—your life is as good as finished." Mistress Knill's voice softened. "I am offering you the chance to redeem yourself in the next. Confess. Admit your Devilry. Turn to Christ, who alone has the power to save you. Surrender your imp."

Jennet gave her a flat look.

"Tell me its name."

Jennet's eyes swivelled to her dress and back again. "Well, now. It could be . . . Gyles. It could be Malkin." Her speech raced, her voice rose. "It could be Johnny Eight-Legs, or it could

be Black-Eyed Grizelda. I couldn't tell you. For 'tis not any creature I know."

Mistress Knill let out her breath. "You are for the gallows,"
she told Jennet. "Unless you confess I will bring Master Makepeace: let us discover what he will say." To Sue she said, "Keep
watch. Don't let her use her creature."

"I pray you, madam," Sue said. "I can't stay here. Not with
that . . . *thing* hidin' in her dress."

"For shame, Mistress Ruddock. I had thought better of you."

"Please, mistress." Sue held up her palms as if warding off
evil spirits. "I'm afeared of her creature, of what it might do.
You can find me some other searchin' task and I'll do it gladly."

"Then go next door to where the Holland woman is being
searched and make yourself useful there."

Mistress Knill went to the door and opened it. Sue almost
tripped on her skirts in her haste to get out. The key turned
in the lock.

———

They waited. Jennet's face was blanched and a blue vein bulged
at her temple. She was young but there was a new wariness in
her face, a dignity also, that made her look older. The small room
seemed to close steadily in. Martha was afraid and sweating,
batting away the discomfort until it was overwhelming and only
then went to the window and forced it open. New air surged in,
bringing a blunt recognition. Father Leggatt preached that Satan
could take many forms. Until today she'd doubted, never fully
believed the village could hold such a variety of evils—not in
the way the priest described. Surely there could be no foothold
for such things. Not in Cleftwater. Not in her own small and

ordinary life. But now: the spider the size of her hand, Jennet's blood. The spitting fire, the too-large lips. They couldn't all be discounted.

All her knowledge—a lifetime's experience, its facts and truths—truths she had assumed were sound and inviolate— all were now strained, on the cusp of corrupting. *Was* Jennet a witch? She fingered the poppet through the worn leather of her pouch while her mind searched out a prayer, a time-worn plea for protection, and began to recite it.

"Martha? Look at me. We ain't got much time." Jennet was standing by the incriminating gown with the fire-iron at the ready. "I got a thing to say to you that I didn't want to say in front of that pricker-woman." Her voice was sharp. "Thing is, Martha, we both know it's *you* as should've been brought here to be pricked. Not me." Colour flooded her face. "I've done nothing. I ain't harmed any babes. You know I got no Devil-imps. I'm innocent as the driven snow." Her tone was bitter. "You know it, Martha, but you don't tell. You could, but you don't. And don't plead—" she hissed, her tone rising, "that you got no voice to say it with. You got means enough when you need it."

Martha's hands hung down, useless as leaves.

Jennet went to the door and covered the keyhole. "So now you'll do as I say. You tell them the truth, the actual facts. I been loyal to you. Now you be loyal to me. Say that you've known me all my life, and that you'll swear on yours I'm no witch. Put your hand on the Bible if you need to. Swear that you never seen me do what they say I did." Her eyes flicked to the dress and back. "You've had a goodly portion of your life, Martha, but I got plenty left of mine, and I want to live it. I'm askin' you to tell the truth, even if it puts you on this table, with your skirts hitched up and that pricker-bitch needling at you." She went over to her dress and considered it. "I'm minded to get rid of that big old spider. Give it a whack with this and then put the whole lot on the fire. We could say as how we never saw it. That it never was. It would be our word against my lady Knill's. What do you say, my friend?"

They studied each other, watching each other's face for clues. "Quickly," Jennet said. "I've given you two choices. You can tell 'em I'm innocent, and take my place on this table. Or you can help me get rid of this creature she's saying is my imp, and take my side and say there never was one." A piercing look. "For you know as well as me, I'm no witch. D'you hear?"

Martha's hands moved, but slowly. *Aye.*

"Good. Then choose now, before that pricker-bitch comes back."

She pressed her temples, a useless attempt to order her thoughts. She no longer knew what to think. Only that she was afraid. *I need to know*, she motioned slowly. Her hands were slow, as laggard as her reasoning. *Is it . . . ?* She tapped with her foot where the creature hid. *Is that . . . YOURS?*

Jennet's face hardened. "Do you *really* think it, Martha? That I'd have such a thing?"

Her mind laboured. The imp's presence signalled the end of cherished things—of goodness, of innocence, of loyalty to her friend. Martha backed away. *Ask no more of me. I can't help you.* She watched Jennet change colour, mottling and turning white. A wave of grief went through her, chased immediately by regret.

Pass me that. The fire-iron was warm from Jennet's grip. Martha provoked the heap of cloth, wishing the tool were longer. The creature emerged—so very black and large. It ran straight to Jennet as if seeking shelter.

"Do it, Martha!"

As she brought down the iron she wondered what mess there would be. But the creature ran out from under the blow, to the chimney breast. She knocked it into the fire and a spurt of dirty flame spat and leaped and died back. When moments later it climbed out she thought her heart would fail entirely. She could hear the faint scrimmage of its damaged legs as it found purchase on the brick. With the rod she indicated it. *Use your creature to save yourself.*

Jennet was staring in that fixed way, the whites of her eyes bulging and threatening to roll, the first sign of a fit. "You know I can't," she said in a part-whisper, as if some of her voice had been stolen. "That thing's nothing of mine." She was beginning to scrabble and pant. "Tell 'em. What we said. *You're* the witch. Tell 'em so. Keep it, Martha. Your promise."

But she'd made none. There were footsteps sounding from below—several pairs—a guard's ponderous tread, Mistress Knill's lighter step. With the fire-iron she hooked up the gown. *Put this on. Haste, haste.* When Jennet did not move she dropped the rod and went to her, wrenching Jennet's gown over her shoulders. At arm's length she tied the first few lacings. The eyelets of the bodice seemed to squint with undisguised fury. Jennet pulled away, her movements large and imprecise, her look crazed.

I can do no more. You must help yourself now, she told her friend, trying to steady herself, or brace them both. *God save you.* The door flung open and the Bullard brothers came in together with the constable. Sue and Mistress Knill followed.

In silence they took in the scene, Jennet's smut-streaked face, her half-done-up bodice, the red incrimination on the floor.

"Take her to the gaol," Mistress Knill said.

"Wait," Jennet shrilled. "It's not me you want. It's *her*," she said, ducking Robert's grasp. "Martha's the one."

"Hear how she blames another for her own Devilry," Mistress Knill said. "Where is the creature?"

Martha pointed. *Up there.*

"Get on, lads," said the constable. "Get hold of her."

"Keep your word, Martha," Jennet cried. "Tell 'em what you swore—"

"Be silent, girl," warned the constable, "or I'll have you bagged."

In the doorway Jennet wrestled Robert to a halt. "I'll not be silent when that one's done worse than anything you say of me," she spat, twisting in Robert's grip. "See her, see *her*, that cursed my sister's babe so he was born marked—"

"She's going to start her frothing," Ned said.

"Then get her out," Constable Napier barked. He slammed the door closed. They could hear Jennet's struggle, the shriek of her protest as she was dragged away.

"You may go also, Martha," Mistress Knill said. She was elated, watching the chimney, walking back and forth. "Your work here is finished for now."

SIXTEEN

In the passageway between the kitchen and the ale room Martha slowed to a stop. Guards and bailiffs were at a late-morning dinner, and the drone of their talk and the clink of cutlery and tankards reached her through the gauze of her thoughts. It was not possible to get purchase on any one feeling, all the urgent jostlings of anger and loss. In her throat a flare of sickness: the worm, restless with its own unsound vigour. Things could mean more than one thing or nothing at all. A spider could be itself or an imp. A woman was a woman, a priest God's servant—until a court or a witchfinder re-named them. Then: a woman could be a witch, and God's servant corruptible. Then lips not made for speaking could cost a woman her life. The difference was nothing or everything, a cavil or a creed.

Through the back door she could see a man relieving himself in the yard. The sky had clouded and in the diminished light she couldn't tell who it was. Then he finished and came back in, fastening his breeches. Master Makepeace. He saw her, halted, seemed about to speak. In his eyes she read a kind of dismissal, a rising disgust. She felt guilty, somehow caught out; was sharply aware of her shapeless girth, her countrywoman's intricately lined face. She was older—old—on the margins of usefulness, incapable of breeding, no longer attractive if ever she had been. Despite her muteness, capable of contradiction because of her knowledge, a lifetime's experience that grew in her like weeds.

At last he made to go past her. The worm thrust and involuntarily she coughed pink spray on them both. He let out a small cry of disgust. Then he was wiping at his sleeve with a square of fine cambric as he went quickly away.

It was suddenly too hot, or maybe it was she who was hot with a spry, lancing anger. She went to the kitchen, saw that it was empty. Undid the pouch-string, dug through the coverlet of herbs, found the poppet in its linen wrapper. Brought it out and revolved it over and over in her hand. The blind side, the staring side. Her everyday self was fading, giving way. She wished to do wrong. She wished to do harm. She eased the splinter from the linen and began to needle and pock, deftly pricking here and here and *here*. If she could slow this evil. Thwart the hunt. Stop the witch man, who'd infected Cleftwater with his special contagion. Who would leave only bile in his wake.

She kept on pricking, aware of the risk but also alive with it, her body thrumming. Let the persecutors sample something of their own justice; let the witch man suffer as the others had— Prissy, Jennet—at the splinter's indiscriminate tip. It was her own lancet, a chastening sword; the poppet its martyr. The tallow's give, the poppet's wounds that didn't bleed, were all strangely satisfying. Her movements got more vicious and more precise; her mind intent but not static. She was less certain now of what she was lancing at, only that it was greater than herself, encompassing all she knew. Nan Dolan's battered copper roasting pan witnessed, showed her who she was, showed her what she did. She was fractured, she was many; all of her was tacitly incensed, all of her was pricking the poppet. Savagely needling; wounding for those already wounded and those yet to be—for all the wronged women, named and unnamed, from this county and the next.

In her ear Mam said, Enough. Martha stopped. Reason rushed in. In her palm the poppet lay, reproaching her with its shocked stare. It was scored all over with marks, some very deep. The splinter was driven into its sex.

She shivered, suddenly repulsed by the doll. What had she done. What would happen because of what she'd done. There was a word for what she was—a woman who had a poppet and pricked it. She stowed the doll away and went out the side door, almost colliding with Sue Ruddock and Liz Godbold, who were watching two men wrestle a hooded figure into the yard.

"Mind out, madams," Herry said. In his grip the captured figure twisted like a small hurricane. Thin bleated protests came from it, outrage mixed with despair.

"Jesu Christ, she's a lump," Thaddeus Spalding said, somewhat out of breath.

"She'll be lighter by the time the witch man's finished with her," Herry said. "Lighter in conscience, if not in body." He called over his shoulder. "Open the stable for us—Liz—Martha."

The door was so unyielding they had to set their shoulders to it. The men's boots rang on the cobbles as they hauled the captive past haybales and empty stalls and a mother goat with four young kids penned against the shit-streaked back wall. When it saw them it retreated, curling its lips in alarm. Beside its pen they pushed the woman to her knees and drew off the blanket. Her face emerged, flushed with fury. The men observed her narrowly, repulsion and interest playing on their faces.

Agnes.

"Well, now," Herry said. "Here's Mistress Crozier all in a heap by the manger. Or *Lady* Agnes, as she likes to be called." He crouched. "Ain't you going to thank us? After the kindness we done you? Bringing you here all covered up so's your neighbours won't see."

"The blanket was a kindness, I grant," Agnes said in a voice like steel. "But that makes you no gentleman, Master Gowler," she said, as she tossed it away. "I see how you enjoy this work— all of you. Aiding Master Makepeace. Tormenting innocents, who've done you no harm." In the pen the nanny goat jostled, its brass bell chiming. "I wonder that you like it over-much. How quick you are to condemn! Yesterday I saw you bring Father Leggatt to our cowpond. How you helped bind him thumb to toe. How you were the first to bring him to the water and push him in—"

"I did as I were bid, Mistress Crozier, no more and no less. And I were bid it by righteous men—Master Makepeace and the justices and the constable—who know what they're doin', who got no axe to grind, who want only to rid this village of its witches. That's what you saw yesterday, my lady. A witch being swum in honest water. Whether he sink or float, that's no care o' mine." Herry drew in his neck, like a swan about to strike. "But float he did, as you seen from your fine window. You know what that means. We all know what that means. 'Tis only a witch as floats." A pause, as he watched Agnes struggling to stay upright. Even so dishevelled—her hair tousled, her bodice coming unlaced—Agnes was compelling. "I wonder whether you would, mistress. Float, I mean. Whether that big belly of yours would drag you down or puff out your skirts." He loomed over Agnes, warming to his theme. "What's gone on in that house of yours, eh? Your mousy Martha here, always watchin', never speakin', keeping your secrets close. Your strumpet cook—I hear she got imps' teats on her chest. Your scullion lad who you send off to church, no doubt to pray for you all—you houseful of sinners." He leaned closer, his face—his mouth—stewing with insult. "What you got in there?" he demanded, stabbing the air above her belly. "Is that Kit's babby, or the Devil's?"

Agnes struck his hand away. Then she stretched out both arms to Martha, who took them and pulled her mistress to a stand. For a moment her mistress stood, scanning her captors, her eyes radiant with fury, her arms folded protectively over the babe's dome. She was sweating, already soiled by stable-dirt. Sideways on, she looked misshapen, the babe's orb slipped low between the horizon of its mother's hips, too great a weight for her to bear. If the babe came now—born here in the stable—what then? No happy nativity, then. Likely the end, for the babe and maybe its mother as well. Martha's mind worked at a furious pace, completing the vivid details of the scene. Blood-soaked straw. Blanched corpses. Kit's eyes, stunned and empty of comprehension. The babe curled in on itself, perfect even in death.

Let her be. Her arms sawed. *She is near time,* she told Liz. *The babe will come soon.*

"What's she wantin'?" Thaddeus asked.

Herry blew out his cheeks. "I dunno exactly. To bring the search-women, I think. But you'd be a fool, Thaddeus, to fall for so simple a trick."

"There's no trick. She has to be searched. She has to be watched." Thaddeus jerked his head at the alehouse. "Don't fret, Herry. I'm a family man, I can see what's what here. Mistress Crozier looks about ready to drop her babe. So you go, find Mistress Knill, send her over. She's been expectin' Mistress Crozier, I'm told. Liz and Martha can keep company with my lady. I don't suppose she'll give us any trouble. I'll keep watch."

Herry went. Thaddeus regarded Agnes with his moth-eaten grey eyebrows hitched high up his forehead. After a time he went out and wrestled the doors closed. Shutting out the day. Martha rocked back on her heels. Her thoughts were shouting in her head. The babe was come full term. It was ready to be born. Where was Kit? Why had he allowed mistress to be taken?

Mistress—Where is master? Why is he not with you?

"He is fallen very sick. I doubt he knows I'm here. His fever traps him in bed even as his wife is hauled from her dinner and carted to gaol like a common criminal." Agnes's mouth curled into a scalding smile. "His house is now empty of all its women. His cook thrown in the gaol for witchcraft. His pregnant wife—so near her term—accused of the same." Her eyes were ferocious, the pupils like seeds, black with anger. She trained them on Martha. "His beloved nursemaid now a servant of the witch hunt. Oh, don't think to examine me, Martha. Who is it you serve now? Which master? Which mistress?" A bitter laugh. "You must forgive me for wondering, where now your loyalties lie?"

She recoiled a little, as if Agnes had struck her. Then made her hands into soft fists and mashed them together while she thought how to answer. She might signal her loyalty all she liked but how much would be understood? By the watchers. By mistress, who had troubled herself to learn only the rudiments of Martha's shaping, relying on Kit for the rest. *Mistress. I mean no harm.* Slight gestures: fingertips batting sealed lips, subtle shakings of her head. *I am true. To you. To the babe.*

Agnes stared and frowned. "I don't know what you mean to tell me, Martha. But I think I cannot trust you . . . your intentions. I pray you: let me alone. We must be enemies now."

Martha stood: stung, motionless. "Stop watching me," Agnes snapped, at her, at Liz. "Do your work or let me go."

Liz said, "Well now, that's a puzzle, Mistress Crozier, for watching and searching is what we're here to do, and we can't let you go until we've done it." She came closer, watching Agnes, talking to Martha. "How near is her babe? If it's born without her confessing, then both her and the child will belong to the Devil, I'm told." She stooped and brought her face level with Agnes's. "Is that what you want, mistress? For yourself? For your babe, that's innocent? Coming into this world of trouble, only worse, for his mother was too proud to say how she's sinned." She waited, very earnest. Agnes only looked away. Liz straightened. "You talk to her, Sue. Maybe she'll listen to you."

"I doubt it."

Please, Martha motioned. *Do everything—all—to save her.*

The stable was quiet except for the restless jostle of the goats. Agnes was plainly in discomfort, constantly shifting her weight. She didn't speak, would not look at any of them. In the pen the kids bleated, pestering for milk. While they fed, the mother goat watched Agnes, wary and yellow-eyed. The stable smelled of summer, the clover in the bales of hay, the goats' earthy tang. Simple smells. Reassuring smells. The scene benign, like the tableaux in the surviving stained-glass window of All Saints.

"You'd best listen to me, mistress," Liz said. "For sure you won't like what I've to say but I'll tell it anyway, for I think you should understand. I don't suppose you've known too much trouble in your life, but you're in a deal of it now. Take it from one who knows. I've had my share of it, same as Sue here, and doubtless there'll be more before our time on this earth is done. But you—you've a chance to put things right for your babe, even if you mayn't save yourself."

She paused, as if waiting for some sign, some agreement from Agnes. There was none. "Madam, this is what we'll do. You don't want Martha near you, that's fair. I think we've all got some doubts about her. How is it that Prissy and now you are brought to the witch man, but not Mistress Hallybread here—"

Martha bridled, felt the retort form in her mouth, and her hands began their protest. *I'm no witch—*

"But listen, madam," Liz ran on, quelling Martha with a narrow look, "you must heed what I say. You must see how your babe fares. Sue and me—well, none of us want him lost if we can help it. Not to this madness and not to the Devil. Even Martha—she wants him to live, that's a fact. So now, mistress, I'm going to take a look, see what's what." She began to peel up Agnes's skirts. Agnes twisted away from Liz's touch. "Gently, madam. I'm not going to hurt you. I just need a little look."

Liz looked, and started. Agnes's freckled thighs were fully on display. Her skin was speckled with them, as if she'd bathed in grain. Martha knew there were other marks—a mole on the back of Agnes's knee, another on her stomach, another on her chest only just hidden by her bodice—too obvious to be hidden from the searchers, too many to be explained away. Days ago they would have been inconsequential. Now they were damning, as good as a judge's warrant. Dread spread over Martha like a scald. While the child was unborn Agnes had protection of a kind; for as long as she carried it she would not be too harshly treated. Liz had collected herself and was beginning to reach between mistress's thighs—careful, questing, intimate. In the delta of mistress's groin the babe's caul bulged. They could see the top of the child's head, dark hair damply plastered against the silver tissue. Liz eased up her hand, ignoring Agnes's complaints. Her look altered as she worked, her eyes widening, then narrowing. "Your babe is nigh on being born," she told Agnes. She considered. "You'd best think on, mistress, and do it quickly. Think of him—put him before yourself. D'you want him born into sin? Branded with it, like you are?" She indicated the moles. "What marks are these? How do you come by them?" Agnes only glared at her. "Well, madam? What will you tell us?"

"Nothing," Agnes hissed. "I have nothing to tell. These marks, as you call them, were put there by my Maker. As for my babe, he's innocent, conceived in God's goodness. That is the truth." She glared at them each in turn, her face lit and defiant, conceding nothing.

Let her be, now. Martha pulled down Agnes's gown. *No more.*

"We've need of Mistress Knill's lancet," Liz said. "But while we wait, the lady can walk. Come now, Sue."

The two search-women urged Agnes into motion, half leading and half pulling her down the length of the barn. Agnes walked slowly, stiff with affront. Martha could hardly bear to watch, her mind toiling, its reason racing, coming again and again to Kit: his last instruction as she'd gone away from his house. Do all you can. Do all you can. Aye, so. She'd done all she could, but her all was nowhere near enough. Trouble was come to Cleftwater, sorrow too, bigger than she knew. Her arts, her skills, were tiny against it. There was nowhere to shelter from it, no safe place. Now Agnes was walking into it with her labouring tread.

Time crawled. Liz was patient, murmuring to mistress, urging her to unburden her soul. They walked again to the stable's far end and turned in a slow circle and began their progress back. From outside came hoof-beats, a grating of cartwheels, shouted greetings from the street; goods of one kind or another being unloaded in the market square. What was keeping Mistress Knill? Agnes was visibly slowing. Frostily she asked for something to drink. Liz denied it. Martha remonstrated. A civil rancour shuttled between them like beads on an abacus. Finally Liz relented. On a bale of silage Agnes sat, wary and exhausted. Sue called through the door for Thaddeus to bring ale. They heard the scrape of the quern stone that he pushed into place to keep the doors closed.

They were penned in, like the goats, in the stable's muted, fly-blown dusk. Beside her Agnes gasped and clamped her hands to her groin, then of a sudden called out—a sharp cry that reminded Martha of the sick cow. Cutting was the cure for bloat. She pushed the thought away. Please God let there be no cutting today. Agnes opened her eyes and then her throat with a roar. She buckled over and then reared up. Water sloughed from her, drenching her skirts.

Her birthing waters, Martha motioned, dismayed.

"Aye," Liz said, watching them run. "Looks like her time is

come." She leaned over Agnes and resumed her remonstrances, a soft harangue at first. Agnes was deaf to them, fending Liz away even as she demanded help to stand. Liz tutted and went to an upturned herring barrel and sat with her arms folded. "Mistress Crozier, let me give you some advice. Your cook's been here the best part of four days, and in that time she's had precious little sleep and even less to eat. So unless you speak out, you'll get the same treatment. If it's help you want," she warned, "you must first help yourself."

The quern stone grated: Thaddeus Spalding returning, with a jug of drink. He regarded Agnes—her drenched face and skirts. "What's she fussin' about?"

Her babe comes.

"What's that?"

"Mistress Crozier's travail has started," Liz said.

"Has it so?" Thaddeus poured ale into a beaker. "Maybe this'll ease her. Her tongue, I mean." He held up the beaker. "Have a sip of this, mistress. And then you talk to Liz here, who only wants to help your babby, and tell her what she needs to know."

"And what is that?" Agnes spat. Sheer light from the open door fell full on her, erasing her face rather than showing it. "You would have me say the very words you put in my mouth."

"I dunno about that, mistress," said Thaddeus. "I do know as you got some toil ahead of you. You can make matters harder for yourself, or easier. That's the choice you got." He passed her the beaker. Agnes seized it and drank. "Mistress Hell Cat. That's what they call you, over in the Scours. Not difficult to see why, my lady."

Peace, peace. Martha's hands flapped ineffectually, like startled gulls. *Let my mistress be.*

"She should go over to the alehouse," Liz said.

Aye, aye, she must. She cannot give birth—

"There's no room," Thaddeus said flatly. "The place is full."

"That's true," Sue confirmed. "They got Father Leggatt in there and two other women besides."

"She'll have to stay here for now," Thaddeus said. He looked about. "I can put down some fresh straw, if you want. Maybe find you a cloth for a curtain, something like that?"

She needs more, Martha insisted. *Ale, clean water—*her hands betrayed her growing panic, pecking at the grudging air—*clean linens, a chair—*

"We'll make do," Liz said, interrupting. "But, Thaddeus, would you go again to the house and find Mistress Knill? Tell her what's happening. We need her. Or Master Makepeace."

"Aye, I'll do that, though they're both shut away with prisoners just now." He turned for the door and then came back, tilting his face to Agnes's. "You may've pledged yourself to Satan," he said gently, as though talking to a simpleton, "but it's not too late for your babe. You can save his soul at least. That's what any Christian mother would do."

"But if she has sold herself," Sue said, suspicious, "she's likely sold the babe as well. Or maybe it's the Devil's own—what she carries. I mean, look you, at her marks." She began to edge backwards, crossing herself and then holding her palms out as though warding off evil spirits. "Don't ask it of me, Liz. Don't ask me to help birth her Devil's whelp."

"For shame, Sue," Liz said. "You are a Christian. Look to your faith. Be strong in it, and trust in the Lord, who will protect you."

"Don't you go all high and mighty, Liz Godbold. Is it so wrong to be frightened? Don't tell me you're not afeared yourself.

Lord knows what she's birthing, but I'll not help bring it to life. And what if she calls on the Devil, to plague *us*?" Sue scuttled to the safety of a stack of empty herring barrels. "I'll keep watch from here. If she do anything untoward, I can call to Thaddeus."

From Liz a murmur of exasperation. "All right, then. Go and stand by, Sue. You watch while I work. Come now, Mistress Crozier. We'll walk again."

"No," Agnes said, through gritted teeth. Martha saw the big belly heave. "Let me rest. I cannot walk any more."

"But you must," Liz said, not unkindly. "We'll walk until the babe comes, or you confess. *Then* you may rest. Get up."

She pulled Agnes to stand. They set off once more, pacing very slowly. Agnes was by turns fierce or pain-racked, mewling indignation as the contractions grew more frequent. Liz was both cajoling and rebuking, pursing her lips when mistress resisted. "What keeps Mistress Knill?" she asked Sue, who shook her head and shrugged.

After a time Agnes wanted the pot. There wasn't one; she must do her business in the corner. Martha held mistress's skirts while she squatted and then was copiously sick. Flies rained witlessly over the mess. Martha kicked straw over it and led Agnes to an empty stall, hoping for some respite. *Leave her be. For the babe's sake*, she told Liz, who reluctantly agreed. In her travail Agnes was furious, rocking on all fours, spouting protests and fragments of prayer, demands for ale, for Kit. The scene was surreal; apocalyptic. If the babe came now and was lost? What would she say to Kit? Martha crouched and brushed back the loose tresses of Agnes's hair. *Mistress. MISTRESS.* Agnes batted Martha away. *Look at me. Heed—heed what I say.* Agnes regarded her sidelong. *For the babe's sake as well as your own.*

The idea surfacing as Martha's hands lifted, their movements quick and conspiratorial. *Tell them.* Eye-pointing at Liz and Sue. *Tell them of your ill luck—of the babe you lost. Last year.* She could see mistress's mind in motion, struggling to understand.

"What mean you?" Agnes panted.

The stall's gloom weighed downwards. *Kit lost the ships,* Martha signed rapidly, seizing the moment, *and you lost the child.* Agnes was regarding her, a succession of looks—puzzlement, suspicion—chasing themselves across her face. *Tell them 'tis YOU who's been cursed.*

"What are you speaking of?" Liz Godbold demanded, standing squarely in the opening of the stall.

Agnes screwed up her face. The moment strained, stretching into an eternity in which Martha blanched at all possibilities, consequences for Agnes; for the babe; for herself.

"Martha is reminding me," Agnes said at last, speaking between gasps, "of difficult times. Last year. When my husband—he and I, both—were greatly afflicted. Martha thinks we've been cursed."

"You think the Croziers cursed?" Liz asked Martha.

I do.

"Perhaps it is so," Agnes rasped, gulping in air. "For months we were afflicted. My husband's grain got rot. Then both his ships sank in that autumn storm, losing all—well, I need not tell you, Mistress Godbold. My husband went away to settle his debts. While he was gone, I—I lost . . ." Agnes halted, on the cusp of revealing a secret. Save mistress and Kit, no one but Martha knew it. "I lost the babe I carried. A boy. Even Martha couldn't save it."

"When was this?"

"Last Martinmas. It was the greatest blow. Though why Martha reminds me now . . ." Agnes finished, her voice breaking. She cradled her belly. "Pray God I'll not lose this child."

Take heart, Martha told her. *This babe is come to term. All is well. It is healthy.*

"Jesus Christ our Saviour was born in a stable. Birthing is natural—look how that nanny goat's done her work in a pen," Liz said. "You have all you need, Mistress Crozier. Clean straw, just as our Lord had at his birth, and three wives to wait on you."

"It is far from what I deserve," Agnes said, incensed again. "God knows I try to live a Christian life, I go to church, I make my confession, I give alms. After the storm I gave what help I could to you and others—"

"My son Judah," Liz said, angry herself, "has not been the same man since. Unlike Master Crozier, my Judah had to help pull those bodies from the sea. His own father, drowned. And what about Tom Archer? Judah near drowned himself getting Tom out, and them both half-dead when they come ashore."

"And neither of 'em the same since," Sue chimed in.

"My husband did all he could," Agnes interrupted, "to make amends for your losses—especially for your husband, Mistress Godbold. As for Tom Archer, we've promised him—" Abruptly she stopped; the contraction built, and her rocking turned to writhing.

"Aye, but only after," Liz said coolly. "Only *after* I came to you and asked for help. Only *after* Marion went to Kit. That's what she told me. She had to beg him—your husband—for help."

"Because we ourselves were wanting," Agnes said, her tone strident, lacking apology. "We, too, had our losses—"

"I don't doubt it," Sue called. "But you still got your man, and Liz don't have hers. And your man lives on in his fine house, with his health and good servants and his fair wife, and new ships as have made him rich again. Whereas Marion's Tom . . . well. He'll never be the same. A young man gone old before his time. Can't work the sea no more because he can't face the water. Can't start again somewhere else because your so-called charity keeps him here, tied to fields he can't own. That's your husband, Mistress Crozier. A Godly man, aye, but not so generous when it come to it."

No! Not true! None of it true, Martha protested, her movements large and emphatic, as though to wipe clean a slate or hold calamity at bay.

"I can't help but think how things have gone wrong in Cleftwater ever since you came here, Mistress Crozier," Liz went on, ignoring Martha. The light was behind her and her thin frame seemed to tower over Agnes. She counted on her fingers, tallying up. "Your rotten grain that poisoned nigh on half the village. That storm that cost my Peter's life. Do you see how I'm reckoning it, my lady?" She fingered the small brass cross at her neck. "Every day I'm a widow, and every day is a trial—harder than you'll ever know."

Martha stepped forward, positioning herself between Agnes and Liz. *Stop. Stop. You speak ill. You vex my mistress. You'll vex the babe—*

"Now you say it, Liz," Sue said, coming hesitantly out, forsaking the safety of the wall of barrels, "I'm puttin' the pieces together. Aye. Like a puzzle." She had ventured closer; now she darted forwards to tap Liz. "Think on Jennet Savory. Going about like an old maid, pious as you like on the Sabbath. But since Tom's been sick, well. We all know what she does in the

Scours. Certain favours she do, for certain men, who'll pay. It ain't Godly. And that sickness she got—frothing and rambling and falling down—all worse since when? Since Mistress Crozier came to Cleftwater. So it's no surprise to me that Jennet's got with the Devil. I wondered at it before now." She leaned into the stall, almost shouting. "Was it you, Mistress Crozier? Did you turn the grain bad? Bring up that storm? Was it you who witched Marion Archer's babby? Were you wanting it for yourself, after you lost your own? Or did you not want another woman to have something you ain't got?"

A shudder like a breaking wave passed over Agnes, who crammed her fist's heel in her mouth. Small gripes of pain came out around it. Sue and Liz watched, unmoved.

"When Mistress Knill comes—if ever she do come—let's see what her lancet finds," Sue said. "Then we'll know." She sucked in her cheeks. "Why is it, Martha, you're so loyal to your mistress, even though she's not kind to you? Has she witched you as well as Prissy? What do you think, Liz?"

"The same as you, Sue. The very same."

For a moment Martha allowed herself to lock eyes with them. They were silent, regarding her and Agnes; Liz pious, fingering her cross; Sue standing with her arms folded tightly over her breast. Strange inquisitors, this pair of goodwives, who were even at this moment convincing themselves of the worst. Martha put up her hands to reply or refute, and found they were balled into fists. A rage was overtaking her, as sudden as a thunder squall: a fury at silence, the perpetual hindrance of this living canker in her throat. On impulse she leaned and took handfuls of mistress's hair, tugging up her head more roughly than intended. With her free hand she made a pair of flapping jaws. *Speak!* The barn's air was thick but her motioning was urgent. *Mistress, you MUST speak.* She shook Agnes by the bunches of hair, willing her to understand.

Agnes's expression contorted, ugly with pain. "Let me alone, Martha. You pull like a madwoman."

Why did mistress not defend herself? For the sake of the coming babe? Martha looked pleadingly at Agnes: saw the white face, the terror on her features. The thought occurred that childbirth was a great leveller. Proud Mistress Agnes, so unprepared for calamity, at her lowest now for all her wealth, for all her position; who had a voice, but could not use it.

She let go. Her arms drifted down and one wrist brushed the pouch. Now was the time to use the poppet, if she could. Invoke—provoke—its power. Her thoughts wheeled in fast loops, alighting again and again on the doll. Twice she had pricked it, but to what end? What help had arrived, what relief? The poppet was a poor thing, a stub of wax, crudely shaped. What if its powers were likewise coarse—slow to work, and ungovernable?

Perhaps then she ought to give it up, as she'd vowed to herself only yesterday. She could expose it, pretend to discover it, with feigned horror. A thing not hers. Foreign. Profane. In her mind's eye a kind of mummer's play started up—fast, flicking—in which she saw the poppet ceded, saw them all exonerated, herself and Agnes and Prissy cleared of blame and threat; her life, village life, returning to its old order. The mumming-show faltered, then resumed, paler now, as if its colour were draining like her resolve. She saw herself caught, then indicted; the noose at the pouch's neck, a noose around her own. And others, too, a growing crowd of noosed women. Frantically she scanned them. Who would be taken? Who would be left? Who would care for the babe?

She knew how she looked, halted, immobile, her eyes fixed on what might be and what might not; alive to the battered doll at her hip. To stop a witch hunt with a witching doll: aye, aye, it was right, it was fitting. There was no better means. Why then did she feel so torn, pincered between these two desires: to surrender it, to keep it?

Because it was hers. A wrong thing, perhaps; but a wrong thing all her own. The extent of its power was still unknown, but hers alone to wield. She was not ready to forfeit it, not yet. Briefly her tired eyes closed: she glimpsed again the attic room, its scant light, Mam folding the doll into her palm.

'Tis all we got, this little power.

Use it scarce. But use it.

———

The barn door groaned open and a long shaft of sun poured in, dousing them all in daylight. Squinting, Martha saw figures advancing. No time: no more time. She bent again to Agnes, her hands flying, urgent and insistent. *Mistress. Say another wished you ill.* She glanced behind her, saw the guards almost upon them; saw relief on Sue's face, a kind of triumph on Liz's. She turned back to Agnes and took her face by the chin. *Say you were cursed. Say it, mistress.* Agnes twisted in her grip like prey in a trap. *I beg you. Save yourself. Save the babe.*

She made her left hand into horns that she put to her forehead, against the dome of bone. *Tell them*—her mind sped, working at a frantic pace—*it was a witch.*

Even as they shaped she was appalled at them, her traitorous hands, that were signing away another woman's life. Innocent Prissy. Ma Southern. The Durriken sisters. Implications;

consequences: they rinsed through her in a shiver of disquiet. She thought again of Jennet, her false accusations, her spider-imp. Her hands moved again, slicing the bruised air. *Tell them*, she wrote—and felt again the soft inward tearing, a rift opening in the layers of herself, beneath the trappings of her bodice and petticoats and hot skin—*tell them it was Jennet Savory. Say Jennet cursed you.*

———

And here they came, Mistress Knill and Thaddeus Spalding and Robert Bullard, arranging themselves before the labouring woman in the stall.

"This is she?" said the search-mistress.

"It is, madam. Agnes Crozier," Liz said.

"But she is heavy with child," said Mistress Knill. "I did not know."

"Her waters have broken," Liz said. "She is in her travail."

"Then she must be brought inside."

Martha helped Robert pull Agnes up. Her own limbs were leaden: impossible to summon strength in herself when she had none. Hours had passed since breakfast.

"Not you, Martha," Mistress Knill said.

The barn's heat struck downwards. For a moment the search-mistress looked broken apart, a mosaic of shifting black.

Not me?

"Your master's errand lad was here just now, asking for you. You're needed at home. It seems your master has taken sick." Mistress Knill studied Agnes, her stained gown, the mess of her face and hair. "Have no worry, Martha. We will see to your mistress. She is in our care now."

PART THREE

PHLEGM

SEVENTEEN

Saturday evening

Outside in the dying day. An incoming tide. Wind, salt air. Big fists of cloud were massed above the Holleswyck sandbar, gathered as if ready to strike. The sun barely showed, a pale ulcer in the caul of cloud. Martha walked uncertainly into the street, then faltered to a stop. Summer had broken, and more besides. She had lost track of time. She had lost track of herself. She had not done what Kit asked: she had not saved a single woman. Possibly she had damned one. Her hands grasped and released themselves, playing out an inner struggle. Home was where she was needed but how could she permit herself to go? When in the gaol and the alehouse innocent women suffered—Prissy suffered, brought into peril by her.

Her legs were reluctant but she forced them into motion, feeling a desire to start again, to correct, to be of service. She crossed the street back to the gaol.

Martin was on duty. "What is it this time?"

One last look, she told him, tapping her eyes.

"One what?"

Look.

"You can look from here," he said. Then he saw her expression and relented.

The gaol's darkness felt somehow crowded. Stirrings. Tattered breathing. Familiar forms gathering themselves, seeming to clot out of shadow and take on substance and shape. Ma Southern, still prone, barely breathing. Prissy slumped beside her, her bowed head curtained by gold hair. Hannah Holland, still in her stall. In the deep shade of the far wall Father Leggatt knelt, his pose familiar, clasped hands with their dangling crucifix, a bowed neck. His eyes were shut but his lips moved, words spooling from them.

Perhaps he sensed her presence or he had prayed enough. "Oh, Martha," he breathed. His voice was subdued, the voice of someone coming out of a dream. "I thought you were with the search-women." His eyes struggled to find focus. "I thought I'd never see you again. See anyone again." His brow furrowed, as if he were considering a complicated problem. "They swam me, like you. With my toes and thumbs tied together. I think this one is almost pulled out." He had been nursing it. Now he held it out to show her.

She turned his palm over for a better look. The thumb was purple, badly bruised and sticking out at a wrong angle. She saw at once that it needed resetting, to be bound up with a splint. She looked helplessly around. There was nothing with which she might aid him. Her hand went to the pouch. A thought arrived and then ignited: she did have what was needed. That finger of wood in the poppet. She had put it there this morning.

Splinter, splint. She was suddenly giddy, as if her blood were rushing to her hands. All her concentration narrowed to them as she turned her back to the priest and fumbled with the drawstring of the pouch. She raked through its contents, her fingers agitated and clumsy, feeling for the poppet. They found it. If she were caught . . . She must not be caught.

The splinter was where she had lodged it. She began to ease it out or try to, but the wax was obdurate and she was concerned not to injure herself with her own improvised pricker.

"What keeps you, Martha?"

She jumped. Martin was squinting through the gate.

"You're not doing your herballing, are you? 'Cause if you are, you must stop. No help for the prisoners. That's orders from Master Makepeace himself."

She nodded, gave a cursory wave. Evidently it did not satisfy Martin; he peered more closely through the grille. "Come now. Finish up."

"Do as he says, Martha," Father Leggatt said. "We will say our goodbyes, take our leave of each other. Christ himself had no succour, no one to bind his wounds. I merely follow His example." His eyes were bright with fervour. "Five times I was swum, and five times I expected to meet our Saviour, but found only weeds instead. By this I know the Lord has some further plan for me, I am certain of it. There will be more ordeals, more tests, before the end," he said vehemently, as if convincing himself. "Each one a blessing, in its way."

She looked at him, astounded. A succession of responses— questioning, unbelieving—passed quickly through her mind. She put her hands to her feet, to her neck. *In being swum? In being hanged?*

"In being chosen, as Christ was, to atone."

She felt a wash of coarse feeling—inchoate, dully rageful. Her arm lifted, circling the four walls of the gaol. *What of the others?* It was difficult to put a shape to the contents of her mind. *These women? Are they also . . . chosen?* She knew she was signing too quickly, too fast for him to follow. *They are fodder—goats—scapegoats—*

The priest put up his manacled hands. "I've distressed you. I didn't mean to. Let us pray together. Shall we do that? Pray to be kept strong in our faith."

She did not want his benediction even as she craved it, his priestly chant, the balm of the ancient words. She knelt, compelled herself to listen. *Our Father, which art in Heaven, hallowed be thy Name.* The words of the prayer falling into the gaol's dusk, the dark of her faith, like stones lobbed pointlessly into a well. Her eyes were closed but weeping. Some part of her knew this to be the last time, their last prayer.

When he finished she got up. The undone pouch yawned open and a fistful of herbs fell out. She kicked them furiously into a recess of the gaol. Then stood hovering by the priest, this good man, her champion, her confessor, who was on his knees, brought low. Let him spend his conviction on someone else—some other woman more worthy. Roughly she pointed, to Hannah and Ma Southern and Prissy. Above all, Prissy. Contrition flamed through her like the flare of a freshly stoked fire. *Pray with them. Pray FOR them. They are more deserving.*

———

On the street the Moot Hall clock struck, five of the evening. An easterly wind was driving in a sea fret that was budging the day too soon into evening. Cool air fluted in her ears that had a note in it, an oscillating ring coming from the village square. She bridged her fingers over her eyes and saw Nan Dolan's stable lad leading a horse into the yard of the Four Daughters.

The horse was a fine one, well groomed, not from the village. Behind it came another—a bay—Nathaniel Whistler's cart horse coming on at a rapid trot, its reins trailing. Nate strode after it, but the horse was picking up speed, making straight for her. As it came abreast she stepped into its path and put her hands out, and it faltered and then made to go around her. She could feel its nervousness streaming in its wake.

She hummed to it, low-voiced. The big hooves slowed and she caught the reins. The creature came reluctantly to a stop, staring at her side-on with a rolling eye. She made to pat its muzzle but it flung away its head, not wanting her touch. What had disturbed it so? She gripped the bridle and leaned against its neck, mouthing things; nonsense, croonings. Mam had taught her to talk like this to troubled creatures. They were all of God, made by Him, but their fear was almost always of man or men's deeds. She put her lips to its coarse chestnut pelt, crooning again, feeling the leap of its pulse. It was foolish to spend what little voice she had on a frightened cart horse but she went on lulling and stroking and fingering its mane, hoping to feel its pulse slow. *So, so. Be still.* It nosed at her with its freckled lips but would not calm, not fully. Her own anxiety was infecting it. Then suddenly it did still. She opened her eyes. Nate had got hold of the bridle.

"How do, Martha?"

She shook her head. *Not good.*

"Oh, aye," said Nate, talking to his beast. "I imagine it's a dirty business—your witch-searching." He held out a proprietorial hand for the reins. "But there's coin in it, even for nobodies like us, eh?" He slapped the horse's flank and read her face. "Oh, you'll get no judgement from me, Martha. So far as I can tell there's plenty of Cleftwater folk happy to help and take coin for their trouble."

She lifted her hand up with curled fingers, shaping the question. *Who?*

He jinked his head towards the alehouse. "Who? Well, there's Nan Dolan for a start, hiring out rooms and stables. She must be minting it. She's got the three of them there now, the witch-hunter and his search-lady as well as that bastard judge, Palfreyman, from Salt Dyke. Then there's all the bread and ale for the gaolers and you search-women—I know, I know, Martha. It's Godly work you're doing, and needed, if we're to rid this village of the foulness that's got into it. But all of us taking coin to put by old friendships. Me included. That's the times we're in now. And Gil Hesketh—selling our timber to the witch man. And maybe our souls as well."

What timber? What for?

But he hadn't seen her question. He began to back away, drawing the reins with him. "Come on now, Walt. Come by." The beast began to turn in a wide arc. "Stand well clear, Martha."

She moved back. A sudden wind bawled, scouring them with grit and bits of chaff ripped from the fields above the village. She cuffed her eyes to clear them and the scene came full into focus; a man and his horse and what they were towing—a thick spar, coarse-hewn, three times her length. They moved slowly off. The spar straddled the whole width of the street and strafed the stony surface as it went. She paced behind, a careful distance, walking as quickly as her fatigue would allow. Nate had parked his old mophrey cart beside the sundial and from it Gil Hesketh's son Clem was unloading timber—flat planks like floorboards as well as longer beams that were higher than the

Market Cross and thicker than a girl's waist. Gil was already at work. Wood rang under his hammer. She watched him placing the studs, fast and precise, how they bit the timber. A frame was taking shape. Gil was working in the middle of it, already dwarfed by the upright beams.

"Christ," Nate shouted, leaping back. Yellow spattered his breeches. "Look you. Walt's blessing the wood wi' his own holy water."

"He is that," Gil said. He gobbed the last of the nails into his palm, regarded the dripping timber. "Not that the town will know it. Nor want this timber back." He bent again to the planks.

"Aye, well. I'll not take it away," Nate said. "Unless the minister's shriven it."

Unease stayed Martha, kept her lingering by their work. She stepped over Walt's yellow runnel to where Gil's son was working, and half caught Clem's eye. He was toying with a coil of rope slung over his shoulder, running lengths of it through his fists. *What are you making?* He came out of his concentration and stepped purposefully through the wooden carcass, to hold the rope to the top of her head. He unfurled it down her body length by length, until he had her full measure.

"Don't mind me, Martha," he said tersely. He was spare-faced and slightly built, like his father, though his birth had cost the life of his mam. Under his heavy lids she saw his thoughts playing. He was reckoning up, calculating.

What d'you measure?

He blinked at her as though she were a fool. "The drop," he said simply. "I been told to make the halters. They're saying as some of the women will hang within days." She could feel panic going through her like a dye. "We've been told to build

the gallows, and that judge from London has just come in—
that's his mare going into Nan Dolan's. I'm thinking, why else
would he be here?" He coiled the rope around his fist. "He
likes a full gibbet—that's what I've heard—as you would, when
you're being paid by the head to rid a place of its witches." He
spat and wiped his mouth with his forearm. "But any ways you
look at it, I'd say it's lookin' bad for your Prissy. And Jennet.
All of 'em."

He stopped and his expression softened. "Eh, now. I didn't
mean to fright you. I thought, being a search-lady, you'd know
already." He grasped her shoulder and shook it. "You're doing
fine work, Martha. If it was anyone else doing the searchin'
I'd have my doubts. But you're a true soul and loyal to this
place, and the folk in it. So I know that while they're with you
those women are . . . well. They got a chance. If that's what
they deserve." He glanced quickly around, to where his father
worked. His voice dropped. "Just watch yourself, Martha. Eh?
Not everyone sees it the same as me. Make sure you do nothing
as will cause you to end up on this." He jerked his thumb at the
gibbet. "I don't like it, but we've taken the coin for it, so I'd best
get on. What's next for you? Are you stayin' to search more?"

She shook her head and pointed down the street, to home.

"That's good. You're safer there than here." He touched his
cap to her. "On you go, then. Get home and see to your master."
He waved at the bruise-coloured evening. "And get some rest
for yourself. You're lookin' half dead."

He went, taking away the comfort of his presence. The fret
was advancing, reaching for the village in long fingers. The
early dark would mean an end to the day's business. Though

not for the alehouse: it was full of trade, its door with its
crazed creak swinging open and closed and open again, each
time with a blurt of noise—gusts of coarse laughter, singing,
a dropped jar splintering on the floor. She turned again for
home. On the beach the fishing fleet was drawn up above
the kelp line, a rank of wooden bellies inclined on their keels.
Mostly their crews were ashore but the Wish Hill guide-lights
had been lit for the boats still due, their narrow rays like paths.
She followed one. Under her skirts her thighs rubbed, their
chafing both a penance and a reminder of her freedom. She
was walking freely—a free woman—not *being* walked. And yet
in her belly there was a tension, as if some inner tether were
pulling taut.

She was treading the right path: home, to nurse her sick
master.

She was going in the wrong direction: away from Prissy
and Agnes.

As if from out of her thoughts a dog barked, sharp jabs of
sound. A light was with it, advancing towards her.

"Martha?" Simon held up the battered storm lantern. She
flung her head away from its glare. "I been looking for you."
His brow was furrowed, his eyebrows threatening to fly off his
forehead. "I went to the gaol but you weren't there. Then to
the alehouse, and they said you'd gone. Where were you? We
must've passed each other?" He was tripping on his words. "God
be thanked I've found you now." The thickening haar streamed
around him, damping his tunic to his ribs. "We must get home
directly. Master is sick, bad sick. He can't take food nor water."
He raised the lantern, shone its stuttering yellow light straight

into her face, read what was written there. "Praise God you're safe," Simon said. "Praise God you're returned to us. I've been praying for you to come safe home."

A pause. She was relieved he'd stopped. Matthew the dog paced steadily ahead of them as if leading the way. She could feel Simon studying her. "Was it bad, Martha? Is it bad . . . for the women?"

Aye.

He was silent, digesting; wanting to know. "How bad?"

She only shook her head. At the back gate he passed her the lantern. "Hold this while I get water." He gestured. "I'm guessin' you'll want to wash." He leaned and worked the pump and brought up the water, then set the bucket down. His look was grave. Of a sudden he pulled her to him, into a crushing hug. She was limp with tiredness and her arms hung down, dead weights. Simon wrapped them around his back. He was sixteen and a man and crying, this lad, the last of her friends, who was so loyal.

"It's been . . . hard, Martha," he said, into her neck. "With all the women taken. Prissy, and then you gone, and then mistress." A waft of liquor rose from his skin. She wondered at it. He was always so correct in himself, a committed follower of the Word. "I couldn't believe it, when they come for mistress. I tried to stop them—I truly did. Master was that sick he couldn't even rise from his bed." He crushed her to him again. She had to make herself keep hold. Some resolve had gone—leached out or left behind in the gaol. "I can't say as master and me have done too well without you," he said, choking on the last.

She freed her hands. *You've done your best.* Their shapes were puny and inadequate, almost lost in the vapour.

EIGHTEEN

Inside the back door she stood, stalled, waiting for the wash of feeling to abate. The house felt familiar but strange, as though some errant spirit had spelled it to a stop. The doors were all open and she could see through to Kit's room where his maps and papers lay in drifts over his mahogany desk. She went on to the kitchen. On the block were the remains of the parsley she'd chopped, how many days since? Two or three: a lifetime ago. Before she'd become a search-woman. The sap had stained the wood green. For some moments she stood in the doorway while the dog licked her shins and fingers, regaining her bearings amid the kitchen's familiar clutter, unwashed pots, wizening fruit and onions, the unemptied slops bucket. Listening for the sounds that made up her life here, trying to summon them through thought. Prissy, humming as she worked. Agnes, calling demands down the stairs.

Gone.

Simon was in the doorway with the dripping bucket. "Where do you want this?"

She waved at the table. *The master—how does he ail?*

"He has a fever. If he eats or drinks he spews, and then he coughs. And he blathers, Martha—it makes no sense.

Sometimes he thinks I am the mistress. Other times he calls for you."

From upstairs, the wet hack of Kit's cough.

A decoction, a poultice: Kit would likely need both. She went to the herb store and brought out some cordial and a selection of reliable herbs: mint, mallow, elecampane for coughs, vervain for fever, crumbling them into her mixing bowl before taking clean cloths from the kitchen linen chest and going to the stairs. Simon followed and then stood on the first stair, partly blocking her way. Irritation rose in her; all her thought was for Kit.

"Tell me first, Martha. What you know. Did you see Prissy? How does she do? And what of mistress? And the babe?"

What, how, was she to tell him? What solace could be found, what small grains of comfort would help break the news or ease it? Simon liked Agnes, who had valued his mild obedience. But he more than liked Prissy—there'd been certain clues— small favours offered, gifts of shells and wildflowers and the thin crooked dolls he whittled from sticks of driftwood. Once, when he thought no one was looking, an attempted kiss.

She looked at him, at his large grey eyes with their black centres and lustrous lashes—girlish eyes—and saw the play of feeling there.

They are . . . being tested. Mistress's babe is birthing, even now.

———

The bedchamber smelled. Kit lay collapsed into the bolster, and for one lurching moment she thought he was dead. The dog jumped onto the mattress and lay with his front legs over master's, whining a greeting. His tail swayed and thumped.

She set down the medicines and leaned over to listen for Kit's breathing. It was thready, very faint.

She stroked his shoulder until he opened one eye. *Master.*

"Mm?" His face was drawn, his breath hellish. "Martha." He struggled to sit up, flailing for purchase. "What news?"

She hooked one hand in his armpit to pull him up, bulking out the bolster with the other. He slumped against it. Lank hair hung around his face. *Be still,* she shaped on his palm. He was so very over-heated. His eyes fixed on her. He grasped her by the wrist.

"How does my Agnes? How fares the babe?"

She freed her arm and brought the cup to his mouth. *Drink.*

The cordial was in the small pewter mug that he had used as a boy. He pushed it away. "Tell me."

Drink first.

He swallowed. The mixture came too quickly and he gagged, drooling liquid onto the sheet. He coughed, once, twice, and then was seized by it. The cough grew, encompassing more of him. In it she could hear a name, not her own. Agnes's. When at last he finished he slumped against her, spent. His lips and chin were flecked with blood like the linen around him.

She wiped the mess from his lips. Simple movements, simple acts; this wiping away of time—thirty years—and here he was, her own Kit, with a faith in her so perfect and redeeming she thought their world might still be corrected. A bolt of love went through her. Mother's love: its strength was astounding. To be with Kit she had remained unwed; had borne no child of her own. Kit was that child, her almost-son. She sat on the edge of the mattress, bathed his face and then put the poultice on his brow, watching his uneasy rest.

He slept. She rinsed the cloth and put the bowl of rust-coloured water in the corner. The room was close and she lit a spray of dried sage, dropping it in a dish that she put on the settle at the foot of the bed. After a time its smoke suffused the chamber. She opened a window and then sat on Kit's chair and stared out. Already the elation of seeing Kit was subsiding and her spirits fell with it. Through the fog the sunset flamed, staining it with burnt colour. Her thoughts lapped, returning again and again to Prissy and Jennet. How many days since they'd been taken? How many nights in the gaol? And what of Agnes and the babe? Simon came with bread and a plate of pigeon thigh and a piece of dry cheese. She hadn't known she was famished until she bolted down the gamey meat. The window kept the darkness at bay but she could feel herself filling with it.

When she'd finished she put the plate on the floor and fell immediately asleep in the chair with her head dropped against Kit's mattress, going in and out, waking, sleeping, stirring again, each shift of consciousness marked by the faint brassy knell of the sandbar buoy as it warned of danger. A time later she came more out of sleep and heard it again. Her breath kept pace with its toll. The sage was all burned, turned to ash in the bowl. She could smell the beach, kelp and salt and wet wood. The tide was full, she knew without looking, its insistent crest and suck, in constant negotiation with the shore. Always, this sound, this pulse. Always this great cathedral dome of the night sky: its constancy, its vastness, beyond calculation. Kit slept on, the dog also, but her soul was restless, feeling through the murk

for the gaol and the alehouse and the women trapped there. As
if she were praying, she mouthed their names.

Waited.

Nothing.

A fresh anguish flared and at the same time the window
shutter banged open. It was very early and the fog was everywhere, pluming right up against the glass. In it was a face: Mam's
face, like the Pieta, mournful and yet somehow accusing, about
to speak. Martha cried out or tried to; one hand clutched at her
hip pouch and found it hanging limp at her side like an emptied
bladder. Frantically she felt through the leather and then inside
it. No poppet. Only a few desiccated sprays of twig and leaf.

She turned it inside out. No poppet. She got up and checked
herself, patting her bodice and skirts. Then searched about
Kit's bedchamber, knowing it was stupid, that she was a fool,
lifting the bed linen, looking under the bed. Her pulse roared
in her ears. The poppet was nothing and everything; though
she quailed at it, she needed it. Without it she was spineless,
boneless, lacking sinew, lacking power.

Her mind worked, back over the blur of the last few days.
When had she last had it? Yesterday? The day before? When?
Go on, Martha. There was a growing recollection—some scene
in the alehouse, nay—

The gaol. It was there. Dropped from her pouch with the
bundle of herbs, when she had gone that last time to see to
the prisoners. Father Leggatt, and Prissy.

A new thought came—as bad, or worse—that someone
would find it and know it was hers.

Behind her the bedroom door unlatched itself. She spun

around. No one there. From the bed came the nonsense of Kit's fever-babble, ending in a cough. After all, she was necessary. She was needed, by Kit at least. The fact was energising, unfroze her from the terror. By his side she brought his hot hand to her lips, savouring him even though he was sick and bad-smelling, the flushed forehead and dark-stubbled jaw and nulled blue of his eyes. In his fever he was praying and to his garbled appeals she added some of her own, *Lord have mercy, Father have mercy, Grant us your grace.* The morning was advancing, she could tell by the whiteness of the fog. There was a bubbling in Kit's chest that wouldn't abate, even when she sat him up with the pillows stacked behind him.

She was bathing his forehead when the coughing started again. A gargling. She balled the damp cloth over his mouth. The gargling built, grew more forceful, went on and on.

Her life, her world, tearing in half.

At last he coughed himself out. His lungs worked but badly, as though they were full of holes. When she took away the cloth she saw what he had left on it. Her spirits were in free fall and she thought how this was more than she could bear, this crimson betrayal she hadn't foreseen.

NINETEEN

Sunday

The day passed. She nursed Kit. Worry weighed on her like a lid. She could not settle, waiting for news, expecting at any moment to be summoned back to the alehouse or the gaol. The house was unbearable with its everywhere reminders of the gone women.

At mid-morning Simon said they ought to go to church, but there was no possibility of her going with Kit so sick. Simon went on his own. She went up to Kit's chamber and prayed by him, over him, instead. When he slept she ventured out, tentative, urgent steps along Tide Lane. The street was empty. People were at worship, their houses shut up, their closed front doors displaying various charms, single shoes nailed to the lintel, a mummified kitten, horseshoes. She went as far as the Market Cross, which was itself wreathed with bay leaves and rowan. A silence lay over the village, a preternatural calm, ancient and unknowable. She made herself go on, half creeping, half running to the Moot Hall, where she hovered under its eaves. The poppet was there. Was it? A nervousness gripped her, claw-like, intense. When, when would it do its work? Then the courage—desperation—that had propelled her here, in pursuit of the poppet, failed entirely. She went back down Tide Lane at a disciplined trot, almost fainting with relief when she reached the safety of her own garden.

In the afternoon Kit's fever waned. She bathed his face and neck and chest and he sat up and ate some boiled egg that she fed to him with the apostle spoon. Once he'd had two but now there was only one, St. John holding his cup with the tiny serpent in it. Kit ate half the egg and then indicated that she should have the rest. Her appetite was scant but she must eat to keep her strength up for him.

Simon was outside on the garden bench and the tune of his jaw harp drifted up, some cheerful sea shanty. She could recollect the melody but not the words. She tried to get Kit to talk. There was an overwhelming need for him to know about what she'd seen, what she'd been made to do—the consequences of their pact. But he was drawn a long way into himself and when he spoke it was only of Agnes; all his mind was for her. She sat in his chair mending a tear in one of Agnes's nightgowns until he dozed again. Then she went out to the field to pick herbs, dandelion and the chamomile that grew like a profusion of tiny suns around the cowpond. Its water was the colour of lead. Here she'd been swum. Here Father Leggatt had been swum. How was it that he'd been accused but not her? Her thoughts were merciless and unrelenting and she looked long into the pond's depths, considering it. Praying or drowning: these were the choices.

She went onto her knees. *God of my rock; in Him will I trust: He is my shield and my refuge; Thou savest me from violence.* Except that He hadn't. Or He had: deflecting the violence elsewhere. Onto Prissy, aye. And Agnes. The guilt came and came. It was difficult to think of aught else. Her skirt was damp and she thought how, when she stood up, there would be dents in the moss, prints of her inconsequential life, badly lived. After she'd gone the moss would correct itself, plumping out to erase her marks. Whereas she must go on and live, tarnished and stained. And how: how was she to live?

In the kitchen the roiling water reminded her yet again. The herbs in their leafy constellations were spread out on the table, and she nipped off the heads and leaves and put them in. The smell was familiar and calming, and she sucked in big breaths. To calm the worm, if she could. The medicine was mostly for Kit but she set by a little for herself. When she took it upstairs its scent seemed to go ahead like a message. Kit stirred as she entered. She laid a fresh towel under his head and combed his hair back with her fingers. He took her hand and held it. Like this the world could pause and in this pause there was contentment. Joy, even. The house and the chamber were briefly still, as if attending to the moment. Then Kit coughed and let go.

She cleaned his face again and went outside and sat for a time on the garden bench. The sun was setting and the sea glowed, different tones of liquid gold. Her own cough nagged, persisting in each breath. The hog came and she fussed him and he eyed her with his marked face. Towards nightfall the sea fog and Kit's fever thickened and her spirits fell. She went around the house closing all the shutters. At supper only Simon could eat. She stewed more chamomile, strained it into a tincture, had Simon help bring her mattress next to Kit's. She lay curled up on the pallet with the sheet drawn over her head, fearful of spiders, of Kit's gargled breathing. Foreboding ran the length of her body, behind her and ahead. How would Kit fare. What of the babe. She thought of Agnes's cared-for body, her smooth white hands that were ignorant of women's work. Her own were ugly with toil but she would choose them again should she need to, these hands that knew how to heal.

In some small hour Kit woke, hawking blood onto the bed linen. He shivered, his skin burned to the touch. His fever was almost beyond her skill. She thought of the doctor; would he consent to come to Kit's aid—to this corrupted house, that had harboured witches? She gave Kit some tincture and sponged him with cool water and took his blood-flecked sheets downstairs, ready for the wash-house. Sleep when it came was fitful, punctured with dreams of the poppet. At cockcrow she came to, desperate to have it. Terrified it would be found.

TWENTY

Monday late afternoon

Kit woke and asked for porridge. They had almost no food. They needed eggs, beets, salted herring. Martha took a basket from its hook and brought it to Simon. He was sitting on his cot-bed, his knees jutting either side of him like the misplaced wings of an insect or angel, whittling a doll from a stick of birch.

"For when the babe comes home," he said, stubbornly. "A present. From me."

She watched his agitated deftness, the doll taking shape, the tell-tale jigging of his left leg. She indicated the basket. *Would you go? To the market?*

He hesitated.

For herring.

Herring was his favourite. He sighed. "I know what you're about, Martha. But all right."

He was gone only as long as it took to build the fire and crumble some stale bread. He came back at a run.

"They're hanging 'em. The women."

Who? Which ones?

"I don't know." He snatched the bread from her hands. "Leave off that. They'll not wait."

Her palms flapped in a panic. *You go.*

He flung the loaf on the table. "We'll go together, Martha. I'll not go on my own." He was almost shouting, anticipating the worst. "Else it'll be me who has to tell master that his wife or his cook or both of 'em has been hanged, and I don't— I can't—do it on my own."

She was skewered, helpless in his look. What he asked was fair, but the prospect of what they would see made her go cold and then hot. Her hand went to her hip and found nothing, only the space where the poppet had been.

Aye, then. Her hands shook.

They went out by the back. Low tide, and the haar had thinned almost away. Surly green waves streamed onto the beach, leaving drifts of scum like curdled milk that blew across the street. The day was untethered, unreal. Simon hooked her arm in his to make her walk faster. Her cloak flapped and she thought it would tear. She could smell the harbour, its tang of wet hemp and landed fish.

They heard the crowd before they came to it.

"Nothing like a hanging to bring folk out," Simon said sourly. As they came up to the Market Cross they saw how people thronged from the alehouse past the Moot Hall to the harbour—a sprawling, shifting mass, like herring from a burst net. There were faces they knew and many they didn't, folk come from other villages, fishwives and net-heavers, the cutler from Sandgrave, gorse-cutters, pedlars, bawds come from Holleswyck, the gap-toothed soothsayer who roamed the coast road, the mayor's spinster sisters rubbing shoulders with itinerant paupers.

"Wait here," Simon said. "I'll try to find out who is for the rope." She watched him work his way through the crowd, eeling along its edge towards the gaol. Gulls circled overhead, screaming to one another. Over the streets an ill force lay, a crushing sensation, like pushing against wet sheep. Already the crowd had its own musk, ale and sweat mixed with sharper smells, of anticipation and excitement. When she looked behind she saw how the crowd had thickened even in these last few moments.

There came a collective indrawn breath. As one the mob went suddenly silent. All she could see were backs. She rocked unsteadily up onto the toes of her clogs: glimpsed the top of the gallows with four coils of rope waiting on the crossbeam, lost her balance and rocked up again in time to see the first rope unfurl and lengthen, supple in the hands of the hangman— a slight figure, straddling the crossbeam—who held up the noose for the crowd's approval. From somewhere in front a man fisted the air, letting out a cry. The mob took it up, part cheer, part bray. Martha fought herself, steeling herself to look again at the gallows, at its row of rope halters. They hung expectant, ready to receive necks.

Moments that might be years went by as wafts of fish-smelling harbour air filtered through the market square, lifting scurries of sand and scraps; lifting a memory, long tamped down, reviving in a blare: the sea placid, the sky an uncomplicated blue, Mam in the stocks amidst a pack of jeering house-holders; Mam plastered in midden filth and muck from the alehouse lane; Mam in the noose as the village clock proclaimed the worst hour, the killing hour, which had stalked Martha ever since, tracking her through childhood, adulthood, servanthood, and was now arrived again. Today, this day, the rope would claim some other wronged woman with its noose that was really meant for her: Martha Hallybread. The heavy-tongued clock confirmed it.

She struggled right, left, wrenching at arms, searching for gaps in the crush. People glanced at her, unseeing. A gap opened briefly and through it she glimpsed a bailiff leading Ma Southern from the gaol, her face a mask of terror. How slowly the lame woman went, puppet legs treading her final stiff paces to the gallows. Some unknown lad darted out and spat before the bailiff jerked her onwards. On the platform she stood forlorn, regarding the ladder and the nooses; the gobbet of spit dripped to her bodice. The town crier sounded his bell before proclaiming Ma Southern's so-called crimes. Ma Southern only gaped at him. Then the constable took her stick wrist and half pushed, half heaved her up the ladder, a cue for the mob to resume its jeering.

Martha pushed on, working slantways to the front, past waving arms and careless feet. The wind raged suddenly, soughing off the beach. A father reached his small son off the Moot Hall mounting block and Martha lunged to claim the spot. The father helped her up. She knew him a little, had delivered his lad. The block afforded the view she sought: the scaffold, the hangman's careful testing of Ma Southern's noose, and the jubilant crowd that seethed serpent-like through the length of the village, spewing its venom into the streets. As if fetched out by the noise the Durriken sisters appeared in the gaol's gate: Joan, throwing up her bound hands to shield her eyes from the too-bright light; Rose, led by Ned Bullard, sobbing her innocence as she walked.

"So young she is," said the goodwife at Martha's knees.

"Aye by Christ, but a good fit for the Devil's bed," swore her husband. He hawked, thickly. "Hang 'em quick," he bawled, "but let 'em die slow."

"No forgiveness," shrieked another voice. A woman's, and familiar. Twenty paces away Liz Godbold stood in the thick of the crowd, white-faced but rageful. "No forgiveness for these hell-hags." The mob took the words and brayed them over and over. No forgiveness, no forgiveness. All around were stamping feet and opened throats, catcalls, prayers, oaths lobbed at the heavens.

In spite of the wind Martha felt starved of air. She got down from the mounting block. A hand reached out and gratefully she took it. Simon jerked his head at the gallows and pulled her in behind him. The wind battened again as the crowd surged, opening, closing, their progress laboursome as birth. They were close enough now to see Ma Southern's wasted frame, Joan's piss-streaked skirts, the hangman moving between the women, placing and testing the rope collars with all the care of a lady's dresser. Joan shook uncontrollably, almost losing her footing on the ladder. The hangman saw it and pulled a band of linen from his belt that he tied around her eyes. Joan's mouth worked, uttering sharp sobs of terror. She was praying, or trying to.

The hangman fetched down the fourth rope and another roar went up. By the gaol entrance the knot of onlookers foamed and parted, spitting and catcalling at the figure who came out. Slowly it came on; hunched, two-headed, passing within yards. Martin Strong, with a bound woman under a piece of blanket. At the foot of the gallows the prisoner stumbled, unable to climb the steps. Martin took off her cover. A quantity of gold hair fell down.

Martha's guts vaulted. She wanted to wail, to curse, to

bargain. To beg for Prissy, even now being led to the noose that surely—rightfully—was meant for her. She clawed at Simon to make him look. *Lad, lad, I pray you. Speak for me now. Be my voice*, she signed. He grimaced at her, not understanding. She flung her arms at the waiting gallows, violently shaking her head. *Not Prissy. Tell them: not Prissy.* Must she spell it all for him? *She's done no wrong.* Her hands were mad with panic. She slowed them, made their shapes larger. *Tell them: not Prissy. Tell them to take ME instead.* Simon's eyes went very wide. She seized his arm and shoved forwards, butting at the bodies in the way. In front of the gibbet the guards stood with raised staves. Robert Bullard saw her coming and moved to obstruct her.

"God's teeth, what are you doing?" he hissed. His face was ashen. "Get back, Martha, if you know what's good for you."

Not Prissy, she motioned. Her fingers raked. *Not Prissy. She is no witch, she has done no—*

Robert shoved with his stave. "Stay back, you daft mare." His eyes found Simon. "For Christ's sake, take her away," he hissed.

Her hands scrawled again, *Hang me, not Prissy*—before Simon caught them, trapping them in his own. She fought him, trying to wrench free. He wouldn't let go. She summoned all her voice; it stretched and cracked, her tongue strained. The truth surged in her throat and died there. The worm ate it all.

Above them the hangman motioned for a knife to hack away Prissy's hair. The constable unsheathed his dagger. Handfuls of golden hair fell to the planking. Prissy's neck showed, white and slender in the O of the noose. She was quaking badly. The town crier's final utterance faded into the thick air; as he stepped down from the scaffold, the hangman arranged the noose. Martha stamped hard on Simon's foot. He fell back cursing and let

her go. Her hands flew up like freed spirits. *Hang me instead.*
I have done wrong. I am the wit—

From somewhere a drum started up, a loud, dry roll. The
constable was reading out the death notice. Time was all run
out. Clemency too: there was no more to be had. To go to the
constable or the witch man and tell the truth would be certain
death, but was she not condemned already? To live on with
Prissy dead: what life would that be? A daily quietus, by the
inch, eaten alive by remorse.

The hangman kicked the first ladder away. Martha let her
hands drop. At once Ma Southern's lame legs jigged and ped-
alled; her face contorted as though she were laughing at some
private jest. The hangman stepped to the Durriken sisters and
deprived them of their ladders. Now it was their turn to gasp
and caper, their faces mottling. The wind belled out their skirts,
twisting the nooses with their gargoyle faces.

"Where's your Devil-husband now, my darling?" bellowed
the Sandgrave knife-grinder. He was asking Prissy.

"Warming the bed, I'll swear," bawled his crowd companion.
Gusts of mocking laughter. Applause, open-throated animal
calls from this mob that wanted Prissy dead. Martha could see
but not hear the hangman's request for pardon, Prissy's ashen-
faced response, her lips moving, Christ have mercy, the Lord
have mercy, her eyes staring and fixed on some great distance.
The hangman moved across and put the noose in position. Then
halted. Martha shoved forwards, but now it seemed that all Cleftwater was solidly turned against her. Above Prissy, the hangman
slid the noose knot under her ear. Then he kicked the ladder.

The mob let out a jubilant howl. With what frenzy Prissy's
life was ending, this thrash and jerk of the rope. Wet ran down

Martha's face. Soundlessly she struck herself, her breast her cheeks her scalp; she would flog herself until she fell. Kin of the dying—Hilda Southern, the Durriken brothers—pushed to the scaffold to take hold of the threshing feet and pull on them, still them, bring their owners' lives faster to a close. Who would help Prissy? She looked around. Simon was disappeared. Why then, *she* would. This much she could do for her friend. This much might salve her conscience, bring her soul some small relief.

The hangman had come down from the scaffold and was being handed—hero, saviour—man to man over the crush. Behind him was Simon, on the platform grasping Prissy's feet, adding his weight to hers. Martha fought to reach him. Dimly she heard the constable calling, "Order, order," but the mob was feral, unstoppable. By now she had been pushed back some thirty paces, more. A balled hand landed on her ribs, knocking her down. Its owner shoved past. There was nothing to hold on to, no purchase on life. She thought to be still and shelter against this thicket of legs and pounding feet. Some primary instinct took over. She rolled onto her knees. To live was to crawl, and she did, without direction.

Someone grasped the hood of her cloak and then her shoulder. "Martha?" Constable Napier pulled her upright. His face was stern, his grip custodial. Judge Bacon and Minister Deben stood either side. They all three regarded her.

"Come," the constable said.

He had her by the sleeve. They fanned out and flanked her and began to walk. She could scarce keep up. The sweat was drying on her body and a coldness taking its place. Where were they taking her? What would they do with her? The Moot Hall loomed, sinister and inordinate.

Wait.

The men stopped. She looked pleadingly at each of them.

"We're bringing you home," said Constable Napier, as if to a child. He softened his grip. "It's an ill evening, Martha. 'Tis not safe, for you or any woman."

What of Simon?

"What's that?"

Simon.

"I don't know your meanin', Martha. But if it's Simon you're frettin' over, have no concern. I've seen him fight. He knows how to use his fists. Now let's get you home."

So wrong it felt, to leave Simon behind. She had thought they would go home together, prepare themselves to face Kit. She twisted to look back. No sign of Simon. No signs of any kind. The sun was declining and long shadows sagged over the gibbet. The crowd had thinned but men still revelled at its base and the rising wind carried the noise of their carolling. Prissy's corpse was swivelling in the current or perhaps it was the air above the body that was moving, a kind of rippling pallor. Oh, oh: impossible that Prissy was gone. Surely she was still here, still present, not yet crossed over?

"This is the worst of days for Cleftwater," said Master Bacon, addressing the others as much as her. "And a bad day for Justice, when old women, aye, and sick ones and those with no kin to speak for them, are sent to their deaths."

"An evil end to evil business," the minister agreed.

"Aye, but not finished," said the constable. "There are yet women in the gaol. Doubtless there'll be more hangings before summer's out."

They had left the market square. Tide Lane was a white

track through this night that was thick with threat. Lights showed in the houses ranged along it. Godbold, the house of her former friend; an enemy now, perhaps. Archer, the house of the dead baby. Durriken, the house of hanged sisters. The house of Thaddeus Spalding, the undertaker. Then the shadowed blank of the field and beyond it, home: the house of the sick merchant, his gaoled wife, his hanged servant. She slowed, reluctant to go on.

Minister Deben said, "Shall I come home with you, Martha? I could perhaps pray with you—your household?"

For a brief moment she entertained the idea. Then balked at it. It was for her to tell Kit. *Nay.* But *I thank you*, she told him, arranging her hands as if in prayer.

On the beach a dim form sat slumped. Its head hung down. A spark of alarm fired across her breast. Was it . . . Prissy's ghost? A strange elation gripped her. Now she might make her peace. She ran across the street. The constable called a warning. She paid no heed. Above, around, the wind vaulted, whipping the surf, casting salt-spray in her face and eyes. The figure lifted its head and looked straight at her: a very mortal Simon. His face and hands were chilled and she took off her cloak and draped it over him. Now it was her turn to lead. She brought him off the beach. The men gave him sidelong glances, falling into step.

The minister touched Simon's arm. "That was a kindness, how you went to Prissy. To ease her suffering."

"I did what any decent man would do." Simon's tone was surly. His jaw clacked with cold.

"There are men aplenty who would rather stand by than take action," Minister Deben said. "What you did today was—"

"Rash, and a risk," cut in the constable. His tone, his face, were grim. "I grant you, it were brave. But you've as good as shown your colours to the witch-hunter."

"Master Makepeace is not a moderate man," said Master Bacon.

"He is not," agreed the constable. He raised a warning finger. "Go careful, young sir. Do nothing that draws attention. Be seen at church. He's marked what you did. Already he has asked in which household you serve. And I could only tell him, in one that's lost its cook to the gallows and got its mistress in the gaol. And whose most trusted servant was seen today in front of the gallows, waving and pointing at herself like someone possessed."

She glanced at Simon. His face was turned down but his mouth had a particular set to it. "Prissy was a true soul, a Christian maid," he said. "She deserved a better death." He looked up, defiant. "That's all Martha was sayin'."

They had reached the house. The light had all but gone. In the yard the ripped sheet flapped, that ensign of her guilt.

"Oh," said the minister, clamping a hand to his chest. His breath was short. "What times we are in, when a flapping sheet can stop a heart."

"Mistress Persore was not so innocent, so I'm told," the constable said, looking at Judge Bacon.

"What do you mean?" Simon asked.

"She confessed," said Judge Bacon.

"Never. Never. Not Prissy," protested Simon. "Not her."

"Even her," the judge affirmed. "I wish I could tell you different." His expression was sorrowful, the look of a mourner. "I admit, I have reservations about Master Makepeace's methods. But 'tis difficult to gainsay his evidence." He loosened his jabot and with it rubbed his neck. "Forgive me. I was up late into the night, and again at cockcrow." Fatigue had put a rime on his voice. "Priscilla Persore confessed to having wedded the Devil, along with several other witches she named. She was marked also—was she not, Martha? And later admitted to having cursed a pregnant mother whose babe was born very sick last week. And then, seeing it born so sick, commanded her imp to cause the child to die. Which it did. So you see, young friend," he said, gentle for Simon, "I had no grounds to spare her."

TWENTY-ONE

They sat in the kitchen in silence. Kit's uneaten supper of bread in milk cooled on the table; they had come home to find him worse. Martha had lit only the one lamp which smoked because it needed trimming, and its light flared and stuttered, causing shadows. Simon was sunk into himself, slumped in the faded green blanket, unreachable. He was gone from her, a long way off, into some exile of grief. He would not let go of the twist of Prissy's hair that he'd taken from the scaffold; Martha had woven it around a strand of red wool, and for a few minutes, sitting with the braid spooling from her fingers, she'd been distracted, escaped from her conscience. But as soon as she'd passed it to Simon—his memento of Prissy, grim keepsake of this day—her conscience had resumed its circling, to Prissy, to Agnes. How did mistress fare? And the babe? Even as she prayed for them she knew there could be no respite. Her bones were heavy, her breathing also. She felt sick and maybe she was: sick from the failure of all her efforts—prayers and cures and Mam's doll—that had kept her safe but brought harm to others.

Sick from her silence, which had cost Prissy's life.

She got up. Of their own accord her stiff legs moved; they were walking across the dark kitchen. All she could do was follow. Her legs went to the fire and she took a taper and lit it before she went. The air of the house was dense and smelling of disease and through it she moved, along the narrow passageway to the study. As she went in she pulled the door to. Her legs kept going and took her to the big window. She knew why and thrust the knowing away. She drew in a large breath and climbed up onto the window seat and, from a crack in the plaster above the window lintel, retrieved a corn dolly.

She'd made it last autumn—one of three she'd plaited from the last sheaf of harvest straw. Their heads were a spray of tiny plaits, their bodies long and thin, with spindly arms and legs. Through the winter she had completed them, tied their hair with ribbon, clothed them in simple petticoats she'd stitched. Then she'd hidden them about the house. Here was the first, in its crude dress of green damask surreptitiously snipped from the hem of mistress's winter gown. She'd put it above Kit's big window, determined to bar harm from reaching him.

There were two more, one tucked into the recess above the back door, the other nailed high up and out of sight, over the front door. Quietly she fetched them down. On her palm they lay inert, regarding her with the same blank stare. Sensations pricked. The worm bridled. She had made them for protection, in the aftermath of the terrible storm, to defend Kit and his household. A sudden heat flared through her, a quick-rushing alarm. The dolls were a transgression, pagan, idolatrous, an offence to religion. While she kept them, while they were in the house, they were a liability—more proof, if any were needed, of her waywardness, her disloyalty to God.

Downstairs Simon was untidily asleep, his limbs lolling. She sidled past his dangling arm and went softly to the kitchen fire.

She offered it the first doll and it caught alight in a dirty yellow flame. Watching it being consumed, a shadow seemed to lift. Perhaps, after all, the dolls had been useless: simple harvest spindles. Under the blanket Simon stirred. In the firelight his face flickered, shadow patched with gold. The hair of the next doll smoked, threatening to catch alight.

"What are you doing?" Simon threw off the blanket, crossing the kitchen to snatch the doll from her. He inspected its damage. "I thought you made these as toys, for Kit's babby?"

She found she had no answer, or not one that would please him. He'd been looking at her questioningly; now he leaned to take the remaining doll and she saw how his humour was shifting, something fierce and wrathful stirring in his eyes. "Only a week ago we were all sat here with no inkling. None at all." He was squinting at the dolls, at the twist of Prissy's hair. "I thought how Prissy was the purest soul in Christendom. I thought the same of you." He looked abruptly up, transferring his gaze to Martha. "What was it, that you was trying to say, back there? At the gallows . . . when you wanted 'em to take you, instead of Prissy? When you said how *you* were the guilty one?" His eyes raked, searching hers. "I'm gettin' to doubt you, Martha. Question what you've gone and done." His voice tapered but she felt the burn of his stare. "Anything you want to tell me? Say it, 'cause now's the time."

He waited. At her sides her hands were still.

"No? Nothing?" His huge eyes flashed, commanding the truth. "That's strange. Seemed like you had plenty to say back there, when there was a rope involved." Her throat made a noise, a protest. He was suddenly damp-eyed. "You been like a mother to me, Martha. All the mother I've known. And up 'til now I'd have done anything for you, anything at all to keep you safe." She sought his hand but he wouldn't give it. In his face his expression was rearranging itself; anguish giving way to something harder. "Prissy's lost, and I never did tell her what she meant. To me," he added, needlessly. "I can't help thinking how she's gone but you're still here. Doesn't seem fair. Doesn't seem right." He shook his head. "I can't help but wonder at your strange ways—what you really do with your herbs and your Popish prayers. What other secrets have you got? Nay—don't tell me. You don't speak and for once that's a good thing, 'cause what I don't know I can't confess, if anyone come asking."

He threw the dolls in the fire. "You should look to yourself, Martha, 'cause of Kit. 'Cause of the babe, God rest him, if he lives. Mistress Agnes too. Pray God they'll let her out of the gaol. Pray God she'll come home safe." The fire burned unevenly, giving out wraiths of smoke. Simon's shadow reared up the wall. "I'll stay on here 'til master gets better, but . . . best you keep clear. You go about your business and I'll go about mine until all this trouble's gone by. And if anyone comes asking, I'll not speak against you. But I'll not speak for you, neither." He was enraged, not quite shouting. Her eyelids fluttered in his blast. "Go your ways, Martha. And I'll ask you to leave me to mine."

He snatched up the coil of Prissy's hair and went.

———

Her life was like a worn-out rope, its strands breaking one by one. She got up and tried to clear the table. Slow, swerving movements; a dry prayer that stuck in her mouth. *Turn thy face again, O Lord, upon thy servant.* The lamp's flame was all but out and in the frail light she sensed the approach of a huge, tidal anguish only just held in check.

In the yard the hogs waited. She threw down the soggy bread and poured out the rest of her ale and watched without seeing as they ate the mess away. Behind them was her garden, tall spires of foxglove and wolfsbane at the very back, their hoods touched by the moonlight that sifted over the yard wall. In the greyness all the losses arrived at once. Lost hopes. Lost lives; including her old one with all its sureties, her place in the house, her portion of earth on which to stand; the future one, with Kit's child. All forfeit, because of her sins.

Mea culpa. Mea maxima culpa: the guilt racked and racked, in waves, in a flood. She was pleading with God for mercy, for forgiveness of her misdeeds, sins of omission and commission.

The sin of her silence over Prissy.

The sin of the poppet.

The sin of the Archer babe's brief life, which she herself had ended.

She had turned him face down on her lap and pressed him into her knees. With her hidden hand, bunched together his nose and cloven lips and held them closed. Snuffing him out like a candle-flame, for while he lived his suffering was her suffering, more than she could bear. A quick death at her hands was a kindness, a mercy. And also a duty, this stopping of blight that was also a stopping of evil. The child was a creature, the product of a curse, and if he were let live he might draw affliction to them all.

After a time his useless flailing ceased. With shaking hands she'd swaddled him in her old blue birthing cloth, just as she would a living child. She'd prayed for him—over him. Then handed him to Prissy.

And this, too, was a torment, another dread reproach, for in the doing of this simple act she had brought disaster on Prissy's head. And now Prissy, too, was dead while she, Martha, lived, and while she did she could never again know ease, not in her conscience, not in her soul; would never again know how she might find solace.

The hogs regarded her, always hopeful. The night breeze touched her neck. She went to the physick bed and waded in. Life's winds would always blow but here among the plants she might still find redemption. They bent towards her, touching, greeting. She sank to her knees, a stain, a shadow among their shapes.

Beneath her breastbone she could feel something physical: her soul, labouring with grief, appalled at herself. To end her own life was a mortal sin, but was she not, in the end, irredeemable because of the blackness at her very core?

On her hands and knees she crawled, crushing the wild thyme she'd let grow all through the bed, its cleansing scent just reaching through her tumult. *Draw nigh to God, and He will draw nigh to you.* Ahead were the poison plants: gracious wolfsbane with oblivion in all its parts—in the long bone of its stem, its fleshy leaves and nodding heads. Let her lie with it, and meet her end in a last dispensation of its green embrace.

TWENTY-TWO

Tuesday

B ut in the morning she woke, and was not dead.

She lay on the damp earth staring at the pillars of the plants. The light was growing and the physick bed was coming into colour. She was not dead. How was she not dead? She touched the cross at her neck. She touched the pouch. It was empty but held something of the poppet, a remnant, like an echo.

She got up and walked distractedly through the yard into the street. She was not dead. The lane, the field, the village, the grey horizon; they reeled about, familiar and strange. Shoeless, she went down the beach to the water. The air felt charged and drained, both. Above her head the sky was flushing with its first colours. Early sunlight fingered her face. She closed her eyes and let them fill with rose and pink. The colour of healed skin. Of health. Today she was not dead. Today she was alive. She opened her eyes and the cluster of pale stones before her seemed to cloud, shift, remake themselves as the poppet: still here and not here. But today, today: she was alive because of God's will. He had spared her, had put out his hand to shield her as He had done ever since the witch man came, from every variety of harm. He must have a plan for her.

She turned and looked at the village. Kit's house—her house—looked peaceful, at rest except for the smoke scribbling from its chimney. Simon was up and going about the morning's business. She must do the same.

Tom Archer's gate was down again and in the street a lone piebald cow stood, calling for its sisters. No-o. No-ow. Now.

TWENTY-THREE

Kit's fever was worse. He was coughing all the time. She sat him up and tried to spoon some medicine into the hot vent of his mouth. He pushed the spoon away. His breath smelled of the bad thing that was breeding inside him. She was suddenly afraid that a serpent had somehow got in him and went to the top of the stairs and thumped her feet to summon Simon. *Come up.* Simon held Kit while she doled in the tincture that Kit promptly vomited over the quilt. He cursed them, not knowing who they were.

She touched Simon on his chest and then the apostle spoon and the bottle of tincture. *You must bring the doctor.*

"I'm to bring the minister?"

Nay. She cupped her hands around her ear and leaned, listening through them to Kit's chest. *The doctor.*

"The doctor?" He hesitated. "I'm afeared to leave you alone with master. Of what you might do."

She glared at him. *Go NOW. Haste back.* Still he dallied. She flapped her arms. *Get gone!*

He clattered downstairs and she heard the front door slam and then his walk turning to a run. Kit slumped against her. If she were to let go he would slide from her, maybe forever. But her own heat was not good for him. He was running with sweat, and she settled him back on the bolster and then bathed him as best she could, his face and neck and under his arms, with a piece of old sheet. She could hear the wind changing again, its whine in the chimney-breast. A great reef of bruise-coloured cloud was coming, advancing over the sandbar. In it a storm was steeping. The bedchamber was filling with a low greenish light and what it touched took on a strange, diseased look. Simon would be through the Scours now, cresting the High Street at a run. Dr. Quinnell lived almost at the top in one of the newer houses with a fine view. Her thoughts ran forwards and then back, frantic, each one ending with a loss. So many people lost. In so short a time. Losing Kit would be the worst. Would be the end. Her eyes filled. Small grains of tears leaked from them. A picture came of Dr. Quinnell bleeding Kit, and she went down to the kitchen and fetched the letting basin and brought it back upstairs. She pushed back the bed curtains and kissed Kit and kept her lips pressed to his forehead. In the bed he stirred. "Godspeed," he said, or seemed to say. His voice was a husk. She pulled up the chair and sat with his hand limp in hers, feeling the heat baking through his skin. Flat morning light picked out the blisters of dark stubble, the waxy gleam of his complexion, his gaze that was inexact and closing up. He was going, aye: nay, he was already gone, beyond the reach of her care, to where the sickness would ransom him. Small quiet prayers came, dredged out of childhood like the beads of Mam's rosary, *Hail, Holy Queen, Mother of mercy, To thee do we cry*. Perhaps Mam would hear and take pity and send some message, some succour across the void.

From somewhere behind her a rood-shaped shadow speared fast across the bed, then crashed against the window. She spun around. On the glass, a print of fanned wings. She got up and opened the window. On the ground, a burst of black, a bead of yellow gazing skywards.

A black bird.

A blackbird, its neck bent at a wrong angle. Already the hogs were coming; they were beasts with appetites and would do as hogs do. She ran downstairs, collecting the yard broom as she went. Cool air met her like a blow. The heat had broken as suddenly as the bird. The tips of its wings shifted in the breeze and for a moment she thought it might still live. She raised the broom and waited. Nothing. It was dead, and here were the hogs, coming to deal with it.

Get away. She swiped at them. The hogs backed off but not far. Their snouts were working, scenting a meal. With the broom she chivvied them to their pen and closed them in. Then picked up the bird, which stared past her with its stunned eye. She looked where it looked—towards the garden wall—and saw various heads assembling there: Simon's with its uncombed curls and Dr. Quinnell's coiffed chestnut wig; the hatless constable—why was he here?—with the Bullard brothers. All of them staring at her.

She could feel herself reddening. Dull Martha. Devil's Martha, with her murdered bird.

Dr. Quinnell said, "What have you there, Martha?"

This. She showed him; read the dismay in his face. Ned and Robert exchanged glances.

"And how do you come by that?"

She motioned to the bedchamber window. *It flew there.* She let her own neck droop in imitation of the bird's. *Broke its neck.*

"Whatever you're doing with it," Simon said meaningfully, "you'd best put it down."

The sky poured its funeral light. Against it the men were shapes only. She did not want to surrender the bird. While she held it she was untouchable; Kit was invulnerable.

"Martha," Simon said again. "Leave that be now."

Dr. Quinnell broke the spell. "Simon," he said. "I cannot delay. Is your master upstairs?" He picked up his medicine bag and came across the yard to the house.

"Aye. I'll take you."

They went inside. The blackbird swayed in her grip.

"Why do you have the bird, Martha?" Constable Napier asked.

His eyes were fixed on her, wary. "Why did you kill it?" He was speaking slowly and clearly, like to a child. *I didn't kill it. It hit . . .* She swayed, suddenly stupid with tiredness.

The constable turned to the Bullards. "What is she saying?" Robert only shook his head. The constable opened the gate. "Drop it now, Martha. Drop it, I say." He motioned Ned forwards. The big lad approached, but gingerly, clutching the coil of rope.

"Come on now, Martha. Let go of that," Ned said, syrup-voiced. "It's bad for you as it is, even without that thing." When she didn't move he shook her, trying to shake the dead bird free of her hold. Her mouth opened, shaping itself to scream. "Let go of it. You've to come with us now." He passed a length of rope around her waist. "I prayed this day wouldn't come. Now it has, and we must make the best of it." He tied her hands gently, with a care that belied his bulk. "Sorry I am, Martha," he said, sorrowful, "to be the one taking you."

Behind him the constable speaking, a proclamation of some kind. On the ground the dead bird. God's sending, His new message, writ in a splay of feathers.

TWENTY-FOUR

Thursday afternoon

After the wind, water. Rain spewing ceaselessly from the gargoyle crouched on a corner of the Moot Hall roof, its stone face screwed up with spite. The tide savage, unnaturally high, threatening to broach the lip of the shale.

All this in glimpses. She has been run and walked without stopping for two days and two nights, bare-armed and shivering in the undershift she put on three mornings ago; clothes from a different time, a kinder world. Shoeless she has shuffled the length of England, the soles of her feet blistering before they bled; from the confines of the Moot Hall she has circled the world. How well she has learned its shrunken topography: the walls with their gleaming flints, the floorboards with their knots and nicks. With every circuit listening for clues from the gaol below—signs however slight of those women who still lived, Jennet, Agnes, the child, though after countless hours her mind could attend only to the exquisite labour of the next forced step. Always there were two others with her, gaolers and searchers. They had emptied her pouch and raked through the herbs and found at the bottom the dried foxglove and poison parsley, the search-women taking it in turns to ask, What have you to tell us? What ills, what witchings have you done? So that she could speak they untied her wrists. With the rope off, her hands at first hung down, stiff and nerveless. She forced them into movement.

How fares my mistress? What of the babe?

"Walk her again," Mistress Knill said, coolly disgusted. "She only flaps like a crow."

———

Crow. Crone. The ceaseless walking was ageing her, uncountable years. The Hall got cold. Mistress Knill put on her cloak. Sue Ruddock went home and came back drenched but with a thicker shawl, gabbling news of the storm: impassable roads, the lower Scours and Kit's field under water. Before Sue had finished speaking Mistress Knill was snapping her fingers at Ned, absently present in the big judging chair. He roused himself.

"The fire," she said. "Light it. Bring kindling."

Ned looked from her to the big open hearth. There were logs but no kindling. He got up and lumbered out.

———

Walk on. More circuits of the Hall, her life, her conscience. She could no longer tell the hours apart. Only her feet left evidence, a trail of red prints in the floor's grime. At intervals the walkers changed. Sometimes she was propped between the Bullards, between Robert's ox-like shoulder and Ned's leaner one. Or jostled unevenly between tall Martin and short Herry with their mismatched steps, Martin matching his to hers, Herry forcing the pace. If for a moment she slackened he would pinch the soft underside of her stretched-out arms. Herry, always Herry:

sneering at her with his stung-looking face, baiting her with muttered taunts and oaths until even he wearied.

For a few minutes at a time they let her sit. Sleep, sag, topple, wake. "If you judge this a torment," Liz Godbold told her, "think what waits you in Hell." Once, Sue Ruddock went out and came back with a full jug of ale. Martha's lips were cracking; Mistress Knill had forbidden her all meat and drink lest Martha feign the need for the pot. Sue drank first, looked furtively around, then poured what was left into Martha's mouth. Ale, ale; its exquisite wetness. Her tongue flapped in the cup.

Martin said, "For God's sake, Martha. If you've done the Devil's work then tell it now and beg for pardon."

What could she tell them? Her hands that were blue-tipped and shrunken, twigs of bone, lifted and fell. Nothing, breeding nothing. For her of all people it was easy not to speak. The watchers said so to Mistress Knill, who came back from supper with coins chinking in her hip-purse. Around her neck was a new green ribbon, beaded with tiny pearls. The search-mistress smiled, showing perfect teeth. "Oh, but she will talk, eventually. Keep walking," she ordered, and they did.

———

Herry Gowler said, "Simon Brock, he's a servant in Knoll House. He knows how she talks, what she says with her hands." Simon was fetched. He came in soaked from the storm. In the fire's big heat Martha could see steam coming from him and also how he sweated. The questions started again: what, why, how?

Simon would not look straight at her; would watch only the trace-work of her fingers. "She swears she has no imps. She serves Christ, not the Devil."

"Yet we have found poisonous herbs in her little bag."

"She says the herbs are for her cough. And also for Mistress Crozier. To help her pains if . . . if she birthed her babe here."

A peal of hard laughter. "How very kind. To think of her mistress in this way. Bringing her herbs to ease her mistress's travail—poisonous herbs, no less. And there is another matter. Of a casket, a witch's spell-box, that was found in her bedchamber. And in it, a variety of evil charms." The search-mistress turned the blue bore of her gaze on Simon. "Did you know of these? Did you see her use them?"

Simon was startled. "She said the casket was her mother's. That's where she told me it come from. She only showed it me once—just the box, not anything of its insides."

He glanced at Martha, his expression perplexed. She knew he was appraising her, and likely finding her flawed. "I know for a fact," he went on, "that box you found is precious to her. She keeps all her special things in it. Not that she got much, 'cause she's not got many things as she'd call her own. What she do have . . . it's mostly what Master Kit's given her, or what she kept from her Mam."

"In the precious box," said Mistress Knill, "we found a crushed frog, and a witching jar with nails in it. And other vile trinkets besides."

Finished: she was finished. Simon was squinting at her, as though her soul's defilement was a too-bright light shining full in his face. How surprising, how fitting, that Simon's testimony would convict her. For a handful of agonised moments they regarded each other, Simon looking at her from his innermost self, a gaze she met with the essence of her own. She could see

the muscles around his mouth twitching, the outward indication
of some hard-fought inner struggle.

"I know nothin' about any charms," Simon said at last. "I
never seen Martha with anythin' like that."

Mistress Knill considered him. Then sent him away.

———

The sky worked through its various tints, a rainbow of dusks
before night deadened their colour. The west windows turned
to squares of black. Perhaps she was already dead, walked into
the shades of Hell.

Praise be. "*Tell* them, Martha," Ned urged, over the draught
of a monstrous wind that bellowed from the sea like a voice.
The fire surged, baptising them in tarnished light. Through
the daze of her exhaustion she could hear the village's growing
panic—cries, calls, shouted alarms, steps floundering through
water, the repeated groaning of the door of the Four Daughters
as its produce and animals were brought into the street.

"What is happening?" Mistress Knill asked, her eyes widening like blue stains.

"Flood's got into the High Street," Ned said, from the opened
door.

As if on cue the wind screamed. Martha listened. From all
around the sound of water, cold, dark; the North Sea, coming
at the land. It was speaking in tongues, in its own language. She
could hear its purpose, its smothering intent.

———

Mistress Knill retired. Then Liz Godbold made her excuses and
left. Herry went out, supposedly to bring ale. The clock tolled:

midnight, one of the morning, two. It was tolling away her life. Sue Ruddock, hanging on for extra coin, went out saying she needed the pot. She didn't come back. Then it was just her and Martin, and he shared his tankard of small beer which she drank down too fast and then coughed up, spraying her dress with bile. When she righted herself she saw Prissy standing in an unearthly light, whole and unbruised but reproachful. The bile made her throat burn but even so a raw noise broke from it. Martin got her up and pulled her arm across his broad shoulders. She could smell the ripe tang wafting from her own pits. They walked again. She knew she was a dead weight, all her limbs exhausted, her head unliftable. Prissy stood by and stood by and then was suddenly not there.

Time went along. The wind's whine was insistent. Once or twice she thought she heard in it a higher note—a high-pitched wail like a babe's cry. She listened hard. With the last of her vigour, despatched some essence of herself—puny, tremulous—into the Hall; sending it below, through the boards and joists, to search them out, Jennet and Agnes and the babe; found the faintest trace of them in the teeming air.

In some small hour before dawn Constable Napier arrived. Martin drew two chairs up to the fire. "Sit down," the constable said. Martha collapsed with her head on her knees and was instantly, dreamlessly, asleep. The constable jogged her awake. With the tip of his rapier sheath—great big pin—he tilted up her face. His eyes, ditchwater brown, fixed on hers. His thin lips moved.

He was telling her that if she didn't confess she would hang like the others, her body would be carted away and tipped without ceremony into some unmarked grave. Or into the reed beds west of the village, to lie nameless and mouldering while the rushes sighed out her story for the rest of time.

She could barely keep up her head. She looked at him or tried to. Her eyes lolled and roamed. Puppet. Poppet. Mam said, Say nothing. Nothing to say.

"Will you not speak, Martha? Will you not clear your soul?" Gravely he regarded her. When she didn't reply he led her to the lancet window that looked out onto the market square. On the gallows, next to Prissy, Father Leggatt's swollen body hung. Rotting laundry on a line.

TWENTY-FIVE

Friday

Herry shoved her in. The day's light was in a narrow shaft that ended just beyond the gaol's gate. Martha stepped along it. It came up to her knees, then her shins, then her ankles. Then no more. Behind her came a grind of metal on metal as Herry locked the gate.

The present rushed at her. There was a vast exhaustion, an emptying all through. To be imprisoned felt somehow correct, a terminus. She was in the right place. Her eyes adjusted. Ranged around the walls were shapes, indistinct in the bosky light. One sat at a drunken angle against the street-side wall, a mess of rags and limbs, its wasted lips ajar. She went towards it but the smell drove her back. Hannah Holland: dead.

Martha breathed through her sleeve. To the right of the brick column that housed the clock tower there was one high, barred window. A blush of light filtered through it—the first of the morning—that picked out three huddled forms. Martha peered. From one of them came a tiny cry—the smallest, piercing wail, a thread of sound in the dark. The sound came again, distinct and unmistakable. A babe's cry. *The* babe's cry: and here it was, the longed-for sound, coming to her through the dark as if from a dream. Her head glanced off the lantern but she scarcely felt it as she crossed the gaol, glimpsed the child nested in its mother's arms; raised it, held it close, kissed and kissed it. The gaol pivoted, disappeared. Returned: its dark was velvet, the child a seraph, a bud of light, a miracle, a girl. Nothing mattered save the fact of her existence, her perfect cry that lit up the world.

The trio of shapes moved as if brought to life by the sound. One of them put up its hand and beckoned: Come here.

"Do you have anything to drink?" Jennet said.

Nay.

"Then go piss in the pot," Ellen said. "Your mistress needs to drink."

She handed the babe to Jennet and went to the pot. Her water was scant. She brought it to Agnes and roused her by stroking her cheeks. Agnes was a sleeping skeleton, cool to the touch, her face caved in, the cheekbones showing sharp through grimy skin. In her bodice her breasts hung slack; her skirts were streaked, fresh blood welling through old.

"I have no more milk," Agnes said. Her voice was a cobweb, an almost-whisper. "The child needs more."

"The babe's taken all she got, and now she's empty," Jennet said flatly. She took the pot from Martha. "Help me." They bent to mistress. "Come on, my lady," Jennet crooned. "It's not nice but 'tis all there is." She dribbled liquid into Agnes's mouth. Agnes moaned and moved her head away.

The wind screamed off the ocean. The rain fell and fell, collecting in pools by the gate and window. They moved to a stall on the town-side wall, huddling in its meagre shelter with Agnes propped between them, trying to keep her warm. The tiny girl they passed from one crooked arm—one bony cradle—to the next. All Martha's look was for the babe—Kit's babe—this perfection of skin and blood and sinew. The light on her forehead, the downy auburn of her hair, her eyelashes. The child slept and woke and cried, opening her jewel lips and snuffling for her mother's breast. Sometimes they put her to it and her little mouth clamped and sucked, but when she pulled away they saw that her lips were filmed with red. Martha lifted the babe from her mother and rocked her to sleep. The rain fell, unrelenting. Its sound was a torment. They were fallen women, discarded women, exiled from care, from God's grace. They were to die of thirst. Martha took the empty pisspot and tried again and uselessly to get it between the bars of the gaol gate. She pushed her hands through and made cups of them to catch the rain's spray that she licked off. The slight wetness only worsened her thirst. She cupped and licked again. Then she went to Agnes and opened her mistress's lips and spat into them and worked the wet around her mouth. These small offices that she could do for mistress. That were kind. That were futile.

———

No one guarded them. No one came. The pool by the gate broadened and lengthened; muddy, undrinkable, a liquid taunt inching into the goal. They were too thirsty to talk. When Martha next got up to piss there was only a dribble in the pot. She shared it out, some for Agnes and what was left for Ellen. Jennet dabbed her fingers in the residue and moistened her lips and then, reaching across, made to wet Martha's. Instinctively she drew back. Jennet's face was grey and caved in, the dents in her cheeks like the result of some savagery. The face of a witch, or of a friend? She batted Jennet's offer away. Towards the middle of the gaol there was a depression in the floor like the burrow of some creature, and she crawled over and into it, lying curled in on herself. Lying where Prissy and Ma Southern had lain before they died; where she had tended to Father Leggatt. The packed earth was unforgiving, and she thought of her garden with its cared-for soil and her body strained towards the remembered plants—their living scents and colours—that she would not see again. Which would come first? The fast drop at the end of a noose, or a slower and more miserable one: Agnes's life draining redly away, the babe falling silent and then terminally asleep. As they all would, one after another, in a series of erasures, their deaths inconsequential as their lives had been.

In the hollow she twisted and her bare heel encountered something set in the floor. All the voices in her head went quiet. She sat up and felt around. Her fingers scraped. The thing was half-buried but showing pale through the dirt. She must dig gently lest it break. Slowly it came free; there was something motherly, almost sacred in the way she prised the poppet from the earth and held it close.

Both of its faces were somewhat damaged, the features a little crushed and one hand almost ground away. The needle and splinter were still there: still pricking. She ran over a thumb and got a nick from the splinter. Her pouch had been confiscated so she pushed it into her bodice. It went easily, as though slotting back into its rightful place, and straight away she felt the climb of some fresh humour all through her body, a bolder force, less afraid. She stood up and brushed herself down and went to the gate, wading through the swilling floodwater to pummel its bars with dull strikes. Nothing. She beckoned to Jennet. They pounded and shook the grille. Jennet yelled.

After many minutes a pair of worn boots appeared on the steps. "What do you want?" The boots descended and the hem of a mole-coloured jerkin came into view.

"Ale," Jennet shouted. "Cider, ale. Anything. We need it."

"I already brought you some."

"That was yester eve. We drank it all. We need more."

"I'm not your errand boy, running to the alehouse and back. Drink the rain."

Jennet swore. "A pox on you, Herry Gowler. We got a dead woman in here and another one likely to go unless we get something to drink." She shook the gate again. "Come down and see for yourself."

He came down the rest of the steps and stood carefully on the lowest one. "Which one is dead?"

"Hannah Holland. Passed away last night."

Herry bent to peer in, his face full of concentration.

"If you want to see her, Herry, come in here," Jennet said. "See for yourself what a hell-hole you keep us in."

"A hell-hole's good enough for the likes of you. Better than where you're going next."

"Take a good look." Jennet pointed. "That's poor Hannah. Dead and beginning to rot."

He squinted. "I don't see her."

"Well, you can smell her, can't you? Or can you only smell your own stink?" Jennet stepped aside to give Herry the full view. "See over there. That's Agnes Crozier. She's not stopped bleeding since she gave birth. She needs proper nursing. And that's her babe, a little girl. Who'll not last the day unless— Herry, don't you turn your face away—unless you help. I don't care what you think of me or the rest of us, whether you think we're Devil's harlots or no. It's too late for us, we know that, and it surely don't matter to Hannah now. But if you let this little babe, that's innocent—if you let her die, that's on you, Herry. On your conscience forever."

He snorted. "My conscience is clean as God's whistle. I do what I'm bid by people better than you. The witch man says to lock you up, I'll lock you. He says, no food or drink for you, you'll get none from me. Anyways, you've got rainwater." He brought his face up to the grille. "You ain't got a bean between you—except for lady Agnes, and maybe Kit Crozier'll settle her gaol fees, or maybe he won't, 'cause he's near dead from what I hear." He drew his head back. "You pledged yourselves to Old Nick, so let him help you. Let him bring you drink. Let him bring your supper and settle your fees." He grinned, showing stained teeth.

"We're not dead yet, Herry Gowler," Agnes said, weakly. "We ask you as a Christian for this kindness." She struggled, attempting and failing to lever herself to her knees. "My child who is innocent needs to drink. My friends, too, so they have voice enough for Judge Bacon." She fell back against Ellen.

Herry laughed. "You can wait all you like for Judge Bacon. He's no use to you. He's taken bad with the coughing sickness. They've brought that other judge instead, and he has no truck with witches." He stood up. "It's as good as over for you. You're dead, the lot of you."

Jennet said wearily, "Just bring us something to drink, Herry. Help us this last time."

"Not me."

Jennet drew a long, hissing breath. "Then I'll curse you, Herry Gowler. You think I'm a witch: I'll be one. I'll put a curse on you as will follow you around for the rest of your life, 'cause I'll be dead and no one will know how to lift it." Her voice shrilled; it was chasing his back, his crude gesture—"A fig for your curses, Jennet Savory"—his boots with loose soles that slapped as he went away.

Again and again Jennet pounded the gate until Martha prised her small hands from the metal. *Go to. Go to.* The fists were red where they had struck iron. There would be weals on them later. She smoothed out their palms. Across the left one Jennet's lifeline was deeply scored in an unbroken arc.

Your hand . . .

"What?"

With her fingernail she traced it. *Your hand says you'll live long.*

"Live long?" A derisory snort. "Aye. Well. Long enough to see myself hanged, if I don't die of thirst." She stared through the gate into the tunnel of grey-blue light. A handful of days in the gaol and already Jennet was leaner, stripped out. "This women's life of ours. Why must we suffer so? Cursed for being women. Prized for our cunts and maybe our looks, but not much else. They *use* us, Martha. They trade us, they breed from us, they trap us. No sooner raise us up than they beat us down." She took her hands back, hooding her eyes. "I can't stand it no more. My life's been all labour. Bangin' at locked gates. Prayin' or pleadin' for what should be mine—ours—by right. And I don't even mean special things. I mean simple things even beasts can get. A bit of bread when we're hungry. Ale when we thirst. Clean rags when we bleed. Ach, don't look at me like that, I don't care if I'm sinning, saying this. I'm a dead woman standing. I may as well speak my mind."

She stepped back on trembling legs. Her face was blotched and slapped-looking, flooding with colour in the familiar way. Martha pulled her close. There was only their breathing and the ruthless needling of the rain. "Let me be," Jennet said. Her voice had shrunk to a whisper. All of her was moving, in the grip of some violent inner weather, her plait snaking around her neck like a living thing, her eyes restless in their sockets. Soon they would roll back and up, as if to study the underside of Heaven.

Cleftwater without Jennet, without this wishbone of a woman, gobby, coarse, impious, who sold herself to men in the Scours, who frothed and shrieked; her tormentor, her accuser, her sometimes friend: the prospect was surreal, inadmissible. Some interruption was needed—a distraction to halt the fit. She grasped Jennet's plait. *Look. Look here.* Tugging the hair not hard but firmly, once, twice. She waited. Still Jennet tremored. She was very pale and the stain on her cheek stood out like a brand. From her bodice Martha took out the poppet. She held it up. *Look.* Jennet's moving eyes widened. *Look at this.* She was gripping too hard and the wax was beginning to give in her too-tight fist. She twisted the doll to show Jennet the two faces, the pockmarked wax, the needle and splinter. With each showing Jennet's fit seemed to ebb.

"What's that?" she asked finally. The poppet's blind face looked at Jennet, whose own eyes were fixed on it. "Where did you get it?" she asked, reaching. Martha snatched it away, suddenly—immoderately—protective of it, angling her body so that the other women could not see. Jennet's gaze followed the poppet. In her expression an idea dawned. "Did you make it?" She sucked in an awestruck breath. "You *made* it."

Nay. Nay. I only woke it.

"You woke it? What do you mean? How? How did you come by it?"

Martha put a finger to her lips. *Speak more quietly.* She glanced at Ellen and Agnes. They appeared to be dozing. *It was my mam's.*

"Your mam's? Did she give it you?"

Aye. And then I . . . woke it.

Jennet frowned. "It's a strange little dolly. I'm not sure I like it. Did it come like that—with those barbs?" She considered it some more, puzzling over it. "Can I touch it?" She put out a careful finger and stroked it. "I never seen one of these up close. People usually hide 'em somewhere. But you got it with you." A long look. "Aye, well, it don't take too much thinking to figure why. So you can use it. Is that it? Make it do what you want?"

Aye. I pricked it.

"What's this . . . barb between its legs?"

The splinter. *My pricker.*

"Your pricker? Where'd you get that?"

A fleet rush of shame. *I made it.* Martha lifted her chin in a small defiance. *The poppet's made for pricking. Like women. Like witches.*

Jennet's countenance altered, softening a little, though her laugh was like a yelp. "You're not wrong, my friend. But what were you prickin' *for*, I wonder?"

Her raised eyebrows, her questioning eyes, fixed expectantly on Martha.

Martha covered her mouth and throat. *I needled it . . . to stop the witch hunt.* She noosed her hands around her neck. *To stop us being hanged.*

"You pricked it to stop Master Makepeace?"

Aye.

"Well so, I can understand why you'd want to do that. I truly can. But it's not worked, has it?" Jennet put out one palm. "Let me look at it." Reluctantly Martha gave it. Something seemed to pass with it, a slight current. Jennet inspected it, turning it over and over. "I always had my wonderings about you. Dear, dumb Martha. Cleftwater's keeper. Where would we be without her? And her little poppet." She chuckled, examining the poppet from every angle. "Seems I was right to doubt you. Seems you really are a witch, Martha Hallybread." She danced the doll up her arm. "It's a fine dolly. Is there another? You could've made a whole family of 'em. Put protection on us all. Then again, just as well there's only one, if this is all the witching you can muster." She walked the doll up and down. "We'll make do with it. Does it have a name? No? Well then, little dolly. You're pricked and spoiled and broken, but what's left of you, we'll be kind to, eh?" She was delighted with it. She went to where Ellen and Agnes lay and held the poppet over their prone forms. Ellen stirred and opened her eyes.

"The kid's soiled herself," Ellen said.

"One more stink'll make no difference in here," Jennet said. She dangled the poppet over the babe. The tiny girl was stirring in her shawl cocoon. "See, little girl—see my dolly?" The child was awake, watching the poppet's dance with a milky gaze.

Ellen hissed. "What are you doin', Jennet Savory?"

"I'm seeing what this dolly can do. Maybe it can help us."

"Or maybe it'll be the finish of us," Ellen said. "Get that thing away from the babe."

"It's harmless enough, Ellen. Martha's mam's trinket."

"That's no trinket. That's a poppet. Made to do harm." She looked at Martha, then at Jennet. "Get rid of it now. If we're caught with it—"

"Ach. Who'll come? They've as good as left us to rot. Anyways. I've taken it off Martha, 'cause she's used it like a witch would. It's mine now."

An anger, hot as blood, engulfed Martha. The poppet was a gift and a talisman: a bile-coloured stalk of candlewax; her inheritance, the last, most physical connection to Mam. *Give it back.* She lunged to snatch at it. Her fingers closed around Jennet's shoulder.

"Go on. Go ahead, Martha. You can hurt me all you like. But I'm keepin' it."

She remembered the spider, the way it had come when Jennet bled. The wrongness of that. The wrongness now of her having the poppet and proposing to keep it. She gripped harder, feeling Jennet's resistance. Jennet's face loomed, homely, marked with its wine-coloured stain. A witch's face.

"You done bad things to it, Martha. I'll use it different."

How?

"I told you. By using it kindly. So it can be better. A poppet that does good."

Was such a thing possible? She no longer knew. Her grip slackened. How weary she was, how spent. Let Jennet have the doll. Let her discover what she could do with it. At least she, Martha, would be free of its taint.

Take it, then.

"I'll do that, my friend. So I will." Jennet twisted the poppet in her fingers, talking to it. "Our Martha don't make a very good witch, do she? But you don't need to worry about her no more. I'll take care of you, little poppet."

"Hold your tongue," Ellen hissed. "They're coming."

Martha's insides turned to water. She snatched back the poppet and went to the small window and threw it but the doll only glanced off the bars. It landed in Ellen's lap. The babe cried out, startled. On the steps were three pairs of knees, a descending assemblage of boots and breeches.

"Hurry," Ellen breathed.

The babe was swaddled in Agnes's shawl and Jennet unwound it down to the soiled cloth. The rank smell came at them. Where the child had lain in the mess her skin was raw. Put it here, Jennet motioned. Martha dropped the poppet in. They wound up the shawl, or tried to. The babe was beginning to fret. Herry was at the gate. He took the key from the belt at his waist, wielding it like some sacred object.

"You wanted help. I've brung it." He flashed Jennet a mocking look before standing aside to let his companions come in. Robert Bullard. Constable Napier. The smell of Hannah's body drifted languidly towards them, as if seeking the way out.

"Jesu," said Robert, making a mask of his fingers.

"That one's dead," said Herry, toe-pointing at Hannah and then at Agnes. "This one's halfway so."

The constable came closer, peered at Agnes and her streaked skirts. "Why is she bloody?"

"She's birthed her brat," Herry said. "That's it there."

"God's blood," the constable exclaimed, looking at the babe. "Even in the gaol they still manage to breed." In Ellen's arms the baby writhed. "How did she birth the babe?"

Jennet said, "In the usual way, Master Napier. From

that place between our legs that you gentlemen are so
fond—"

"Close your mouth," the constable told her. "I'll not have
any more of your filth." He leaned over Ellen to look at the babe.
"What ails her?"

"She's a new-born," Ellen said. "And hungry. This is no place
for a babe. She shouldn't be here. Nor her mother, Mistress
Crozier. She'll die if she don't get to the doctor."

"I can't do anything about that. The mother, I mean. She'll
stay here until she's seen the judge. As for the babe . . . aye.
Maybe she can come out."

"Take her to a wet-nurse, I pray you." Agnes's voice, barely
audible, floated up from where she lay.

"You must," Ellen said. "Take her to Liz Godbold. Her
daughter has milk. She can nurse this one until . . ."

Constable Napier chewed on his bottom lip. "Aye. Aye. I
suppose that's possible." He jerked his head to Robert. "Do that.
Take her to the Godbold woman. Make haste, man. Give her
the brat and then come straight back."

*Wait, I beg you. Please. Please. Let her mother bid her fare-
well.* Martha rocked her arms to show an empty cradle.

"Go on, then," the constable said.

Martha took the babe and kissed her again and again as she
refastened the shawl. *Go well, Kit's girl. Be well and thrive.* She
could feel the grief emerging, expanding in her like something
burst. She pushed it hard down and went to where Agnes lay and
put the child to the mother's inert lips. A last kiss. A mother's
benediction. Agnes's hand was limp as she put it on the child's
belly, wanting the mother to have sensed the girl or the girl to
have known the feel of her mother, however slight.

"Enough now," Constable Napier said. "Robert—take her."

Robert put out his arm—his large, coarse arm that was better used to holding a plough or a pike. As Martha handed the child to him the stink of the soiled shawl came also, foul and sharp.

"Must she come in that stinkin' cloth?" With his big fingers Robert began to peel away the shawl. The bulb of the poppet's head emerged and then the rest—the torso with its damaged arms, the ruined legs—as though the doll were birthing from the child. Then it fell to the gaol floor.

Robert took a step back. Gingerly he toed it. "What's this—that she's shat?"

The constable crouched to look. "Last evening when I left Hannah Holland was alive. Today, the girl witch is dead, and Mistress Crozier very sick. And now we find a charm. This . . . this is a poppet. I seen such things before. Foul charms made for bad purpose, with evil spelled into them." He looked at each of them in turn. "Whose is it?"

The moment enlarged, its seconds passing slow as hours. In Robert's arms the babe fretted. Pray God for help. Pray God for the babe, for Jennet's silence. Martha grasped her own hands to steady them. The constable saw. "Is it yours, Martha?"

In her chest her heart sped up, its beats teeming and uneven. She shook her head. *Not mine.* This much at least was true. The poppet was hers no longer. Jennet had claimed it.

"No? Not yours?" said the constable. She could hear the doubt in his voice. "I don't know as I can believe you. What can you tell me as'll put my mind at rest?"

Her lips parted, her voice strained. *'Tis nothing, 'tis only—*

"What does she say?"

"I can't tell," Robert said. "Maybe she's tryin' to distract us."
She caught his eye. A mute plea. "I know some of how she talks,
wavin' her hands like she do, but not all. Until yesterday I never
had reason to doubt her," he went on, with his bullock's slow-
ness. "But then, on Monday, at the hanging . . . Well. She was
flappin' her hands like she was right desperate to tell something
about Prissy Persore. And then again, when we come to Knoll
House. So strange, to find her master lying sick, real sick, in his
bed, and her outside with that dead bird. I don't know any more,
what she's about." He looked at the poppet. "And now *this.*"

Her hands were frantic, reshaping what he implied. *'Tis a
doll. A child's plaything.*

"What now?" asked the constable.

"Something about the brat," Robert said. "The brat's toy."

"A toy?" The constable's lips narrowed and his in-drawn
breath hissed through his teeth. A look of intense suspicion
flowed into his face. "'Tis a strange toy for any babe, with those
barbs in it. Tell me, Martha. How do you come by it?"

She opened her mouth—useless, futile. The constant effort
of moulding silence, the strain of being always misunderstood.
She put up her unreliable hands. *I found it.*

The constable looked at Robert. "She says she found it."

"You found it? Where?"

There. In the floor.

"Some other poor bitch must've dropped it," Jennet said
swiftly. "Ma Southern, maybe. It's the kind of thing she would
have. Like a magpie, she was. Always one for trinkets."

"That's true," Robert said. "I've seen her selling them."

"Aye," Jennet said. "She was always trying to sell 'em. Special
stones or sprigs of things she'd picked from the hedge—"

"But this one," Constable Napier cut in, "is not so harmless. This is no charm. 'Tis a witching doll, and already put to use by the look of it." He eyed it, and then Martha. "You say you found it, and perhaps that's true. But having found it, why did you hide it? Unless you were thinkin' to use it yourselves?"

A silence, in which the babe briefly quieted and then resumed her squalling. Constable Napier raised his voice over the infant's din. "Will none of you own it? Will none of you confess, so's to spare your sisters?"

With two fingers he took up the doll, pinching it between his thumb and forefinger, his expression curdling with distaste. By turns the poppet's two faces revealed themselves: blind, sighted; keening, mute. Martha could hear it clearly now, its descant cry, its embryonic plea, though the sound was faint, from very far away. Confess, confess: it was urging her—was it? She looked at Jennet and then at the wailing babe, searching their faces for the answer. As she did the poppet's keening changed; its cry was the babe's, or the babe's cry was altering, growing louder and more forceful.

The cry of Kit's girl, insisting on living.

"What a pack of firebrand's darlings," the constable proclaimed. "What a coven. All of you are for the rope, in spite of your bad little poppet." He gave them all a disgusted look. "Well then, this is what we'll do. We'll agree 'tis the babe's—for 'twas found on her, after all. That's the bare fact of it. That's what I'll tell Master Makepeace, when I bring him this witching doll."

TWENTY-SIX

Saturday night

He sat looking gauntly magisterial in the high-backed judging chair of the Great Hall. Light from the ring of burnt-down candles on the judging table cast a nimbus of wavering light around his head. Before him was a parchment and beside it was the poppet, half covered with a cloth. Martin steered her to the empty chair opposite, instructing without speaking what she was to do: sit, wait.

Ellen and then Jennet had been brought to this very chair and questioned to the point of collapse. Now it was her turn.

Master Makepeace ignored her. He was writing on the paper. She watched him work, the quick flex of skin and bone, staring at his hand until it became an entirety, the centre of Creation. At last he set down the pen, stretched his fingers. He sat back. His gaze lifted, found his supper—a part-eaten meat pasty on a pewter plate. He finished it absently, still engrossed by the paper. The smell of cooked meat was overwhelming, a taunt. She would go mad with hunger. How long since she had eaten a proper meal? Too many days.

"Mistress Hallybread. I have saved you some labour." The witch man smiled, his strangulated grin. "You need not trouble yourself to devise another pack of lies." He angled the paper towards her. "I know what you are. See here, where I have writ down your true nature."

Her heart laboured like a failing clock. What had Jennet told him? What had Jennet said? With huge effort she forced herself to look. The lines of his writing tracked across the flesh-coloured parchment like the stitches of a wound. A list: he had composed an inventory of her assumed misdeeds both mundane and surreal. Everywhere she had wrought Satan's evil: she had blighted crops, sent imps to curse her neighbours, honoured Satan with other witches.

"What more," he asked, "must you tell me? What more should I know?"

What more? What else? Her mind was reduced to scurries that fled even as she grasped at them.

"Tell it all, Martha," Martin said. His jaw trembled, as if it had been hit. "Whatever you've done, tell Master Makepeace. Clear your conscience. Then this business will be at an end, and you can make your peace with God, and find a home in His mercy."

"She has no home," said Master Makepeace. "Unless it is in the arms of the Devil. She has forfeited her earthly home. Because of this." He uncovered the poppet. "Tell me its name."

She looked at him, blank. *I don't know it.*

"She's sayin' she don't know its name, sir."

"I can see that, Master Strong. She must know what it is called."

She fanned out her hands. *Nay, sir. I don't.*

The witch man made a sound, a snort of derision. "I believe," he said slowly, "that you do." She was skewered in his stare; saw again his contempt for her, the consuming blaze of his zeal. With the blunt end of the quill he pushed the doll towards her. The doll was very scarred. Was it her that had so injured it? Who had been so vicious?

"These marks on it," Master Makepeace said, bringing a candle closer, "are where it has been cut and pricked. By its mistress. By its witch." He was talking slowly; a careful laying out of evidence like a man of law. "And here there are deeper marks, where it has been savaged. On the throat and here across its chest. And here at the top of the legs." His eyes shifted, from the poppet to her. "What nature of person would own something like this? Would *use* something like this? To cause harm to another?"

To everything its season: a time to keep, and a time to cast away; a time for silence and a time to speak. She looked down at her hands, each one a hundredweight, unliftable from her thighs.

"Mistress Hallybread. Pay attention if you would save yourself. It was found on the Crozier babe, but I think it cannot be hers. She is born of a witch but is too young, I believe, to be one herself. To be one *yet.*"

He waited, important, prideful. Still she looked away. What did he know of this speechlessness—of powerlessness, of barricaded lives? Her head dropped, her eyes lost their focus, and on the screen of her lids she saw a lacework of poppets, each one strangely illuminated, each one with its null lips moving, their soundless entreaties lost in the thinning air.

"I put this question to your sister witch, the Savory woman," the witch man continued. "She denied any knowledge of the doll. So now, Mistress Martha, I ask you. Whose is this poppet?"

Careful now. Go careful. She opened her eyes and gripped

her hands and held them, as if by stilling them she might prolong the amnesty of this moment, though its end point was foregone.

The witch man's eyes were widely open and fastened on her, like judas holes, enticing her to peer in. "Come now, mistress. One of you must own it. One of you has used it." In the black of his pupils tiny bonfires burned; white fires of power, his privilege, his pride. "Mistress Hallybread. Unless you answer I will take your silence as a confession. 'Qui tacet consentire videtur.' It is Latin. It means, 'Silence is consent.' It means, He who is silent is taken to agree. Do you understand? If you stay silent I will presume that the poppet is yours. So I'll ask once more. Whose is this poppet?"

Again his raking glance: demanding, dismissing. In its brilliance she was reduced—one more nonentity in a host, a multitude, a legion of women; old, young, virgins, crones, clever, simple, luckless, thwarted, sick, raped, maimed, vilified, crushed; oh, countless women, those who had been and those yet to come; those already dead and those yet to die at his hands. A vast, ticking anger came up in her, a fury to rival his. Let him presume her corrupted, witless, duped by Satan. Let him christen her "witch," as he had so many others. She would own this title, make it hers. With it, she would defy him.

She blinked. Saw again a vision of the luckless women— fleet, spectral, unmistakably present—all of them demanding to have counted, to *be* counted: to count. She took in a breath, let it go. With a large movement gestured to the Hall, the village beyond it; to the floorboards and through them to the women trapped below.

We who would deny you. We who would halt you. Who would indict you, in our turn.

"What is she saying?"

"I . . . I'm not sure," Martin said. She could hear the hesitation in his voice. "In truth, sir: she got no words except what she makes with her hands, and they're simple ones. So whether it's that she got no shapes for what you ask, or that I don't understand 'em, I don't know."

"But *I* must know. I must have the truth. For the record. For the magistrate." He looked at her. "Speak again. Answer again."

The doll . . . the poppet . . . is of us all. FOR us all.

"You toy with us, mistress," the witch man said, unmoved, unmoving. "My question was simple. It needs but a simple reply." He leaned towards her, his expression severe, his bloodless lips moving slowly and deliberately as if he were addressing a child. "Yes or no, madam: is this your poppet?"

The worm was awake and fully uncoiled now, its whole choking length unfurled into her throat.

It belongs to us all. All us women.

He looked expectantly at Martin.

"She's saying it belongs to them all."

"To who all?"

"All the women."

"All women?"

"Aye, sir. That's what she's saying."

The witch man rocked back in his chair. An expression of vast triumph overtook his face—storm clouds parting to admit some unearthly light—a brightening that showed his true nature. "A coven! Cleftwater has a coven! And you are one of their number, are you not? And this vile doll is likewise an instrument of your Devilish circle. I had suspected so much, and now God has confirmed it."

He snatched up the quill and began to write ferociously, his pen raining words onto the paper. Its noise was apocalyptic, scratching out all truth, scratching down the stars. She understood she had loosed something in him, some force not meant to be discharged.

"Tell me now, Mistress Hallybread. The names, if you will, of your sister witches."

Nay, nay! I meant—I mean—the poppet has no mistress. It governs itself. There is no coven—

But he was only looking through her. Her hands stopped, as if they, too, were stunned with dismay. What had she said? What had she done? Her head, her thoughts, swarmed with self-blame. Too late now. Futile now. Noise—gaol noise—seeped from below: a woman's retching cough, the babe's piercing wail. Frantically she gestured. *Not them. Spare them. Spare the others.*

"What does she say now?"

"Somethin' about the other women. The ones in the gaol."

"What about them?"

"She wants you to spare them."

The witch man's laugh was a bark, coming out of the side of his mouth. He put down the pen and turned the paper towards her. "See here, Mistress Hallybread, where I have set down your words. And here—" his finger moved; where the quill had leaked his skin was stained, the colour of dried blood—"here is where you must make your mark, to own that this is your testimony."

He saw her hesitation and misread it. "You reconsider, perhaps?" He waited. "Now is the hour, Mistress Hallybread. You are out of time and I am out of patience. You may tell the truth or stay mute as is your habit: the choice is yours. You say the poppet belongs to all your coven. You point to those in the gaol—Jennet Savory, Ellen Warne, your own mistress, Agnes Crozier. I believe you are all damnable witches. Unless you tell me otherwise, I will commend each of you to the rope. For the last time, Mistress Hallybread. Whose is the poppet? Write it. Write it here."

He dipped the quill and presented it. Ink brimmed blackly from its tip. But it was Martin took it, who prised open Martha's fist and forced the pen into her hand.

"It's time, Martha," he said. His voice cracked, threatening to break. "You've done some wrong things and in the doin' of them you've wronged yourself. That's the truth. But Master Makepeace here—he's showing you how you can redeem your-self. Sign what he's writ, I'm beggin' you. Confess all you done so you can clear your soul in the eyes of God. He will look on you with mercy, maybe even with forgiveness. That's what I wish for you."

The worm was balling, refusing to be swallowed down. She had to open her mouth to breathe around it. Poppet. Puppet: Martin's big hand closed over hers. He had forced the quill to the paper; now he moved her hand. A blemish appeared—a rough-drawn X—a crude substitute for her name. Above her head Martin said: "That's done. God save you, Martha Hallybread."

He took his hand away; took his loyalty away, and in the same moment she thought how she was finished, as good as dead. Nothing achieved. Truths, still unsaid. The worm like a noose, ready inside her neck.

Nay. Nay. Not like this. Not yet. Mistress Knill's lancet, Master Makepeace's pen: they lied, they were lies in themselves. She had used one to prick the poppet; she would use the other to make her mark, her very own—a last, late correction. The pen brimmed, its nib scratched. There was something proper, almost holy, in crossing out the names: Jennet Savory, Ellen Warne, Agnes Crozier—prized women, betrayed women— before she struck through her own.

The witch man hissed, craned his neck back, then opened his mouth. A storm came out of it, a veritable blizzard of damnation. She fought him as he tried to wrench the pen away. It twisted, zigged, bled, then scored a long blaze of shining ink, a dark comet's tail, across his catalogue of lies.

She let it drop. There was a sense of an inner cleaving, a ripping in her lungs. The worm vaulted. It was everywhere inside her, insisting on an outlet. She opened her mouth and let it gust. A cough ripped, and then another. Then another that bent her almost double with its force. She was shreds. Tatters. She fought to keep herself within herself, but still her lungs went about their desperate business, drowning from inside. She opened her eyes expecting to greet Mam and saw instead the poppet, sprayed now with red. As she reached for it the next cough threatened; her fingers closed around the living wax as the cough welled and then erupted. Over it she heard the witch man's yelp. Too late he'd stepped away. Across his cheek a viscid string hung, quivering as though it were alive. The worm! The very signature of the worm! Its red was brilliant, the colour of joy.

TWENTY-SEVEN

Monday

O ver here," Jennet said.

Behind her Herry locked the gate and waded away.

The gaol seemed crowded, full of pale forms. After a moment she could make out the woman-shaped clump spraddled against the gaol's far wall. Time, the lost quantity of it, surged at her. She went towards it, bunching her skirts in her fist. The floor was uneven and it was difficult to find purchase, to keep from slipping. The floodwater was like a living creature, fitting itself to her shins. There was something drifting in it, its fat tentacles beckoning in the current. She peered. Hannah's body sculled sideways, the bloated lips like those of a sea-monster, broaching the surface for air.

Below the clock-tower window the ground rose and there was a shelf of dry dirt less than two arm-spans across. Enough space for three to sit if they were jammed together; now they would be four. As she approached Jennet levered herself stiffly upright. Water drained from her hem.

"You've been gone so long," Jennet said. She was racked by shivering; her jaw clacked. "We didn't think we'd see you again. I was thinkin' maybe they'd finished you like they finished Prissy and the others, poor sods. But somehow you're s-still here." Her voice was hoarse. "Budge up, Ellen. Make room for Martha."

They huddled together. In Ellen's arms there was a bundle of filthy cloth that made a feeble noise like an unoiled hinge. The babe was fitfully dozing, swaddled in Agnes's damp shawl.

Jennet saw her astonishment. "Aye, so. Seems as they've condemned the kid. Seems as they're content for her to moulder on in here, like the rest of us," she said. "All of us being witches."

Martha held the child close, put a crooked finger in the girl's mouth and felt the strong suck. For a time she felt peaceful, heavy with gratitude. Then it faded. She could feel the warmth leaching from her body. The babe must have what was left of it. Agnes must have what was left. She edged closer to mistress.

"We'll have to take it in turns to sit," Jennet said. "Two of us always with Mistress Crozier. She's weak, she's got that cold."

Martha had lost all track of time. The rising floodwater was the only measure, creeping relentlessly up, threatening the dry ledge on which they stood. From time to time they changed places, edging around each other and with Agnes, incapable now of standing, in the middle.

"I need to piss," Jennet said. "Will you hold your mistress? Else she'll fall in."

Martha took Agnes in a kind of embrace. Mistress's neck rested against hers, corpse-cold. Jennet did her business and came back. She felt Agnes's wrist, shook her head. "She's slippin' away from us. We must try to keep her awake. Keep hold of her. That's all we can do." Her tone was contrite, apologetic.

She would thank you. If she knew.

"I never liked Agnes Crozier, that's a fact. But I can't see as she's a witch. I can't think she did any of what they're saying.

She's a very prideful lady, no doubtin' it, and that makes her a sinner like the rest of us. But that's all she is, surely?" They clustered again around mistress and the babe. Jennet spoke into the press of bodies. "Who is it, that's spoke against her?"

"Not me. I said naught," Ellen said, through rattling teeth.

"Nor me. I said nothin' to no one, not when they walked me, not even to the witch man," said Jennet. The words jerked from her mouth. Martha freed one arm and draped it around Jennet's thin shoulders. "We got no witches in Cleftwater. Leastways, we had none, until the witch man came. He's poisoned us all." She lowered her head. "I'm sorry I thought ill of you, Martha. I'm sorry for all I said. I never meant harm to you—not to anyone, not a single Cleftwater woman. I don't know what got into me, after my sister's babe died. She so wanted a child. We all did."

The reminder of the dead babe was like a pain returning, an ache starting up after a lull. Martha put Jennet's hand on the living one, Kit's living girl. *This one. THIS one.*

"Aye. Aye so. We got to do all we can for her, little mite. We got to stand to the end if we have to. Keep her warm." Martha pulled Jennet closer until their foreheads touched. Jennet's was clammy. Like this they stood with Agnes and the babe sheltered between them while the foetid water swilled at their feet. The window showed a portion of the outside world. A thin moon, showing intermittently in the storm-marbled sky. Dead feet hanging from the gallows, swinging like pendulums in the turbulence, as if they were kicking at heaven.

––––––––––

The clock marked off the passing hours and her strength ebbed with each tolling. She stood with her head dropped on Jennet's shoulder and Jennet's head resting on Ellen's. Cold invaded her body. Each time she woke there was more floodwater and less dry ledge. In intervals of wakefulness her body made known its many complaints. Her muscles going rigid with cold. Her stomach, curdling with hunger. Her swelling feet, which filled her clogs and then bulged outside them, the flesh forced tight against the leather. Finally she kicked them off. The tiny girl woke more and more often, hungry and wanting to feed. They all had teats among them and yet there was nothing to suck. They took it in turns to wade to the gate and fill their mouths with moisture. The wind had lessened but the rain fell unabated and the tide rose still, in and outside the gaol. They could hear its wash and swill in the street. Their ears strained to the noise of the flood and the village's alarum, the bleats of frightened animals and people calling to each other as they went about saving their possessions, their lives. The wind freshened again and the rain fell heavier, cold and with a maritime smell while the outside world dissolved. Agnes began to retch. It was more and more effortful to prop her up. Sometimes she talked, mumbled scraps of nonsense.

———————

A time later, Constable Napier: his purposeful tread through the torrent cascading down the steps. He unlocked the gate.

"Give me the child," he said, beckoning to Ellen.

She looked at him, mistrustful. "Where are you taking her?"

"She's to be nursed," the constable said. "That's all I know."

"By who?"

"Liz Godbold." A grimace overtook the constable's face. "Ach, Ellen, hold your tongue. It's taken me all this time to find someone. No one wants to nurse a witch's brat—no one but Liz Godbold, and her only for pay."

"What of Mistress Crozier?" Jennet demanded. "She's practically dead."

"I got no instruction for her," Constable Napier said. "The judge and Master Makepeace left at first light, wantin' to get out before the road flooded. They'll be halfway to Seachurch now."

"What of the rest of us? Are you going to just *leave* us here?" Jennet said furiously, kicking the water.

"It's that or the gallows," the constable said. "Would you have me clear a rope?"

The babe started to cry. Jennet pulled the child to her and then hooked Martha and Ellen into their embrace. For precious moments they all three stood, hugging one another close, while the babe's crying covered the sound of their own.

Constable Napier clapped his hands. "Come now. Time's up. The child must go to her nurse."

He took the little girl, draped the filthy shawl over Agnes, then turned and went swiftly out of the gaol. The babe's crying changed pitch as it faded. There were no last looks; no fatal looking back. It was she, Martha, who was turning to salt; she could feel it, running down her cheeks. Kit's girl, saved. Kit's girl, gone forever. More than she could bear. Her gullet was tight and strangely full and she thought how the worm had not left her, not fully; its mark, its imprint was still there, scarring her throat.

———

They were roused by a cascade of water through the high window. A small boat was passing, towed by a pony led by a drenched form. Jennet shouted to it. The figure halted, looked around. Jennet called again. Somehow it heard them. Its approach sent another gout of water through the window that flooded the last of their dry ground. The angular face of Nan Dolan's stable lad came into view.

"What do you want?"

"Food," Jennet shouted. "D'you have any? Anything— a crust, a bit of cheese—anything at all."

"Who is this?"

"It's Jennet. Jennet Savory. With Mistress Crozier, who's starvin'—"

"I got nothing spare," he said. "I only got what's in my pockets, and I need that for myself."

"Come on, Will," Jennet said, beginning to be strident. "You can spare something. You come straight from Nan's, you must have more than just crusts."

"That's no business of yours, what I do or don't got," he said. His sparse beard had been washed into wisps by the rain. "And anyways, I got no reason to help witches." He began to turn away.

"Wait!" Ellen cried. She had got feebly to her feet; now she swayed back and forth. "Please, Will. There's four of us trapped in here. We've had no food, not even scraps, for days. I'm askin' you as a neighbour—a Christian neighbour—to remember all those times I've helped you."

He brought his face right up to the grille. "Who is that with you?"

"Agnes Crozier. She's all but dead."

He let out an oath and crossed himself. His head disappeared from the window. The water sloshed as he went away.

Minutes later he reappeared with a heel of bread that he forced between the bars. "That's all I can spare."

"God bless you, William Frobisher," Ellen breathed.

"How bad is the flood?" Jennet asked.

"Bad. It's right through the village, up to Wish Hill and all the way across to the Scours."

"What's happened to the folk along Tide Lane? What of my sister?"

"Those houses are well flooded, but folk had time to get out," Will said. "Some are sheltering in All Saints and some gone across to St. Hilda's. Your sister's with them—gone to the church."

"She still lives?"

"She's still sick, but aye, she lives."

"And what about us?" Jennet asked. "Who'll get us out? Or are we to rot in here?"

"So far as I know you're for rotting, though whether that's in the gaol or on the gallows I couldn't say." Behind Will the pony whickered. The gibbet rose severe and monumental in the early light and on it the bodies bellied; restless, bloated ghosts. "Any ways, you'll be waitin' a while. Your judge has gone, your man Makepeace as well. The road's under water. No one can get in or out of Cleftwater—no judge and no hangman, that's a fact." His face was emotionless, his voice factual. "You got a few more days, I reckon."

"What day is it today? Is it the Sabbath?"

"Today's Monday, but there's plenty of prayin' still goin' on, I can tell you. You lot'd do well to pray the water don't get you first."

TWENTY-EIGHT

Undifferentiated time, hours blending one into the next. Martha gave up trying to count. A torpor like a weight that she could barely push away. She stopped being able to feel her legs. Then her arms, too, were numb. The shelf of dry ground she shared with the others shrank to inches. Water threatened their feet. She leaned her forehead against the gaol wall and went in and out of a frigid swoon; dozing, rousing, dozing, losing all residues of herself, of the others, apprehension clinging like her soaked shift.

She woke to the black streaming of the flood. The shelf of ground disappeared. Her feet disappeared. A distance away, beyond the window's ellipse of light, Ellen lay face down in the water, her splayed fingers floating easily on its surface. Agnes, too, was collapsed, racked with cold, a faint, animal moaning coming from her. Martha hauled her up and with Jennet took it in turns to stand with Agnes in a kind of lover's embrace. Martha felt for a pulse. Not dead: not quite.

Jennet patted Agnes's cheek. "Agnes. Mistress Crozier. Waken up. You must waken for us."

She's too cold.

"I know that. What are we to do?"

Martha looked around the gaol, at the uprights of grilles and stanchions showing like the trunks of naked trees in the stale light. Then, a crack of thought; some memory of Tom Archer or maybe Gil Hesketh crutching a sheep, the ewe propped in a makeshift cradle.

A last chance for Agnes. A last chance to redeem herself. Her numb fingers worked at her jacket hooks, unfastening them. She took it off and passed it to Jennet.

Put this on.

"What? But then you'll be cold."

No matter.

Somehow she forced her fingers to work, to undo her bodice and fasten it to the shawl, twisting both garments to make a crude rope. She went to Agnes. *Help me with her.* They half-dragged mistress to a post in the middle of the gaol. The rope of clothing they passed under Agnes's arms and tied to the stanchion: this, her final act of service for mistress, now hanging martyr-like in her improvised harness. In Martha's mind a memory played, an anguished rehearsal of their last quarrel and mistress's unkind words. Old Martha. Mute Martha. Country nurse Martha, with her curing weeds. Agnes slumped heavily against her, her head dropped as though for comfort against the lump in Martha's bodice.

She took it out. Jennet gaped. "Sweet Christ. How do you still have that poppet?"

I took it.

"From the witch man?"

Aye. He left it behind. So I took it back.

Jennet stared, then shook her head. "Ach, Martha. All these years and still there's no knowin' you. Not truly."

They held Agnes. Despite the harness she was still collapsing, her small weight threatening to slide towards the flood. "I can't hold her much longer," Jennet said. "I got no strength left."

Time now, to take out these barbs.

"Aye. You should do that, Martha. You put 'em in; it's only right you should take 'em out. I can understand why you woke it. I'd have done the same, most like. Waken your mam's witching dolly, even just for comfort. But prickin' it—that's where you gone wrong. Made yourself no better than the pricker-mistress, by doin' that." The poppet seemed to regard them both, its wounded look upon them. "There now, lovely. You been pricked and marked like we are. But no matter," Jennet sang, husky and tuneless, "you'll soon be free of your barbs. Then you might just turn. Maybe you'll do some good."

The night sifted, thick in the gaol. In its grey Martha could see almost nothing. She brought the poppet right up to her face. Blinked, and in an instant the gaol was void; was the tavern, its rough beams attic beams, its frowsy tavern air stewing with need and lust. Uncles stupid with drink humped over Mam in the stale bed; Mam at her rosary; Mam crooning over a poppet in a cradle; over a stub of tallow. The poppet, the child: both of them shaped by Mam, by deeds as well as sins born out of want and desperation.

'Tis all we got, this little power.

She sees her mother's witching chest and its adulterous contents, beads, nails, talismans of leather, plants, of dead creatures—vole, bird, toad. Sees shadow-women making them, gifting them, handing them on; hears their soft chanting; feels their scant presence, air moving by her face as they come rustling into the present.

Sees the poppet put up its nubs of hands, that beckon to her, that sign to her, blunt shapes.

Do not think we are nothing. Do not forget. Do not forsake our little powers: our skill in healing, our ministry with herbs.

It shows her great sheaves of cuttings, yarrow and valerian and goldenrod, spires of mullein waxed into candles. It shows buzzards picking at churned ground; waste land, where graves have been dug.

In her upraised hand the poppet, too, is glowing: a firebrand, wielded against oncoming fate. A torch to light her way.

————

It took an age, an aeon, to ease out the barbs, the pin from the poppet's throat, the splinter from its groin. In a nervous stasis she waited. Hopes flared like kindled embers: the jeopardy of their present would roll swiftly forwards, into some shining reprieve.

Agnes would rise, hale with new vigour, milk brimming in her breasts. The babe would feed and be warm.

A golden key would appear in the gate.

Her own throat would heal; she would call for help, speak up for Agnes; tell her truth.

Moments passed. From the harness came soft sounds. Martha raised mistress's sagging head. In the smudged light Agnes's face had a blurred dignity, some light-of-God coming from her eyes. That faded like a stoppered candle, a taper going gently out. The rain fell and fell, sieving through the window, mortality in every drop.

TWENTY-NINE

Tuesday

Dawn, and movement at the gate. Men arriving with keys.
"What?" Jennet said, thick-tongued.

They're here.

Herry Gowler with his lopsided sneer, swearing softly as he stepped into the filthy water. A few steps behind him, Ned Bullard, peering in.

"Those of you still livin', come out." Herry opened the gate. Water muddied in his wake. "Just you two?"

"Just we two," Jennet confirmed. "Are you bringin' us our last meal?"

"Is that what your Devil-master promised you?" He guffawed. "Far from it, my ladies. We're bringing you to the gallows."

"But why?" Jennet cried. "Master Makepeace has gone, the judge has gone."

"Hold your trap. The constable's said to bring you upstairs, so that's what I'll do. Now get up."

"Give us one more moment," Jennet said.

"What for?" Herry asked. "You've had days in here all cozied up."

"Aye. But now we've to say goodbye. Ah, Herry. Give us that."

He sighed. "Go on, then." He turned his back. Dread clung like their wet clothing as they clasped each other close.

"You birthed me, brung me into life. We'll see each other out of it. Seems about right," Jennet said. Against Jennet's waxy complexion the mulberry birthmark stood out like a blow. She pulled Martha close and kissed her, on the cheeks, on her fore-head, crushing the poppet's small bulk between them. "God love you, Martha."

And you, my dear. I'm sorry, I am so very sorry.

She thought to ask for Father Leggatt and then remembered: he was gone to the place where she would soon be.

———

Her bones were lead and she walked with an old woman's cap-sizing step. There was no footing to be had; she and Jennet had lost their claim to the earth. Constable Napier stood at the top of the gaol steps and shook his head as they passed. Outside in the frail light all looked serene. The oneness of the sea and the flood, unbroken to the horizon. The village sheeted in water, all its imperfections covered over. Ahead the gallows were waiting, empty, expectant. No bodies now, only fresh nooses. One of them was hers. At the tavern window a pair of women stood, Nan Dolan and Liz Godbold with Kit's daughter cuddled on her shoulder. Her whole being flowered. Godspeed Kit. God bless his little girl. Part of her was desperate to keep going, to live on and see Kit's girl grow.

For the last time she turned and looked along the street or where the street had been. Where her life had been.

She cast around for the hangman but there was only Judge Bacon, who came towards them with a parchment that he carried upraised. The sun was behind him and the quick-moving clouds cast stripes of light and shade across his face. He opened his mouth and began very earnestly to speak; a fast flow of ungraspable words. She stood and watched his lips moving, not able to take in what he said. Beside her Jennet folded, fell to her knees, and began to thresh. Martha's heart went on with its frantic pounding; between each beat it was stopped. She could feel herself dispersing, fleeing from the hour. Adieu, adieu to her small life with its myriad small deeds, to this goodly world and her short time in it. Adieu to sickness, muteness, suffering, joy, Kit's company and love, his daughter's cry, hopeful dawns among the fragrant herbs, calm evenings on the lulling shore, long nights studying the stars, dull hours of choring, brief times of ease, the scent of Prissy's new-baked bread, Kit's dog with his perfumed fur, Simon's reassuring, perennial cheer, the loyal hogs, memories of Mam, the troubling comfort of the poppet.

All of it going, almost gone. *O Lord, be still our defence, unto the end and in the end.* She wondered how long death would take, which jig her legs would dance, which part of her would die first, her head, her hands, her pulse. She was suddenly aghast, terrified that not Mam but Prissy or the Archer's dead boy would be waiting to bear her away to Limbo. The judge talked on, grave and earnest, though what he said was dissolving. All her thought was for what lay ahead: the choking rope, then death's embrace; she would ease herself into them both. In the lively breeze the noose would twist, one way and then another. Revealing to the world Martha Hallybread's two faces: the doomed one, the dead one; their vacant eyes, their silenced lips. Oh, oh. How false it was, how truthful, this two-faced work of dying.

PART FOUR

BLOOD

Wakes to a dream of herself coming through the village, from the gibbet through the market square and along the sweep of beach. Tide Lane is white under summer sun: a direction, a route. She goes along, propelled by some unfamiliar compulsion. As she walks she seems to lighten and lift; there is a new sensation of spaciousness, a shucking-off of burdens, of guilt.

Beside her the sea is peaceful, a guileless blue. Then from it—over, out of it, walking quickly across its placid expanse— is Mam, who calls to Martha with a bell-like cry, steps to her with outstretched arms. Martha reaches, finds only fevered air. Encounters instead the poppet, standing scarred but woman-sized in the lane, that draws Martha into its smooth embrace.

A stalledness. A stoppedness. The present, eddying into the past. A sense of her body softening, her self thinning. In this unmaking she and the poppet become welded, fused. She is the doll and it is her: her shame in its wounds, its desire in her pulse, the steady beat of its purpose.

Use me scarce, but use me. For justice. For good.

In panic, in shame, Martha tries to pull away, to divorce

from the doll or give it back, to the past or to Mam, but Mam is now earth, vapour, sky. Phantasm. Soul.

———

In the lane, herself and the doll. That lets go of Martha as it starts to billow, its wax plumping, its limbs sprouting, until there are a thousand poppets, each one a woman, distinct, countless. The women crowd about, regarding Martha with hopeful stares as they gesture, urging her to turn around. So purposeful they are, even with their damaged gaits, as they shepherd her along the white road. Tide Lane is a crossing, a causeway back to the obverse world, its scuffed materialities, its hateful facts. Martha lags, tries to delay, but the women urge her on. As they go they one after another speak; she hears them in her pith, she hears them with her soul, their voices chiming like tones in a sound box.

We are bitch. We are chit. We are slut. We are wench, harlot, bawd, madam, jezebel, whore, daemon, sorceress, doxy, cunt, slattern, jade, hag, Madonna, quean, tart, sow, vixen, bee, shrew, bird, mutton, maiden, harpy, succuba, dame, mistress, hellion, crone. We are repugnant to Nature, contumely to God; We are monstrous, legion; We are too many, We are never enough.

The women teem in every direction, they crowd through the village, they surge in the sea, Martha sees how they flock to the horizon. Together they come to Kit's house. At the gate they halt. All looks as before. Here is her physick garden with its emerald lure, the careless hogs dozing in their pen, Kit's dog basking golden and sleek on the flagstones by the back door.

Behind and around the women wait, clear-eyed and expectant. It is not for them to give counsel; it must be her choice, to open the gate and go through.

The poppet, a doll again, smarts in Martha's hand.

Already she can feel the signs of her own remaking, her fabric densening, her name—names—returning: Martha the Sinner, the Spinster.

Healer. Witch.

Aye, aye: she is all of these, knows all their treacheries as well as their gifts. And what choice has she? What choice remains but to try once more to use them for good?

THIRTY

One day later

The sky was mackerel, a mottled rose. Tom Archer's cow was on the higher land at the top of Kit's field. Its udders bagged with milk. Martha put the tether over the animal's head and began to lead her down. Damp air reeked of the flood. The field's seaward end was still submerged and strange shapes floated in the dead water: a drowned shrew, a child's cap and mitten, a piece of ripped sail, rafts of stinking muck. But the cow came steadily enough, pacing clear of the slew. On the beach many villagers were working, forking up great bales of rotting kelp. A weak risen sun cast its light over Tide Lane, and Martha led the cow along and into it: obeying this primal instinct, to come home.

―――――

Bread sopped in warmed milk: Simon was holding out a dish. Martha knew she must resist its lure. To eat, to sup food would be to choose to go on and slow her passage to the next.

Kit's room and its contents grew into focus. An apple core, browning on the window seat. The room's oak panels glowing, honey-coloured in the late-morning sun. Simon and Jennet, her two loyal friends, were watching her, she knew even with her gaze turned down. Simon's face loomed, a portrait of bafflement. His moving jaw, his wagging lips: with his words he was trying to reach her. He took her hand and shook it, trying to dislodge the poppet, to coax some signal from her.

"Is it this . . . idol that's made you sick?"

Nay. Nay. The two poppets—the doll and the babe—they were the only true things. Mam had gifted one, Agnes the other; they were all that held her to this earth. Simon prated on, full of proposals, for her, for them all; how they should continue. Worry made him talkative, determined to see God's hand in all things. She half-listened, not indifferent but not willing to be gulled again by words.

At last Simon set down the food. He spoke over his shoulder. "Why don't she answer? Is she ailing?"

"Maybe," Jennet said. "Aye, maybe. A sickness in her soul."

"Then what should we do? Should we bring the doctor?"

"Ach. He'd only want to bleed her. Let her be. All her life she's laboured. Now let her sit. There's worse things for soul sickness than sittin' in the sun." Jennet took off her shawl and draped it over Martha. "You could ask Kit to come and talk to her. She loves him best—except for the babe. Maybe he'll cheer her, bring her back to herself."

"He's only just strong enough to sit up."

"Well, if he cares for Martha, he'll have to, won't he? Just this once, bestir himself. Make an effort for her sake. How many times has she stirred herself for him? Numberless times, for him and Agnes and all the others. So I'd say it's his turn. Let him comfort her now."

They waited. In her chest her heart beat on, her lungs kept up their hateful pumping. Through the open window came the toll of the sandbar bell, a summons of some kind, though she had neither strength nor will enough to respond to it. After a time her friends went away. She drifted again, straying to some timeless place. Found something of the women there: a mark like a fingerprint in wax; an echo like a struck bell.

THIRTY-ONE

Martinmas, mid November

Two months passed since she'd dodged the gallows, re-prieved by Judge Bacon at the last. Sixty days as a freed woman though in herself she was not free. Too much had been witnessed, too much gone. Her life had lost its former shape, its old definition. Nights were an ordeal, a restless moving in and out of wary sleep, always listening for Kit. Days were a blur, the hours within them passing in smudged succession. She rebuilt the kitchen fire, brewed medicine, made bread, fed the hogs, changed the sheets, drew water and boiled it, bathed the dog's gummy eye, helped Simon scrape a path through the flood detritus that had filled the yard, washed Agnes's petticoats and draped them to air in the kitchen. When they were dry she folded them carefully away in the upstairs linen cabinet with sprigs of lavender between their folds. Every action, every breath, was an opportunity for self-reproach. The babe was gone, sent to the Godbolds for wet-nursing. Kit was not gone, alive—praise be to God—though a shade of himself, thin as a child and adrift in the great marriage bed. She must steel herself to go up and tend him, and often it was Simon who tramped the stairs with the teas and tinctures she brewed for Kit's damaged lungs. After a time it got easier to be near him again, the grain and musk of him: two more reasons to keep going.

———————

On the dawn shore she found herself scanning the horizon. Looking for the women. Hoping for them, maybe. Saw instead the waves' muscular shift, the foetid water receding, each day exposing more and more the imprint of the flood. Wreckage. Decay. But also: new growth, vivid in the brackish water—green birthing out of black.

THIRTY-TWO

In her physick garden she stood taking stock. A profusion of dulling colours. Mildewed stems crowned with seed heads, each one seeded with reproach. Behind their hurdle the wolfsbane and foxglove reared in untouchable spires. Somehow she must reckon with them. She took out her knife and began to cut, a harvest that turned into a cull. Raspberry leaf, motherwort: birthing herbs planted for Agnes, not needed now. Maybe even forbidden. The plants clung to the ground, resistant, scratching as she pulled them out. That was their protest.

She threw them into heaps in the yard and turned to go back to the house. Simon was there, Jennet beside him with the babe nested in her arm.

"Come sit with us, Martha. Rest awhile." Simon went to the garden bench and patted it. When she didn't move he came and fetched her. They sat as three, close together on the bench. It was not so pleasant as it had once been, to sit and idle. In such pauses the thoughts could restart, her conscience resume its chiding. The babe squawked and for one fractured breath it was the Archer babe protesting, then Jennet crooked a finger and put it in the tiny girl's mouth. The child sucked, ferocious, asserting her claim on life.

"She's hungry," Simon said.

"She's growin'," Jennet said bluntly. "As a babe should." Martha watched the play of expression on Jennet's face—tender, soft, rueful. They looked well-matched, the starveling child, the unlikely Madonna. "Have you thought more? Who's to take care of her?"

Simon said, "*We* will, Jennet. It don't need thinking about. She's lost her mam but she still has a father, and she's got *us*—Martha and me."

"It's not quite so simple, though, is it, Simon? Her father's still weak—in more than one way." A muscle in Jennet's jaw worked. "I don't know as Kit's done the best by Martha. Not always." She threw Martha a rueful look. "But that's between Kit and his Maker. What I know is you're a man now, Simon. Soon you'll be wanting to find yourself a wife, make a home of your own. Is that not so? Ach, save your blushes. We all know it. A good-looking man like you. It's only time before you're wed." The tiny girl was quiet, her eyes fixed on Jennet's face, her pale eyebrows which shuttled up and down as she talked. "And that'll leave Martha and Kit, both of them not fit nor young, trying to care for this babe. That's how it looks to me."

"That's how it looks," Simon agreed, "but 'tis not how it *is*. The Lord has put out His hand and sheltered this child and brought her safe home to us. He will succour her. He will not take away his hand. Martha and me, we'll tend this babe like she's our own kin." Gently he pulled at Jennet's arms, lowering them so that they could all see. The girl had the likeness of both parents, her father's forehead, her mother's hair, a feathery mass of it, dark red. "We served her mam. We'll tend her daughter. She's our master's girl and we're loyal to him. We'll not shirk our duty."

"That's all to the good," Jennet said. "You keep your lofty thoughts." A brittle laugh. "Your babe needs milk as much as she needs prayer, Simon. Mother's milk, and plenty of it, if she's to thrive." She gave Martha a searching look. Then: "My sister still has it," she said quickly, running on. "So much milk she don't know what to do with it all. Oh, I know there's herbs to stop it, dry it all up. But I . . . I had another thought." Her voice had got low, urgent, the words meant only for Martha. "I don't need to remind you of what's gone past, Martha. If you catch my drift."

Overhead, the gulls' racket. It was an effort, like lifting a weight, to persuade her mind to attend to what Jennet had said.

"What are you meaning, Jennet?" Simon asked.

"Martha knows what I'm meaning. I'm speakin' to *her*," Jennet said, a little strident. She drew the babe to her chest, holding her very close. A rush of some feeling—affection? devotion?—had brought colour to her face. "Liz Godbold says our little girl here feeds strong. Like she wants to live." She breathed nervously, the dull blush of her birthmark moving as she spoke, as though it were alive. "I'm askin' for you to let Marion nurse the babe. Just for a time—until she's weaned." Jennet's cat eyes were unblinking. "I'm hopin' you'll find it in your heart, Martha, to do this for Marion. So she can find out . . . so she can know what it is, to mother."

A longing to be away came over Martha. She got up, showed Jennet the empty cradle of her own arms. *The child's not mine to give away.* Unseeing she went across the yard, then lost momentum and stood by the back gate, battling the clamour in her head. How was it, that she was still here? The noose should have taken her, pinched off her breath. An eye for an eye; her life's account settled, its reparations made.

She let out a breath and discovered she'd been holding it, this one breath, for an age. A thin crescent moon was showing over Psalm Cliff, starkly pale, like a nail pared from some woman's hand. Woman. Women: as if the thought had summoned them they came, they were everywhere here, behind and in front and around her, enfolding her; she sensed their cool heat on her skin, the collective sigh of their breathing. Somewhere among them Mam waited, the taken women also. It was trance-like and instinctual—like feeling for a birthing babe—this searching of her conscience for some good in herself, some redeeming aspect. An array of memories played before her eyes; recollections of service, of Godly acts, each one arriving in a small flare of self-kindness before it faded.

From the bench behind her came some notes, the first of a song, from Simon's jaw harp. "Hark, hark, the lark," he sang in his boyish tenor, so surprisingly pure. What a puzzle fate was; what a puzzle was her life; was Simon's music, its bright melody weaving through the caul of her anguish. Hark, hark. She had survived the witch hunt, the loss of sisters, the gallows. She had not won honour, but she had not died. Kit lived; his daughter lived. Hark, hark, Simon sang again. The tune rose and her spirits rose with it. Perhaps, aye, perhaps: there were reasons to be hopeful.

THIRTY-THREE

In Kit's day room she sat, patching the sleeve of his shirt. From outside, faint but clear, came the sounds of the Martinmas hiring fair, snatches of pipe music, the dry rill of a drum. The fire was low in the grate but on the wall above it the ornate silver mirror—brought at vast expense from the Low Country, wherever that was—held flares of afternoon sun. The door swung open and the dog came in, padding noiselessly over the rug to put his muzzle on her thigh. Kit followed, a ghost in a nightgown, carrying a bundle of things: Agnes's berry-coloured shawl, her household keys. A pair of her slippers.

"These are for you." He swayed, doubled over, coughed for too long.

Sit. You must sit. She got up and brought him to the big chair. Weeks since he'd been out of bed. His legs were like spindles growing out of the cambric. She stoked the fire, feeling the climb of that old instinct to mother him. Bone broth; there was a portion left, he should have it. *Let me bring you—*

He caught hold of her. "Please, Martha. Sit with me. That's all I want just now. These are my gifts to you, my most loyal . . . my dear friend. I want you to have them. All my gratitude comes with them." His hand strayed to his lovelock and fingered it. "For bringing home my daughter. For giving your all for my poor Agnes."

Agnes. The same Agnes who, two short months ago, had sat in this very chair, fiercely alive. Guilt welled. Had she truly given her all? She could no longer tell. Let God be the judge. Kit was urging her to take the gifts, the dainty shoes, the fine shawl. Too fine to work in. Too fine for her, Martha Hallybread, who was unworthy.

But you should keep these. For your daughter.

He shook his head. His face bore new lines that had not been there in the summer. "It will be years before she has need of them. I have kept other things aside for her."

His cough came again, raw and wet. From the cellar of her mind the thought crept that his cough was her cough—irreversible, permanent—an accidental dowry.

She went to the cool-safe and fetched out the broth, which she put on a trencher with a piece of bread. Kit supped it slowly, pausing every few mouthfuls to breathe. When the bowl was half empty he thanked her and she put it aside. She went upstairs and brought down mistress's summer quilt and tucked it around him. She drew up the footstool but Kit asked her to sit in a proper chair beside him.

The room's air was close, freighted with things too difficult to say.

"I'm minded to name her Agnes, after her mother," Kit said, after a silence. She turned to look at him. His gaze was blue and piercing. "To remind me. All of us. And I will—we will—cherish her, just as her mother was cherished."

She nodded. *Yes. Yes.* A tear formed and welled. Kit reached and thumbed it away and then took her hand. His clasp was warm and firm. Like this they sat for a long time. Forging in silence some new compact, an agreement to keep going for as long as they could.

Kit's head began to sag; he was falling into sleep, the dog Matthew too, their breathing one with the waves' tempo. The house was quiet. The room's glow, the scent of Kit's tobacco, Matthew tranquil at his feet—all seemed drawn from before; a gentler, more hopeful time. She allowed her mind to drift, her thoughts to skim. But she couldn't settle; could feel the motion of her conscience, a certain pressure at the back of the mind from where bleak feelings leaked.

Dangerous, to give way to them. She got up and moved quietly about the room, fingering things, Kit's tinderbox and compass and the pearl of the lovelock he'd worn when Mistress Agnes was alive; picking them up and putting them down, as if by touching them she might somehow retrieve something of them both—master and mistress—or the essence of her life with them.

A movement in the mirror caught her eye. Its glass was flashing. She forced herself to look. Here was her reflection and, behind it, not fully visible, the poppet—or a poppet version of herself—shaking its head, displaying its two faces: the blind side, the sighted side; an aspect that healed, an aspect that destroyed. A deep shame rinsed through her. She longed to look away but the looking-glass stayed her, and even as she watched, the poppet drifted towards her, breaking over—through— her in a kind of paroxysm of connection.

Surely a trick of the light. Yet something persisted, some partial truth, rising to the rim of her awareness. She blinked. The mirror blinked back. She went to the window and opened it. New air flowed in and with it a medley of noises, shovelling, hammering, birdsong, the fair's cheerful racket. She made herself listen. Cleftwater went on, repairing itself. She must do the same. As if in confirmation a gull cried and it was the sound of baby Agnes crying, and she thought how the slender stock of time remaining to her was not so much, but a gift nonetheless.

Behind her Kit stirred. She turned to him. *We will need*, she began, and in the same moment Kit said, "A cook, and someone to help Simon. Both of you go to the fair. Speak to Tom Archer. Marion as well. Ask if she's content to keep nursing our girl. And find us another Pr—" He'd almost said "Prissy"; he checked himself. She brought him the small chest where he kept money. He unlocked it and counted out a quantity of coins. "These, for Marion Archer, with my thanks." He counted again, chinking more coins into her purse. "Find us the people we need. Only the best, Martha. Only those as fine as Simon and yourself."

———

At the back door she put on the new shawl. Mistress's scent was still in the wool. Simon followed as Martha led the way, walking gingerly along storm-pocked Tide Lane. A track had been trod into its layer of silt. Coming up to the Market Cross they fell in behind a party of herring women, distinct in their striped skirts and gleaming with fish-scales. It was mid-afternoon and the fair was in full cry. The street was packed with stalls and trestle tables. Buyers and penny-hawkers moved slowly among them, looking and bartering. Simon stopped at a baker's table to buy a currant biscuit, ate it, grinned, and handed one to Martha. The smell of roasting mutton, the crush of bodies, the waves of noise;

Martha felt bilious, in spite of herself, recalling the executions. In the village square the gibbet was gone and a large dray had taken its place. All around it were ranged those folk available for hire: men, women, lads, and lasses. Scanning the sea of faces, she recognised many of them—Scour folk whose livelihoods had been destroyed by the flood, looking now for new work. Each displayed some tool indicating their skill or trade. The wagoner stood before his dray, a piece of cord twisted elaborately in his cap, working on a part-constructed wheel. Next to him stood two gorse-cutters, polishing their sickles and scythes. A few paces away a group of shepherds stood, leaning on their crooks, one with a tuft of wool tucked through his buttonhole. Tom Archer was among them, deep in conversation with a well-off Holleswyck farmer. Martha pointed him out to Simon. Even as they watched they saw Tom and Judah Godbold strike some kind of deal, shake hands, accept the farmer's proffered coin. Then they looked across in the direction of the tavern.

"Judah will be looking to spend that," Simon said. "And no doubt Tom will cheer him on."

Go you and speak to him.

"Which one?"

She made a T with her hands. *Tom. Tell him Kit has work for him. Plenty of it.*

"We're too late, Martha. He's spoken for."

She showed him Kit's purse. *Master will pay. Good money.* She fished out two coins and gave them to Simon. *Bring Tom. Bring a jug. We'll drink to his staying.*

She watched Simon follow Tom to the alehouse and then turned and made her way through the square. The women hires were clustered on the seaward side, housemaids with their mops and brooms, dairymaids with stools and buckets. She walked slowly among them. Marion Archer was sitting on her milking stool cradling the Crozier babe in one arm and a rolling pin in the other. When she saw Martha she got up. There was very little of her; her shadow was a thin line. Martha went to her, took her by the shoulder.

You bleed.

"What?"

You're bleeding. There was blood on Marion's skirts. *You bleed . . . here and here.*

Marion groaned and bunched the cloth in her fist. "I can't leave. I can't go until Tom and me find work." She looked distractedly about her, scanning the scene. "I don't know where he's gone. I'm afeared that the soldiers'll take him. They're after men. They've been going through the village looking for any hapless lad, 'cause there's coin for every man they get." She glanced down at the babe. "I'm that thirsty. This girl of yours feeds enough for two, and then some."

Tom'll be all right, Martha shaped, inscribing a large S in the air. *He's with Simon. In the alehouse.* She took off Agnes's shawl and tied it apron-like around Marion's skirts. The stains were loudly red, like shouts. Where to find a more private space, when the streets were so jammed? They were two women; there were so many men.

Come with me. It was her turn now, to lead. She clasped Marion around the waist and they made their way across the square. Marion walked in small, cramped steps, leaning against Martha like a cripple. On the beach they sat with their backs propped against Judah Godbold's coble. Warmth came from its timbers. They sat in a silence that was almost companionable.

Marion unfastened her bodice and put the child to her breast: this babe who was an enthrallment, the crux of all goodness. As she fell asleep the child's bud mouth fluttered, as if she were about to speak.

But it was Marion who spoke. "We were that joyful," she said. "For our babe." She gazed, unseeing, eastwards towards the horizon. The sea was restless, a smudged infinity, and the breeze carried a fine tilth of salt. "After all we been through, Tom and me. All our losses. And then I got with child, and that was a prayer answered. A gift from God bringing some light back into our lives. And then I go and lose him . . . our boy."

Not you, Martha told her. *Not lost by you.* Her throat throbbed and then constricted. The worm lived on, dwelt in her still. *Taken by the Lord. Called to Him.*

"I'm afeared for him. For his soul," Marion said. "He died that quick. Tom had him buried so quick." She had begun to pluck at herself, pulling at her eyelashes, her lips, loose tendrils of hair. "I didn't even see him. Jennet and Liz, they wouldn't let me look. I know he was born . . . wrong. I do know that," she said again, as if giving herself an instruction. "Tom said our boy never would have lived. Not more'n two days at the most. But I never did see him living. That's the worst of it. To have birthed him and not truly *see* him. My own son! Losin' him, that's bad enough. Losin' him without mothering him, though. That's . . ." Her voice tremored, threatening to break. "I can't make my peace with it." She looked straight at Martha, her expression defeated, her face sagging like an emptied bag. "How am I to live with it, Martha? Tell me. For I don't know."

In the lee of Judah's boat all seemed still, a perfect stasis. Martha's hands lifted as though pulled by phantom strings. The psalm was running through her head. *A time to weep, a time to laugh*... Marion watched; softly she chanted. "A time to mourn, and a time to dance." Her voice lapsed away.

For a long moment they regarded each other, two devastated women, hurt shining in their eyes. "You tried your best, Martha," Marion said gently. "Jennet said how you did everything to save Agnes and this wee girl. Just as you done your best for me and Tom. Healin' him after he near drowned. Helpin' me when I fevered. When I was sick after our boy. Tom says, I still live because of you." Kit's girl slept in her arm, and Marion rocked her. "That's a life for a life, whichever way you figure it. You've a good soul, Martha. That's what I believe, anyhow. No matter all that's passed." Marion stopped and felt the blanket. "Ah. She's wetted herself. I tell you, this girl of yours, she's set to live." She grasped the boat to pull herself up. "Ach. I'm weary. And thirsty. I'm off home. I can't wait any longer for something to drink."

Martha stood quickly. *Come home with me*, she motioned, seized by some fresh energy.

"That's all right," Marion said. "We've got some small beer brewed."

I mean, Martha told her, in ample, generous movements, trying to make sure Marion would understand, *come to Kit's*.

"To Kit's house? Why would I do that?"

To live with us. Help us raise the child.

"Help you ... what?"

Martha made a cradle of her arms. *Nurse this girl.*

Marion gaped. "But she's ... she's as good as yours, Martha. And if I did stay with you for a time, then what about Tom? And my sister?"

Them too. With a circling motion she pointed to the alehouse and then up the street, towards the Archer house. *You
and Tom and Jennet.*

"All of us?"

Martha steepled her fingers to make a house, which sagged
as Marion stared. *Your house is not good. 'Tis no place to live.
Not for this babe.* She could feel Marion's attention fixed on her
face as well as her hands. *Kit wants the best for his girl. I want
it, for you as well.*

Marion didn't move. *Come now.* Martha took her sleeve.
It was damp from the babe's wet. A wrong woman leading a
wronged one: there was symmetry to it, a rightness. They came
up the slope of shale to the street where their people waited—
good people, *her* people—in time to see a young man clam-
bering onto the dray: Ralph—Herry's jug-eared accomplice,
resplendent in a pot helmet and orange sash, which he showed
off to the crowd. Herry shinned up, bowed, and put a pipe to
his mouth. There was a rill of bright notes, then Ralph winked
knowingly at the crowd before he sang.

"Women, women, love of women,
Make bare purses with some men.
Some put themselves out for hire
Others bait men in every shire.
Some be lewd
And some be shrewd;
Go shrewes where they go."

The pipe chirruped, Ralph capered and sang again.

"Some be brown and some be white,
And yet others be cherry ripe.
Some of them be trew in love
Beneath the girdle but not above.
Some be lewd
And some be shrewd;
Go shrewes where they go."

The song finished. There was some half-hearted cheering, a smatter of applause. Herry swung down off the cart and Ralph followed. Together they began to work through the crowd, holding their caps out for coin.

"That pair of wastrels'll get no coin from me," Marion said. She laughed, but harshly. "Let's get home, Martha. Your girl needs feeding, and I . . ." She looked down at her skirts. "I need clean petticoats. And a wash. And that cup of cider," she said, rolling her eyes, "that Tom promised me more'n an hour ago."

The babe was over Marion's shoulder, and with her free hand Marion held Agnes's shawl tight to her skirt. Across the street the Four Daughters looked to be doing lively trade, its front steps and ale room crowded with drinkers. Of Tom and Simon there was no sign. Martha hoped they were out back, striking a deal to have Tom come to Kit's; raising tankards to the future. Because of the crush they must walk in the gutter, negotiating all the wastes of the fair. Nan Dolan's back gate was unlatched, and as they went past the kid goats ran out, tethers trailing. They were making for the heap of spoiled vegetables in the market. Martha jogged after them. The kids began to sprint and she chased them across the street, emerging at a jog from the arch of the Market Cross and coming face to face with Jennet.

"I been lookin' for you," Jennet said. She smoothed down her skirts. "I've just come from the alehouse. Tom's there, soused as a herring and spoutin' some half-baked tale of us coming to live at yours—with you and Simon and Kit. Is there any truth to it? Or is Tom talkin' his usual crock of nonsense?"

The goats skittered past. Jennet caught one. *Aye. Aye. It's true.* There was more to be said, a future to be affirmed, but she wanted Marion to witness it. Martha turned to beckon; found instead a coarse-haired soldier standing in the way.

"What a sight," Herry said. "What a show." His speech was slurred. "Look you, Ralph. See this pair of doxies."

"Here's another," Ralph said, indicating Marion, who was approaching. "See this goodwife who nurses a witch's brat."

"Ach, not again. Leave off and let us be," Jennet said, her cat's eyes flashing.

"Oh, we can't do that," Herry said. He swayed. "No. We can't let you witches pass."

His breath was rancid. They made to go around him; he moved, they moved again. Chess, dancing. Herry was determined to bar them.

Jennet said, "That's enough, Herry. You're that drunk, you don't know what you're saying. But hear this: we got no more quarrel with you. So go your ways and let us go ours."

"But that's just it, you dense mare," Herry said. "Leavin' you be is what I can't do." He wiped his mouth with his wrist. "I said before and I'll say again," he said, propping himself on his cutlass, "there was none gladder than me to see the witch man come, and none sadder now he's gone." His sigh turned into a belch. The cutlass swivelled. "Still, I learned some right good lessons from Master Makepeace, so I did," he said, correcting his balance. His eyes shuttled as he looked from Marion to Jennet to Martha, his face flushing, his look rinsed with rage. "I learned how there's little enough rightness left in this world, no justice 'cept for what you can deal out yourself." He lowered his gaze and fixed it on Martha. "That's why I got business with you, Martha Hallybread."

A flare of fright went off inside. Herry raised the cutlass, putting its point to her chest.

"I've heard tell of a certain witchin' doll," Herry said. "That you was caught with, in the gaol. So Master Makepeace told me—I heard it from the man himself. Said as how he seen it with his own eyes—a bad little poppet, all stuck through with pins." His lopsided grin reappeared: mocking, baleful. "That's not nice, Martha. That's not a nice thing to have, for a dull old maid like you." His grin disappeared. "I want to see it, witch. Show it me. Now."

Under her shift she could feel sweat beading, threatening to run down her neck. In Herry's face she could see some instinct showing, ancient, pitiless. She put up both hands; put one on the blade of the cutlass while with the other she reached into the pouch and took out the poppet, which she held up between them.

"Jesu," Ralph said, shrinking back, Herry also, their eyes snagged on what she held. "It's true, then."

"Aye. Aye. Now she shows herself," Herry said, recovering, his tone strengthening, tinged with triumph. "Now we know. All this time she's been for the Devil. All this time, a witch." He let the tip of his cutlass rest on the bones at the base of her throat. "I'll tell you plain, mistress: there's a goodly part of me as longs to finish what Master Makepeace didn't." For a moment he let his weight rest on the cutlass. Its point threatened to puncture her skin. Then he sighed. "But that'll have to keep for another time. So this is what I'll do today," he went on slowly, voicing the thought as it arrived. "I'll trade you, Martha. I'll let you go home to your witch's nest, your witch's ways, leave you to raise your witch's babby, grow your bad plants—all what you do. And for that you'll give me your witchin' doll. A poppet for a poppet. I think that's a fair trade. 'Cause if I got your bad dolly, you can't do no witchin' with it." His goat's eyes were wickedly lit, the pupils like darts. "Give it me," he ordered. "Then we'll go our separate ways."

The street teemed with its countless transactions: trades, purchases, provisos, pacts. Behind Herry a man in a pristine jerkin lurched from the alehouse yard, to vomit against its gatepost. How often, how many times, had she contemplated this moment, this giving up of the poppet? Now it was arrived. *Bless them which persecute you: bless, and curse not.* How fitting, how wickedly perverse, that her enemy should take the poppet. Let Herry relieve her of its burden. Let Herry draw its consequences to himself, as a poultice draws poison from a wound. That was the poppet's lure. That was its trap.

Her hand extended, reaching across the gap. The rest of her felt curiously detached; the moment passing slow and fast at once. She dropped the poppet into Herry's outstretched palm. His fingers closed proprietorially over it. He went very still, his gaze fixed on what he held but did not understand.

She looked away. Felt immediately that familiar rending,

that ragged inner cleft. Jennet seemed to read her mind. "Do you mean him to have it? Are you sure?"

Aye. Nay. She was suddenly exhausted. It was an effort, to make the necessary shapes around the blade. *I can't fight more.*

"Leave off your dumb show," Herry said. He was holding the poppet a small distance from himself, twisting it between two fingers. Regarding it as though it were something sacred; his expression open, wondering, almost reverent. For an instant his face was clear of its malice. "Look at it, Ralph," he breathed. "So small a thing, for what it can do. I can keep it in my pocket. We can bring it to the war, use it to keep us safe. Use it on our enemies—put a curse on 'em, or some such. What about that?"

Abruptly his face hardened again. He looked at Martha. "Show me how your witchin' doll works—how it do its magic," he hissed. "Then we'll let you go."

She stared at him. Felt a thrill of outrage as sharp as the cutlass. Base Herry, vicious Herry. And, he was a dolt. She gestured to the poppet, pointing out the scoring in its waxy skin. With one finger mimed a gouging motion. *You prick it.*

He eyed her, suspicious. "You scratch it?"

She nodded. *Aye.*

"That's what these marks are? Scratches—to make it do your bidding?"

Aye. She tapped her temples. *Think—think of what you want. Then prick.*

"Is that it?" he asked. "Is that all?" She could hear his surprise, the tone of the credulous boy that still dwelt in the man. He turned to Jennet. "Is she trickin' me?"

"Nay, she's not tricking you," Jennet said evenly, catching on. "Why would she? She got no reason to." Her tone dropped as she leaned towards him, as if to disclose a secret. "But what you got to understand is there's a catch to this dolly."

The kid goat strained and bleated. They were close enough to see Herry's mind working, the slow grind of its machinery. "A catch?" Herry said, wondering at it.

"Aye, a catch," Jennet said. "You must treat it right. You must use it careful—right careful. 'Cause if you don't—if you use it wrong—that'll come back on you."

"What do you mean?"

"I mean just that. Use it in a wrong way, that wrong'll come back on you. Use it for ill, you'll get some yourself. If you doubt me, Herry, think on your witch man. He comes to Cleftwater full of vigour—a gentleman in his prime. He's here a week, he catches Martha, and he gets this poppet too—for a day. So how is it that he's gone away so quick, with his work not finished? And how is it that Martha and me are still here—still alive, still standing—when others have been hung by their necks? Why would that be? That's what you got to wonder at. That's what you got to keep in mind. 'Turn ye not unto idols.' That's what it says in the Bible. So you be careful. That's all I'm sayin'. Think hard. Do you really want to keep a poppet—a good Christian like yourself?"

"You'd have me give it back," Herry said, incredulous, "and let a witch go free?"

"But she's not, though, is she," Marion said. "She's not a witch. Nor my sister. That's what Judge Bacon said, and I'll take his word over yours any day." Agnes's shawl untied itself and poured to the ground. The stained skirts were plainly in view; Herry recoiled but Marion made no attempt to disguise them. "What's wrong, Herry? It's only a bit of blood. Plenty of that where you're going. Truth be told, you're a nobody desperate to be somebody, going about preaching justice with your gob full of scripture but hate in your heart. So what if Martha's got a bit of old wax doll? So what if she pricked it? But you—you'd happily see her hang for it. My question is, why's that wrong, but it's lawful to prick a woman? And why is it lawful that you should have it, but not her?" Marion had raised a finger; now she brandished it, jabbing at Herry's chest. "Let me tell you, Herry Gowler: the moment you prick that poppet—the moment you use it—well then, it's done its trickery, and made a witch of *you*."

The air bristled. Herry's expression contorted, passing quickly from disbelief to dismay, his mouth opening into its familiar gape. In his confusion, in the curious pause, Martha reached across. The doll was hers alone, was nothing and everything; the sum of her history—her own as well as Mam's. She plucked it from Herry's grasp. At once time seemed to start again, the fair going on with its cheerful din, the waves resuming their break and ebb. Sunlight poured over her—over the three of them—as she linked arms with Jennet and Marion and bore the poppet away. Herry's shouted insults followed them down the street, inconsequential trinkets of noise.

THIRTY-FOUR

Mogg's boat was called the *Costly*. It was surprisingly heavy. They brought it to the river in a series of shoves. At the waterline the bow floated and Martha clambered in. There was a moment of nothing, of pure suspension, and then the current nudged the boat ashore. Jennet shoved it off again, bunched her skirts, and got in.

They took an oar each. Mogg came from his house at a run, barrelling onto the jetty to roar his curses. Their first few strokes were hurried and mismatched, slewing the *Costly* side on. They rowed hard to right it, the wash from their efforts wetting them both. The water was cool and mud-coloured, scumbled with sludge. Something floated nearby: a half-sunk fishing coble, its blue stern lifted above the surface.

The storm had been drastic, had radically reshaped the shoreline. No perch of low-lying land had been spared. Looking downriver to the mouth of the Cleft, Martha saw the great lip of banked-up shale that now partly blocked the river. On both banks there were mounds of kelp and dead sea-birds, washed into rotting cairns by the tide.

Their progress was slow. After a time there was something steadying and mesmeric about their rhythm, the pull and give of the oars. Already Mogg's insults had faded, the view of the Scours dwindled, cottages and boats and the alehouse receding, becoming toy-like. On either side the gorse-covered banks grew less steep, sloping gradually down, the gorse giving way to grassy fields. The river spooled through them, a glossy shifting serpent.

"Mogg's face," Jennet said. "Did you see it?"

Oh yes, she'd seen it. Jennet's laughter overtook her. She crumpled over her oar. Martha felt her own welling: decades since she'd heard it, and its sound when it came was dry and hoarse, like a hinge in want of oil.

They came to the first bend and had to pull harder. The river had energy here, its current funnelling determinedly eastwards out of the Cleft to the sea. A skittish breeze had got up and for some moments the stoked water seemed to gain purchase, pushing the *Costly* onto a reef of gravel. They'd run aground. Small waves battered the boat. Martha wiped her face with her sleeve. Cold water lapped at her hem, climbed her skirts. Not again. Not the climbing water, again. For a few panicked seconds she was back, too far back, in the gaol, its stinking, implacable tide.

"All right?" Jennet asked. "We can turn around if you want."

Nay. Keep going. She mouthed a prayer—to Mam, to St. Cecilia—and fresh resolve came with the saying of it, which she used to wield the oar like a lever. The mudflat was there and then it wasn't, shelving steeply down.

"Here," Jennet said. She untied Mogg's bailer—a cut-down leather bucket—from the rear thwart. "You bail. I'll row," she said, reaching for Martha's oar. "A bit farther up, and we can find some calmer water." Jennet rowed in short strokes, her slim hands like a pair of low-flying birds as she worked the oars. "Never thought we'd have an outin' in a boat, Martha. But then, life's full of surprises, ain't it so? *You're* full of surprises, Mistress Hallybread. I know that, for certain sure."

Martha managed to smile as she re-fastened the bailer. To either side of them the river branched into smaller watercourses like the fingers of a hand. Jennet steered the boat into one of them. The quiet, the stillness, were immediate. The boat drifted, edging into the lattice of reeds.

Jennet rested on the oars. "Is this what you were wanting?"

Was it? Slowly Martha stood. Above Jennet's head the sickle moon hung, its nether tip pointing. To here. To now. She took the poppet from the pouch and for some reason offered it skywards. Late-afternoon light slanted obliquely, clothing everything in gold. The river rocked, close and inviting. Into its depths the sun's rays furrowed: each one a possibility, each one a door.

Wax doll, witching doll, poppet: whatever its name, whatever its purpose, it was not for use by any man. Let the Cleft's waters hold it, shelter it, keep it safe for some future mistress yet to be known.

She brought it to her lips and kissed it—a kiss for Mam, another for itself—and then she let it go. Jennet made a soft cry; what she said the rushes ticked away.

The poppet dropped, briefly luminous in the gilded light, then pierced the river's skin, disappearing in a plume of spray. Martha leaned all the way out, over the boat's gunwale. Like this she watched the poppet sink; saw how the doll's shocked stare seemed to relax, its wounds fade. In the water's prism the doll refracted, each portion twinning itself, each twin multiplying, the poppet becoming poppets, becoming Prissy, Agnes,

Mam; becoming the women, uncountable, inestimable, a sum in which every part storied the whole, a great shoal of women shining in the river's fold. Then it became one doll again. She could feel her custody of it ending, its hold on her dissolving, growing faint as a fable or second sight. The riverbed received it, pillowed it, quilted it in silt.

A warbler called. The boat lilted. The gauzy after-lingerings of the poppet were all she could see and then they too faded into the amber.

She lifted her eyes from the water. With what rapture saw the world's living details and was pierced again and to the quick by its wonders: the damselflies' jewelled flick, the healing breeze, the steady warmth of Jennet's hand on her back, the reeds' dry chatter. The reassurance of the constant tide, its take and give, which neither rebuked nor absolved her.

ACKNOWLEDGMENTS

I am indebted to numerous historians and biographers whose work informed and inspired my research. Of the many books and articles consulted for this novel, I would like in particular to acknowledge Malcolm Gaskill's detailed and compelling *Witchfinders: A Seventeenth-Century English Tragedy* (John Murray, 2017), which became a touchstone while I was writing my own book; also Ivan Bunn's excellent *A Trial of Witches: A Seventeenth-Century Witchcraft Prosecution* (Routledge, 1997). I am grateful to both these historians for their time and advice— as well as their generous attitude to historical novelists. Scott Eaton's *John Stearne's Confirmation and Discovery of Witchcraft: Text, Context and Afterlife* (Routledge, 2020) provided invaluable context, especially of the social dynamics surrounding the witch hunts, as well as insight into the mindset of the original East Anglian witch-hunters. For information about early modern midwifery, humoral medicine, and contemporary uses of plants and herbs, I drew extensively on Jane Sharp's *The Midwives Book, or the Whole Art of Midwifry Discovered* (ed. Elaine Hobby, Oxford University Press, 1999), a title in the Women Writers in English 1350–1850 series. Jane Sharp's book has been a rich, moving, and endlessly fascinating resource; I consistently find inspiration there.

Readers of these scholarly works will discern that, in shaping historical material into fiction, I have in places made full use of writer's licence. For example, while certain events described in this novel occurred over the period 1645–47 (the time of the East Anglian witch hunts), I have in places compressed events that actually unfolded over months or years into just one season. I have also made selective use of details from various witch trials that took place across Suffolk and Norfolk, though key scenes, in particular the searching and pricking of accused witches, are based on contemporary accounts. While all my characters are invented, some are closely based on key figures from this episode in history. Similarly, the village of Cleftwater is my own creation, a composite of several towns and villages on the East Anglian coast, including Aldeburgh, Dunwich, Great Yarmouth, Lowestoft, and Thorpeness.

———

It takes a village to write a novel. So, I have many people to thank.

I am exceptionally fortunate to be represented by Peter Straus (and the superb RCW team) here in the UK, and in the US by the equally wonderful Kimberly Witherspoon: to both of you, huge thanks for your many kindnesses and unstinting championing of this book. Likewise, to all at Phoenix Books and Scribner: thank you all for your inspiration and effort, especially Frankie Banks, Becca Bryant, Alainna Hadjigeorgiou, Lucy Cameron, Cait Davies, Georgia Goodall, Joie Asuquo, Ashley Gilliam, and Clare Maurer. To my truly brilliant editors,

Francesca Main (Phoenix) and Kara Watson (Scribner): your insights and astute editing have made this a better book. My particular thanks go to James Nunn for his uniquely magnificent linocut illustration.

Thanks to all my UEA tutors especially Tom Benn, Giles Foden, Jean McNeil, and Jos Smith, who gave early encouragement.

I am very grateful to Dorothy and Ray Meyer, who made the MA possible.

Special thanks to Arts Council England, the Francis W Reckitt Arts Trust, and the Norfolk Library and Information Service, whose timely project grants afforded me precious writing time.

To the many friends who have provided beds, laughs, wine, and pep talks at crucial times, especially Maxine Altman, Karen Angelico, Emma Bamford, Kate Baker and Peter Middleton, Caroline Brazier, Catherine Gaffney, Mary and Alastair Snow, Jillian Stewart, and Stephanie Tam: thank you, all.

I would like to take this opportunity to express my gratitude to Christabelle Dilks, Linden Hibbert, Delwar Hussain, and Bec Sollom, whose creativity, wisdom, and friendship have been great gifts in my (writing) life.

Last and above all, thanks to my family for their several years of tea-making, laptop-fixing, map-reading, proofing, unswerving belief, and patience, especially when my attention stayed too long in 1645. Michael, Imi, Fraser, dearest and most discerning readers: this book came into being because of you.